Development

A Novel by Paul Backalenick

Copyright © 2015 by Paul Backalenick
Copyright © 2016 Revised by author

All rights reserved.

ISBN: 1518794866
ISBN-13: 978-1518794865

DEDICATIONS

For Karen, whose belief in me nurtured my own.

And for my Dad, Bill Backalenick, who helped me to learn compassion.

And lastly, for Ann Craig, a beautiful soul who died much too young.

ACKNOWLEDGMENTS

Thanks to Cliff Hirschman, my most astute and diligent reader. Cliff's wise and thoughtful suggestions improved this work immeasurably. And special thanks to Peter Gambaccini without whose advice and support, this novel would not have been completed. My gratitude goes out as well to my many readers who loyally plowed through drafts and parts of drafts providing support and feedback every step of the way. That includes Karen Loew, Susi Cohen, Moe Shore, Lynn Backalenick, Bill Cramp, Christine Poolos, Larry Weinberg and Debbie Cohen.

Also, I want to acknowledge my parents. My mother, Irene Backalenick, is an extraordinary writer and editor. Her comments helped clarify my writing and greatly improved my dubious grammatical skills. And finally, I wish to thank my dad who managed to read a draft before his death. I am grateful that he did.

Thank you all for enduring the struggles of this first-time novelist.

Paul Backalenick
November, 2015
New York City

CHAPTER 1

12/13/71 – Monday

The money was gone. That much was certain.

Four weeks earlier, when Hank got it, he hadn't been able to think clearly. Not sure where to put it, he had anxiously stashed it in his garage. $20,000 in hundred dollar bills. Two hundred of them. So much cash in his hands. It couldn't go in the bank. They would have to report that much cash. Maybe a Swiss bank, but he hadn't investigated that. So temporarily, he had taken a shoebox from his closet, put the money inside, and placed it on the top shelf in the back of his garage. Nobody ever went up there. It seemed safe enough.

But now, the box was gone. He scoured the shelves, looking behind and under every possible object. It simply was not there. *Why in the world did I put it here? Why not a safety deposit box? Stupid, stupid, stupid! Who found it?* Fuming, he began turning over possibilities in his mind. Maybe someone had followed him home from the site that day, watched him from the woods and then snuck into the garage when it was dark and taken it. It might even have been Holden. The garage was never locked.

Or maybe one of his daughters, Dora or Amy, had come in here, looking for something and discovered it. Perhaps Norma, his wife, had actually noticed a shoebox missing from the closet and found it in the garage. That seemed unlikely. Or could it have been one of Dora's shifty friends? Or even a neighbor looking to borrow a rake? Or the kid who cut the lawn? *Jesus, it could be almost anyone.*

Feeling frustrated and furious, Hank left the garage and stalked into his house.

CHAPTER 2

9/13/71 – Monday, three months earlier

Madison Hixon smoothed her skirt and marched into Hank Latour's office in County Savings Bank. He'd seen her before, on the tennis courts at Longshore Country Club, among other places. She was about his age or maybe a few years younger, he thought. People in town knew her. She hadn't lived in Westport long, but already she'd made a name for herself in local real estate. She was trim and athletic, not especially tall, but well-proportioned. She wore a tight skirt that ended above her knees and showed off her hips to advantage. Her arms and legs were tanned. Hank caught himself staring and looked up at her face. A short haircut framed a pair of deep blue oval eyes.

"Maddie Hixon," she said thrusting out her hand. Her grip was firm. It felt to Hank as if they had an agreement already. He knew he was expected to grant her a loan for the Newport Lane housing development. He clung to her hand for a moment before letting go.

With her was Mike Holden, the developer. A big grinning, red-faced man, Hank had known him for years. Dressed in a gray unzipped sweatshirt that loosely covered his hulking body, Holden seemed too big for the office. Everything about him was thick. Thick hands, thick shoulders, a meaty face. With a throaty laugh, he launched into a joke.

"Hey Hank, you know why Puerto Ricans don't want their daughters to marry Negroes?"

"No," Hank said warily.

"Cause they're afraid the children will be too lazy to steal." Holden laughed loudly and slapped Hank's desk. "That one kills me," he snorted.

"Okay," Hank said, after a moment. "Why don't you both have a seat?"

Hank's office was small, with two armchairs facing his desk. Maddie sat primly in one while Holden, still laughing, squeezed himself into the other.

"Well. We've started clearing the land," Holden said after he'd settled in. "Everything's in place, the permits, the variances, power, septic. All good. We just need the financing for this next phase."

Maddie joined in. "We need to have a model home built. That's how we'll sell them."

"And there's something in it for you when you get us all the money we need." Mike grinned.

"What?" Hank winced. Feigning ignorance, he asked, "What are you talking about?"

Mike leaned across the desk and said "Remember. We'll give you twenty grand if you make this happen. No one has to know."

Hank felt himself blush. He had expected the offer. Holden had alluded to it months ago when Hank first became involved, when he made his initial investment. Hank knew that raising capital was a problem for Mike. It had not surprised him that Mike implied he would grease his palm if Hank secured the loan. Still, it made him squirm to hear it out loud, especially here, in his office. He nodded assent and said "Shush. Quiet."

Holden looked at Maddie and winked.

"Well, ruh… right," Hank stuttered slightly. He turned to Maddie. "Mike and I have been in on this thing since day one. You're going to be the realtor?"

"Yes. I'm the agent. It's my exclusive. Once we have a model home up, it's full speed ahead. I can sell all six in a few months."

"At what price point, do you think?"

"They're big. All in the one twenty-five to one thirty-nine range."

"That's true," Hank agreed. "They're not small. I hope there's a market at those prices."

"Absolutely," she replied, smiling.

Her bright white teeth distracted Hank for a

moment. "So how much are you looking for right now?"

"We'll need three hundred thousand total. Fifty for now," Mike said.

Hank nodded slowly. "Let me give you the application forms. Fill these out. Apply for the fifty and we'll worry about the rest later." He turned around and faced the file cabinet behind his desk. Inwardly, he gulped. *I'm going to have to go to Walsh on this, since we're really talking three hundred. Damn.* Hank steadied himself as he opened one of the file drawers. *Don't let 'em know you're nervous. Be a man, for God's sake. Take charge.* He found the right folder, pulled out the forms, turned back around and dropped them on his desk.

He slid the papers across to Maddie. At the same time, she reached for them. Their hands collided in the middle. "You ca... can review it with Hennessy, right?" he said, "I have to be arm's length on this."

"We know." She gave Hank another toothy smile and he smiled back, wondering why he was so drawn to this woman.

Hank had his own money in the project. He had given Holden $50,000, almost all he had, for a 33 per cent stake in the development. As part of the deal, he was supposed to secure the financing. It was a sensitive issue, mixing his personal investment with a loan from his bank, but he wanted the action. He wanted to be on the inside for once, to make some real money.

Hank felt frustrated. He knew life's gifts had come early to him. But as the years went by, he felt he had done nothing of importance. He had not lived up to his early promise. Now he needed to show himself that he was a man of consequence. He felt he had something to prove. *If you don't have something to prove, you won't do anything important*, he guessed.

He shook his head. This loan was a problem. Of course Ray Walsh, the bank president, didn't know of Hank's investment. It was dicey, a conflict of interest. Hank had to remain quiet on the subject. It was between him and Holden, and now this Maddie.

"Well, come back when you're ready with the application. Any time," he said.

"It'll be soon," said Maddie. "Time is money."

They all stood up. More handshakes and they were gone.

Hank sat back down. He stared at the gold Cross pen he'd bought himself a few years earlier as a reward for five years at the bank. It sat at the front of his desk in a gold holder on a white marble base, a testament to his ambition and pride. He felt a little better. Still picturing Maddie, he imagined himself alongside her. He was probably almost a foot taller than she. It was not a good match. He shoved her image aside and thought about Holden and the development. *Damn loan.*

He regretted getting in so deep, but he couldn't back out now. He knew that Walsh was not keen on

Holden. There had been some trouble with him a few years back, something about misrepresenting collateral. Hank wasn't involved and didn't know the details. *Plus it's $50,000 now and $250,000 more after the first phase, after the model home is done.* Hank did not have the authority to approve such a large amount. *Would Walsh possibly approve it? Sure, the market is improving, but how many people want a house that size? How many people need five bedrooms?* Hank had certainly believed in the project before. Now, he was not so sure.

CHAPTER 3

Driving home from work that evening, Hank peered through the drizzly mist as he negotiated the curves of Greens Farms Road. Steering with his right hand, his better arm, he glanced at the empty fields as he passed them. They didn't hold his attention long. His thoughts returned to Newport Lane. As a senior commercial loan officer, it was his job to initiate a big loan, not approve it. Sooner or later, he knew he would have to present it to Walsh. Hank put his other hand on the wheel and gripped it more tightly.

They needed the loan. The prospect of failure was dismal. It was a great opportunity for the bank, he had believed, as well as for himself. Maybe it was reckless, but he had big dreams. He could triple his money. Not only would it get him out of the hole he was in, it would start him on his way. On his way to becoming someone important, someone to be reckoned with. But now his bright future was in jeopardy. He was feeling increasingly worried those six houses would never get built. Not only would he not make money, he might lose everything, including his job. It was too late to turn back now. Examining his original decision, he thought *ambition clouds judgment.*

As he watched the unlit road, he braced himself for seeing his family. He never knew what to expect, especially from his wife. Norma often would have downed two or three tall glasses of vodka during the afternoon. Would he be faced with the angry, accusatory Norma, a tumult of rage, for which he could not prepare? Or would it be a gloomy, depressed Norma sitting on the couch, staring at the television? Sometimes he would find her passed out on the living room sofa, sleeping soundly. On rare occasions, she might be alert, with dinner prepared, awaiting his arrival. He could not know.

And then there were his two children. His older daughter Dora, now almost 17, always seemed to be either silent or surly lately. If she were there at all, she would likely ignore him, her face masked behind too much black eye shadow. She had changed over the past year. Her once cheery demeanor was a fading memory. He ached at the thought.

Only Amy, his younger daughter, might brighten his mood. But Amy tried too hard to please her father, to be perfect. And she nearly was. A good student, she worked extremely hard in school. At everything, really. He smiled sadly. She was so beautiful, but very timid and tentative; she didn't make friends easily. She spent most of her time by herself doing homework or walking in the fields behind their home.

Thinking about his troubled family, Hank felt his chest tighten. For a moment, it was hard to breathe and impossible to relax. He thought back to his promising beginning. He had been an athlete at Stanford, at least until the injury in his senior year. He was a good student, with a bright future. Everyone saw him that way. He had been ambitious. He had felt special, if a little insecure, at the same time. Now he had mounting credit card bills and he was overextended everywhere. He found himself holding his breath. *If I can't make this deal work...*

Hank had gone to college on a partial football scholarship and majored in Finance. On the team, he was a good wide receiver, though not first string. He was tall and lean, with black hair and blue eyes. Girls liked him even if he seemed a bit aloof and unapproachable. In truth, he was shy. He had various brief girlfriends during his time at college, but none had really mattered to him until he met Norma in a coffee house at the end of his junior year. The moment he saw her, he was transfixed. She was beautiful. She looked like a goddess to him. Hiding his nervousness, he had approached her and she had responded happily. Being with her gave him confidence, a feeling that he was where he wanted to be and if she didn't say much, Hank didn't care.

That was a long time ago. He had not advanced as far and as fast as he had hoped. He simply expected he would be more important by now. True, he had moved east, to an upscale community, with a good position in a local bank, but he thought somehow he would be running a bank or a brokerage firm by now. It was not so. He was a small-town banker with a lot of bills to pay and a boss who could crush his dreams in a moment.

Hank made himself exhale as he entered his driveway and pulled into the garage. He took his briefcase from the car and walked in the back door leading to the kitchen. It was dark. He passed through to the living room where he saw Norma seated on the couch, smoking with one hand, a tall glass of what he knew to be vodka in the other. The only light was from the table lamp alongside her. "Any chance of dinner?" he asked.

"On the stove," she muttered, gesturing with her chin toward the darkened kitchen behind him. Norma had once been lovely, her Irish good looks accentuated by wavy red-blonde hair. Now her skin was mottled and her hair frizzy and unkempt. Though still strawberry-blonde, her hair had lost its luster as though an inner light had gone out and it had somehow become dimmer and coarser over the years.

Hank grunted assent and made his way over her bare outstretched legs to the hallway where he dropped his briefcase and keys. He returned to the kitchen and turned on a light to find a steak in a pan on the stove and soggy string beans in a colander in the sink. He assembled these items on a plate, poured a glass of water, and sat down to eat by himself. "Dora here?" he asked.

"Nah. With her friends somewhere."

And Amy, he knew, would be studying in her

room. Hank did not want his wife to join him. In fact, though it was never mentioned out loud, nobody wanted to be around Norma when she was drinking.

****

Amy was not studying. Standing in front of her small bedroom window, she gazed at the oak tree behind her home. Only an hour ago, she had climbed that tree, up to the second large branch, where she sat for a few minutes, catching her breath and gazing at the open fields. Now, as darkness gathered, she watched a wisp of smoke drifting over the treetops beyond her yard. Sighing, she sat down at her desk. Tomorrow, she'd go back out there. She was puzzled by the smoke and she was anxious to investigate.

Amy was 14. She was the younger daughter by just over two years of Hank and Norma Latour. Others thought she had a beautiful face, with lovely eyes. But she was also considered by some to be too thin, too tall, and too studious. She thought she was not enough of anything. She certainly wasn't too thin. In fact, her widening hips and budding breasts only made her feel fat. Her older sister Dora was popular. Dora was somewhere with her friends now. Amy could never be like Dora, missing dinner, staying out late, doing dangerous things. Amy stared down at her English homework. She had to write at least three pages about the symbolism of the river in Huckleberry Finn. It would be hard work. She had better start soon.

She heard her father come home. She wanted to

see him, but imagined her mother snarling at her, interrupting and ruining whatever connection she might make with him. Instead, she stared again out the window at the dark fields behind her home. She loved the woods and marshland in those wild acres. She liked nothing more than walking in that open land startling pheasants and occasionally deer or walking along the edge of the small pond, seeing a turtle dive under water as she neared it. She looked down at the blank sheet of paper and told herself *stop daydreaming and get to work.*

She heard the front door slam and knew Dora had come home. She listened as a car pulled away from the house; probably Dora's friend Katie was driving. She heard her father ask Dora where she'd been, but she could not hear Dora's reply, if any. A few minutes later, she heard Dora climbing the stairs to her room and slamming her door.

Amy was unhappy. She often felt this way. She did not like being home, even in her room, and preferred the solitude of nature. That was where she fit in; it was a place where she felt safe. At home, and even more, in school, she felt fearful and out of place among people. She hated getting fat and tried hard to be the slender girl she had always been. Her home felt like a battleground, some bombed-out village in Viet Nam. Everyone was a prisoner in solitary. They didn't speak. They had separate cells. In her last year of junior high school, her friends no longer seemed to be her friends. Their interests had diverged from hers. They talked endlessly of boys, clothes, drugs. She focused instead on her schoolwork and pleasing her teachers as much as she could. She was an awkward, gangly girl who still felt the pull of her tomboy youth.

She would spend four hours tonight on her homework, foregoing television and eating as little as possible. She knew she was not as smart as many in her class, but she made up for it with relentless study. She felt a powerful compulsion to please her teachers and her father. She achieved good grades, but she knew she could do better if she only worked harder.

CHAPTER 4

Dora walked past her mother without a word and saw her father in the kitchen eating by himself. She walked around him, opened the refrigerator and heard him ask from behind her "Where were you?"

"Driving around," she said, without further explanation. She took out a piece of broiled chicken and poured herself a glass of milk. Holding these items, she said "I'm going upstairs." Hank watched her go. A black sweater and short dark skirt was all he saw as she walked out of the kitchen. For a moment, he thought of the lively, bright child who used to run to him. She had been his favorite, his "Dorable." Now, she never approached him and only spoke when spoken to. It broke his heart and bewildered him.

After eating in her room, Dora dressed to go out. Where her sister was considered beautiful, Dora would be better described as "striking," or worse yet, "interesting." When her outfit was complete, she went to her parents' bedroom. She found her mother's purse and removed the car keys. She put the purse down momentarily, then picked it up again, found the wallet and removed ten dollars. She quickly put the wallet back, snapped the purse closed, and crammed the bill in the front pocket of her shorts. She went downstairs, past both parents and without a word to anyone, walked out the door to the garage. In her mother's Volvo, she made the fifteen minute drive downtown and parked in the big lot off Main Street.

Now, shivering on the damp sidewalk, bouncing from one foot to the other, she waited for her friends, Katie and Dick. She was wearing small black leather boots above which the top inch of white lace socks peeked out. Her long legs were covered in black tights leading up to short blue jean cutoffs followed by a thin black sweater with rhinestone buttons at the collar. Her black hair was cut short and severely combed over so it parted just above her left ear. She had a gold stud in each earlobe. She carried a small black purse in her hands which were clutched together over her crotch. Her nails were painted deep red, almost black, and they were chewed to the quick.

She had been standing on the Main Street sidewalk, in front of Coppersmith Kitchenware, for nearly twenty minutes. Finally Katie and Dick drove up in Dick's Honda hatchback. In the front seat sat an older guy Dora did not recognize. He turned out to be someone none of them knew, a drifter Dick had bumped into, simply known as Hibbard. Dora climbed in back with Katie, as Dick resumed driving. Heading north up Main Street, they spotted Jared Appleton wandering alone on the sidewalk. He joined them, squeezing in the back seat next to Dora. The subject turned to drugs. Jared had with him speed, pot and some acid.

"Check it out. Black Beauties," he said, showing them a handful of black capsules. "Pharmaceutical speed, man. The best. Two bucks each," he added.

Everybody fished in their pockets for money, except Hibbard who turned to Dick and said "Front me the two bucks, man."

"Sure."

They each took a capsule from Jared, passing around a can of Coke Jared had with him.

"Where you wanna go?" asked Dick.

"The beach," said Katie.

They headed toward Compo Beach, turning right at the Minuteman Statue, passing summer beach houses and driving by the unmanned gate house as they entered the beach access road. The beach officially closed on Labor Day, but one could still drive in. A large empty parking lot was to their right, the beach itself on the left. They drove to the end of the road and parked facing the water. It was a cool, misty night. Aside from two other cars some distance away, it was dark and virtually deserted. A pale half-moon in an overcast sky provided the only light.

They got out, waiting for the speed to hit. Dora walked with Jared toward the water. They'd both lived in town since childhood. They met when they were in tenth grade at the start of high school. She had always liked him. He was smart, she thought. He seemed to have purpose, a sense of direction, plus he was cute. She looked up at him in the moonlight. He was smiling, bouncing along, with an extra skip in his gait.

"Can you feel it yet?" he asked.

"Yeah, it's coming on. Love that rush," she replied.

With that, he whirled around and kissed her, laughing. His damp hair fell across her cheek. She was pleasantly surprised and pushed him away, laughing as well.

"C'mon" he said, "Let's go out on the jetty." He ran off toward the rocks that thrust out fifty yards into the Long Island Sound.

Dora was excited, really feeling the speed now. A surge of energy flowed through her hands and feet. She took off after Jared, running. She caught up to him at the water's edge. The dark rocks stretched out before them in the dim moonlight. Relatively dry here at the water line, the tumble of boulders looked wet and slippery further out. Jared climbed on the first of them and began picking his way along the spine of rocks heading away from the shore.

He turned to her. She was still standing in the sand. "C'mon," he said. "It's cool." Tentatively, she climbed up the first few rocks. They were an array of large boulders, with flat surfaces and sharp edges jutting in all directions. *I'm not dressed for this,* she thought. She tried to be careful, but the speed made her walk quickly. She stepped on the tops of the rocks, trying to avoid the sharp parts, trying to maintain her footing. She caught up to him. He grinned at her and she smiled back, feeling tingly.

He turned and continued out. She did her best to follow him until they were standing on the last few large rocks at the end of the jetty. The black surfaces out there were wet and glistening.

"Wouldn't want to fall in here" he said, looking down at the waves striking the rocks below. Dora felt frightened. For a time, it had been exciting, but it had grown increasingly ominous. She wanted to get back to the shore urgently. She reached out for Jared's hand, partly to steady herself, partly to feel less isolated. She looked down at the roiling black water. She imagined big fish, sharp rocks, herself slipping and falling in.

"Let's go back" she shivered.

"Okay, sure," he said, still smiling.

He let go of her hand and deftly jumped to the flat surface of another rock, heading back.

"Wait," she said. "Wait for me." He turned and looked back at her. She was shivering. She looked cold. And she looked scared.

"It's okay," he said. "C'mon. You're okay." He reached out his hand. She grabbed it like it was a life preserver, her one connection to safety. He pulled her and she slipped slightly, but caught her balance in time.

Breathing heavily she joined him on his rock. More slowly than they had come, they returned to the shore.

When they got there, she turned toward him, her heart thumping. He threw his arms around her and tried to kiss her again, but she buried her head in his chest instead. He held her like that for a few moments. She was shaking. He said "Let's go back to the car. You can warm up." Gratefully, she walked with him up the beach and back to where the car was parked.

Dick was sitting on the hood, smoking a joint. He said dreamily "It's really cool here." Then he added "I was watching you guys out on the rocks. I could barely see you at the end of the jetty."

"Yeah, we walked all the way out," Jared said. "Pretty intense," he added, almost to himself.

Dora was rubbing her shoulders vigorously. "Let's get in the car," she said. "I'm freezing." She walked around to the door and saw Katie and Hibbard making out in the back seat. *Oh well,* she thought, *they won't care if we're sitting up front.* "C'mon" she said to Jared. "Get in." She climbed in the passenger side as he got in the driver's seat.

She could hear the rustling noises of clothing and kissing in the back seat, but she didn't mind. She only wanted to feel warm. The keys were in the ignition, so she said to Jared "Turn on the car. Get some heat in here." He obliged and in a few minutes the car was much warmer. She felt jangly from the speed, but at least she wasn't cold. And she finally felt safe. She shivered for a moment, thinking again of the dark water, the slippery rocks, her fear and Jared helping her. He reached for her again and this time she kissed him back, relieved to be in the car, happy to be with him.

Things were progressing fast in the back seat. Dora could hear Katie moaning and Hibbard laughing quietly, whispering to her. Dick got off the hood of the car and got in the front seat, sliding in alongside Jared, who moved that much closer to Dora, pushing her up against the door. It was awkward to keep kissing and he stopped.

"Let's go," said Katie huskily, from the back seat. "We can go back to my house. My parents are away all week."

Dick put the car in gear and they headed toward Katie's house on Minute Man Hill Road. It was only a five-minute drive. Katie Price's family was relatively well off. Her father was a wholesale jeweler in New York City. He had bought their large home in Westport ten years earlier. He was a regular commuter to the city and would often spend the night in New York, where he maintained an apartment. And he travelled on business. At the moment, he was somewhere in Europe with Katie's mother. Her two older sisters were away at college.

When they arrived at the house, Dick said "I can't stay. Gotta get home. Anyone need a ride?"

Jared and Hibbard shook their heads. Dora thought about leaving, but realized she'd much rather stay with Jared than go home. "No," she said, looking hopefully at Jared. They watched as Dick drove away.

It was a modern ranch house, painted bright yellow, perched high on a hillside. There were big plate glass windows lining the front. From inside, Dora knew, you could look out at the Long Island Sound. Both Dora and Jared knew the house well. There was a swimming pool in the back. Katie opened the front door and they all headed to the living room. There was a stone fireplace in the center of the wall directly opposite where they entered from the foyer. Two beige leather couches faced each other from either side of the fireplace. Katie flounced on one with Hibbard following her. Within seconds, they had resumed their embrace.

Dora and Jared didn't sit down. "I'm thirsty," she said. They walked through the living room and came to the kitchen. It contained a rectangular table with six chairs in front of sliding doors opening on to the deck and the pool area. Jared sat down and Dora opened the refrigerator. She wasn't especially hungry, but she found orange juice and poured herself a glass. "Want some?" she asked.

"Yeah, sure."

She poured him a glass of juice and sat down. The speed was wearing off. They were starting to crash. Jared reached in his pocket and took out his handful of black capsules and said "You wanna do another?" Dora looked at his hand and up at him. She just liked being with him, speeding or not. "No," she said. She didn't like the way her body felt now. She ached and wanted to feel normal again.

"Yeah, okay. I might do some acid. You want a hit of that?" Dora had not taken LSD before. She was interested, but a little fearful. People had jumped off roofs on it, she'd heard.

"Nah, not now." She didn't want Jared to know she'd never tried it. She'd do it soon, on another night, she decided. She watched as Jared put a small piece of paper on his tongue and took a sip of orange juice. She didn't know what to expect from him, but she was starting to feel tired. "I gotta lie down," she said.

She walked out of the kitchen, back to the living room. There was no sign of Katie and Hibbard. She stretched out on one of the couches. Her body ached and she struggled to get comfortable. Gradually, she drifted off to sleep.

CHAPTER 5

Jared remained seated at the kitchen table. He had taken acid several times. He loved the feeling, the disorientation, the sense that the world was plastic, flexible, visually fascinating. He waited for that feeling. The speed rush from before was gone. He sat at the table, remembering the night, thinking about Dora on the rocks. *She really was scared*, he thought. *No reason to be. Nothing was going to happen.* And he thought about Katie and this new guy Hibbard. *What was his story anyway? Where'd he come from? Oh well, he seemed okay*, Jared decided. He sipped his juice and waited.

The acid began to wash over him. He got up from the table and opened the sliding doors to the back yard. It was a clear night. The earlier mist had disappeared. Jared stood a moment in the doorway. He relished the feeling of his body changing, his perceptions altering. He looked down at his feet and they seemed a mile away. They carried him out the door on to the deck. He gazed at the shimmering water in the pool and had the thought that he could just glide across it. He glanced up at the Japanese lanterns that were strung above the pool apron. They were alternating yellow and sky-blue. They swayed slightly in the cool breeze. He thought they were extraordinarily beautiful. He walked out and around the pool, feeling as though he were floating. He passed through the yard and on to the next door neighbor's property. He looked up at their darkened house. There was one light on in an upstairs room. He thought *I can go anywhere. There isn't anything I can't do. There isn't any place I can't go.*

He reached out and touched the wood shingles of the house. The bumpy texture surprised him. He touched his own face, tapping with his fingers. He touched the smooth glass of a window. He had never realized how varied these different textures were. It was almost like they were parts of himself that he had never discovered before. Feeling like a king floating above his realm, Jared walked around the house and out onto the street. He gazed down at the lights below. He was tripping and he loved it.

****

The next morning, Dora awoke in her clothes, finding herself curled up on Katie's couch. She felt stiff and sore. Her clothing clung to her. She stretched and got up. She heard Katie's voice in the kitchen. She walked in. Hibbard was sitting at the table drinking coffee. Katie was at the counter pouring herself a cup. "Want some?" she asked Dora.

"Yeah, thanks."

Dora stood by the sink and looked at Hibbard. He was a big rangy guy, with long straggly brown hair that needed combing. He wore a white tee shirt, untucked, and blue jeans. His feet were bare. Dora thought they must be cold. Hers were and she had on boots and socks. She looked down at his slightly bloodshot eyes. "So where you from?"

"Yeah, where *are* you from?" repeated Katie, as she handed a cup of coffee to Dora.

"California. I've been hitching across the country."

"You're kidding! Wow, that's cool," said Katie.

"It's okay. I like it here. I might stop."

Dora glanced at Katie, standing alongside her at the counter. Katie looked a little uncomfortable.

Hibbard said "I'm a poet, a traveling poet." He had his knapsack with him and he pulled out a pen and a brown paper bag. He began writing on the bag. He became absorbed in the effort.

Dora turned to Katie and said "I wanna get home. Can you give me a ride back to my car, in town?"

"Yeah, sure. Gimme a minute."

She left the room. Hibbard was still scrawling intently. Dora drank her coffee, idly watching him. He stopped writing and looked her up and down. "No question. You are the best looking bee in the hive," he said, with a grin. Dora grimaced and rolled her eyes. *And you're a pig,* she thought.

Katie returned, with a coat on. "Okay, let's go," she said. She faced Hibbard. "You can't stay here."

He looked up at her. "I'm almost finished." With that, he dashed off a few more lines. "Here," he said presenting her with the bag. He got up and left the room, presumably in search of his shoes.

Katie looked at the poem and read the first few lines.

> *What was in the mail today?*
> *Look in the dresser*
> *or up in the attic.*
> *The answer is there.*
> *It's everywhere.*

It seemed incoherent to her and she put it down. "I'll read it later," she told Dora.

Hibbard returned wearing desert boots without socks. They all went out to Katie's car. Katie asked Hibbard where he wanted to go. "You can leave me in town too," he said.

Katie swung through downtown Westport, left Hibbard in front of the movie theater and headed around to the big parking lot along the Saugatuck River, looking for Dora's car.

"You like him?" asked Dora.

"Not really. I thought I did, but after I came down, nah."

"Did you guys...?"

"Yeah. It was okay, I guess. Speed always makes it better, you know?"

"Yeah, it does."

"What happened with you and Jared?"

"Nothing. He dropped some acid and I fell asleep."

"Really? He's tripping somewhere? Where is he, do you think?"

"I have no idea. I just crashed and he was gone."

"Yeah. Acid's like that. People can go anywhere."

"I hope he's okay."

"Yeah, really."

They arrived at Dora's car. "See you," Dora said, getting out.

Dora returned home. She put the car back in the garage and quietly slipped into her house. It was 10:30 in the morning. Her father and Amy had already left for the day. Dora walked through the screened porch toward the kitchen. She only wanted a glass of milk. She had no appetite. She thought momentarily about school and dismissed the idea. She wondered again about Katie and Hibbard. Katie was pretty loose, but that Hibbard was weird. *What was Katie thinking?* She guessed he was harmless enough. She hoped so, for Katie's sake. *A traveling poet.* She smiled.

And what about Jared? Where had he gone, tripping in the middle of the night? She'd heard stories about acid and the strange and dangerous things people sometimes did under its influence. She was a little worried for him. She thought about her night. She had trouble remembering exactly what she had done, but told herself she had had fun.

She entered the kitchen and was a little surprised to discover her mother there. Norma was wearing a brown, fluffy sweater, washing the dishes. She looked at Dora as she came through the door. "You look like you slept in those clothes," she pronounced.

"I was at Katie's."

"All night?"

"Yeah. No big deal."

"What were you doing? Smoking marijuana? You shoulda called. I was worried about you. Your father thought about calling the police. He didn't though."

"Jeez. I was fine. What's the big deal?"

"You're not supposed to stay out on a school night. Why aren't you in school anyway?"

"I'm going. I'm just a little late. I have

homeroom first period anyway. I gotta change my clothes."

"Jesus Christ. I'll drive you."

"Okay."

Dora had no intention to stay in school and no intention to tell her mother that. She went to her room to change clothes. She pulled out a pair of blue jeans and a black rayon shirt that buttoned up the front. She laid these on her bed and walked into the bathroom. Seeing herself in the mirror, she stared at her eyes. They looked small and ugly to her. *Pig-eyes*, she thought. She applied more eye shadow, over what was already there. She returned to her bedroom and dressed.

Downstairs, she found her mother in the hall, putting on her coat. It had gotten cooler and Dora took a windbreaker from the closet. Norma glanced at her with a frown. Turning away, Norma walked out to the garage with Dora trailing behind her. They drove to the high school and Dora was dropped in the school parking lot. She began walking toward the entrance to the school, but as soon as her mother's car was out of sight, she turned around and headed toward the road.

CHAPTER 6

9/14/71 – Tuesday

That morning at her school, Long Lots Junior High, Amy was walking to her French class when she was confronted in the hall by two boys blocking her way and forcing her to come to a stop. She was a head taller than both. One looked up at her and said "How's the weather up there?" He elbowed his friend, laughing. Amy could not think of a response. Blushing, she fled to an empty bathroom nearby. She looked in the mirror. Where others would see a slender pretty girl, Amy saw only a puffy face on a pudgy girl of no consequence. She wanted to go home and climb her tree again.

In the afternoon, in English class, Amy considered telling Miss Olsen that she needed more time because she wasn't finished with her essay, but she couldn't bring herself to make the request. So she reluctantly handed over her paper, distressed that it wasn't better. She expected to get a C on it. She was an honors student but that only made this pathetic paper that much worse. She smiled at her teacher, but she felt terrified inside. Miss Olsen tucked her paper in with the others on her desk and smiled back at her. Amy heard the bell for the end of the period and the end of the school day.

She walked out front to the waiting buses and boarded hers. She sat near a window and hoped no one would sit next to her, but it was crowded and a younger girl she didn't know sat alongside her, chatting excitedly with another girl seated across the aisle. Amy stared out the window until she reached her stop.

At last, Amy was back in her tree. She had come home to find her mother oddly alert and anxious to talk. But Amy immediately felt confined. She mustered her courage and told her mother "I need to go out," and ran past her. The last she heard was her mother saying "But Amy…"

Sitting comfortably at the intersection of two big forked branches in her oak, Amy looked in the direction of the smoke she had seen the day before. Only now it wasn't there. Something bothered her about it nonetheless and she decided to investigate. It was still quite light out as she scrambled down the tree and dropped to the ground below. She walked to the back edge of the Latour property and came to a small stone wall. It was more a tumble of rounded grey stones, no longer really much of a wall. She stepped over the rocks and passed through a small wooded area and then emerged into the light. She was in an open field. Summer was over and no more flowers bloomed. A flock of geese passed by overhead, squawking loudly. She started walking in the direction of the smoke from the day before.

She passed a small pond and stopped to look for turtles or frogs, but there were none this late in the season. She felt she knew they were there, hidden, buried in the mud, securing themselves for the colder weather to come. She strolled easily through the tall grass. There were woods on either side of the field. Here and there, she encountered prickly raspberry and blackberry bushes. She made her way carefully around these as she reached the far end of the field and entered the woods.

She was back among tall trees. There were still leaves on the maples and oaks; a few were beginning to change color. She loved it out here. Without thinking why, she felt this was where she belonged; this was her real home.

After a few more minutes, she emerged from the woods to what she knew to be another large open field. But it was not as she expected. There were men cutting brush and trees. She wondered how she could have failed to hear their chainsaws. A dirt road now cut through the field and led out to Clapboard Hill Road. A bulldozer was clearing the land of rocks and vegetation. Smoke burst from its smokestack as it pushed mounds of muddy soil into large piles. She thought that maybe its exhaust was the smoke she'd seen the day before. She remembered a stream had run through this section of meadow, but she couldn't pick it out among the muddy mess before her. She understood what was happening. Houses were to be built here. She turned and walked slowly home.

DEVELOPMENT

It was dark by the time Amy arrived back at her house. She let herself in quietly. Her mother was dozing on the couch. Careful not to wake her, Amy quietly climbed the stairs to her room and shut her door.

CHAPTER 7

9/19/70 – Saturday

One year earlier, Dora, about three months shy of her 16th birthday, and her friend Katie, went excitedly to Pete's Tavern, a bar behind the Westport Country Playhouse. They were celebrating the fact that Katie had just gotten her license. They entered the big bustling Tavern room, not expecting to be served drinks. It was enough merely to be there surrounded by loud chatter and laughter over a background of Rolling Stones music. They wore tie-dyed tee shirts in rainbow colors and blue jeans, thinking they looked like sisters, though Dora was taller with dark hair, while the shorter, bustier Katie had dusky blond hair, worn long and straight. Around their necks were beaded necklaces they had bought for the occasion.

They were excited and soon separated. Dora gathered her courage and walked to the end of the bar where a handsome man with long auburn hair was busily serving drinks. She smiled and caught his eye. He smiled back and resumed working. She watched his arms, shirtsleeves rolled up, as he gathered the dirty glasses, coasters and tips. Nobody else at the bar seemed to notice her. She could see Katie off in a corner talking animatedly to two young men, one a black guy with an afro, the other, an earnest looking boy with a ponytail and glasses, holding a beer.

Dora turned her attention back to the bartender, who at that moment, seemed to be free. He was at least 25, she thought. She smiled again and this time he walked toward her.

"A little young to be here, aren't you?" he observed.

"Oh, I'm not drinking," she said quickly.

"It's okay. Lemme get you something. Wanna ginger ale?"

"Okay, sure."

He poured it and handed it to her. "On the house. Name's Randy," he added. "Randy Carson."

"I'm Dora Latour. It's my first time here." She smiled, feeling shy in his presence. "Thanks. I'm Dora" she repeated.

"Hang on. Gotta take care of some customers."

"Okay."

A few minutes later he was back. "Jerry's due in soon. Then I'll have a little more help. This place, they don't hire enough staff. Cheapskates." Someone at the other end of the bar called for him and he was off again.

Dora looked around, sipping her ginger ale. It was fun here. People were crowded together in groups, talking, drinking and laughing. She liked it, even if she felt a little bit alone. She looked across the room. Katie was still talking with the two boys. *Probably doesn't even remember I'm here*, she thought, but she didn't really mind. She liked sitting at the bar, drinking her drink and maybe talking some more with Randy. She watched him. He seemed friendly and she liked the way his long hair fell across his face when he leaned over the sink.

Just then, Jerry, the other bartender arrived. He was out of breath. "Sorry man," she heard him say to Randy, who merely nodded and kept working.

At another lull in the action, Randy came back to her. "So what are you doing here, Dora?"

Surprised he remembered her name, she giggled and said "My friend Katie and I thought it'd be fun to come here. I've never been here, but like we'd heard about it. It's really cool."

"Stick around. I'll show you some stuff later."

"Okay." She wondered what he would show her…maybe backstage at the Playhouse, she speculated. She'd like that.

He again moved down the bar, picking up glasses, bottles and napkins. She watched as he handed two beers over a couple seated at the bar, to a man standing behind them. At the same time, another man bent in and asked for a Heineken. Randy pulled one out of a cooler and deftly popped it open, handing it to the guy and taking the money, seemingly all in one motion. Dora was entranced. She couldn't take her eyes off him.

****

Their plan had been to stay the night at Katie's house. Her parents were away. It was not yet ten o'clock. Dora thought she could stay out awhile. Katie didn't seem in any rush to go. Dora felt content sitting there and she enjoyed watching Randy.

He came back to her again and said "Man, it's busy tonight. But I'll take a break in a little while and show you around."

"Yeah," she said, "okay."

She watched him whisper something to Jerry, who glanced slyly at her and nodded. Randy worked a little longer and then returned to her. "C'mon" he said.

"Where we going?" she asked.

"Through here." He had walked around the bar and taken her hand as he led her through a door which opened on to the parking lot. It had gotten colder and he drew her quickly around the back of the building to another door. "In here," he said.

She felt a small cautionary premonition. "What's in there?" she asked.

"Oh, a lot of offices and stuff," he answered

vaguely. They entered a long hallway, poorly lit, and very quiet.

He stopped at the first door on the left and turned the knob. It was not locked. "No one will bother us in here," he said. He walked in and turned to her. She was lingering in the doorway. "Don't worry. It's all right. We won't do anything you don't want to do," he promised.

Not at all sure what that actually meant, Dora found herself entering.

He stared at her. "You're beautiful, you know," he said, once again taking her hand.

She giggled and said "Oh, I don't think so," but she was pleased, though that inner voice persisted, scaring her a little. "I should go," she said, but she made no move to leave. Not yet.

Randy put his hands on both her shoulders, looked down at her and repeated "so beautiful." With that, he reached behind her and shut the door. He began kissing her. It was sudden. Dora thought *I should have known this was coming.* She allowed herself to be kissed. She felt herself being drawn in. She was nervous and a little frightened. At the same time, it felt exciting. And she liked Randy or thought she did. She kissed him back. He whispered "I love you" and she shivered. He kissed her neck, repeating that he loved her. Dora had had some experience with boys. She wasn't new to sex, but she was still a virgin. Randy stroked her back and pulled her to him. She felt his hand slide under her tee shirt. She shivered again as he slid his right hand up her back and deftly unhooked her bra. Holding her with his left hand, he squeezed her breasts and nipples with his right.

Frightened and excited, Dora felt her body respond. "We should go," she said breathily.

"Not yet," he replied. "We're fine. I love you. Mmmm, I love you."

Randy's hands dropped to the front of her jeans. She felt the button open and the zipper slide down. Both his hands were on her exposed hips now.

"Nooo," she said, but still she didn't try to leave.

"Feel how turned on I am, how much I want you," he said, taking her left hand and pressing the back of it to the front of his pants. She let it stay there, intrigued, despite her reservations. He took that as encouragement and said "Oh yeah."

He pulled her closer to him. Her hand fell to her side as she felt his body press against hers. He leaned her back. They were in a store room. There were shelves on either side of her. She felt the door behind her. A harsh light came from the bare bulb above them. With both hands, he slid her jeans to the floor. Now, in her panties, and tee shirt, her bra loose under it, this felt like a moment of decision to her. She wondered if he would let her dress and leave if she wanted to. She thought he would. She made an effort to bend forward and pull her jeans back up. He caught her and said, "Oh no baby, stay here with me. Let me love you."

Dora's life seemed to hang in the balance. For reasons she barely understood, she let go of her pants, stood back up and whispered "Okay." He smiled at her and hooked his fingers in the hem of her panties, sliding them down her legs. He bent over and lifted one of her feet so her panties lay gathered around her other shoe. Rising, he looked into her eyes again.

"So beautiful," he repeated. Almost before she knew it, he had unzipped his own pants and dropped them along with his underwear down to the floor. He put his foot between hers, spreading her legs. At the same time, his finger found her wet pussy. In the next moment, he had his penis poised to enter her. Holding her hips and separating her legs further, he suddenly entered her. He groaned.

She said "No," feeling the pain. He was already thrusting urgently. Within seconds, it was over.

Afterward, Dora could barely move. She looked down at herself and then up at Randy. "I'm bleeding…a little," she said.

"Oh man. Wow. You were a virgin, huh?"

Dora looked away. "Yes," she said quietly.

Not knowing what to say, he looked at her, naked below the waist, still standing in the same spot. Finally, he said "we should get dressed, get back."

Dora remained paralyzed for a moment and then bent over and pulled up her panties and jeans. She reached behind her back and rehooked her bra. She found she couldn't look at Randy; she didn't want to. He was fully dressed, waiting for her. "We should get back," he repeated. He opened the door and Dora followed him out.

Walking behind him, she returned to the tavern. As they entered, he turned, leaned in close to her and whispered "That was great." He gave her a smile and returned to working behind the bar.

The crowd was even denser and noisier than before. She looked around for Katie. She wanted to talk with her, tell her what had happened. But Katie was nowhere to be seen. She suddenly felt terribly anxious. She realized she couldn't stay any longer in the tavern. It was too crowded, too noisy. She couldn't think clearly. *Where was Katie?* She tried to walk through the room, looking for her friend. It was so congested; people jostled her from all directions. She could not see over them. Finally she gave up and left the bar, saying nothing to Randy. He seemed busy anyway. Outside in the parking lot, cars were coming and going. There was no sign of Katie or of her car. Looking up at the night sky, Dora stood there a moment. The moon was a blur. She had tears in her eyes. Finally, she began the long walk home.

The next day had been a Sunday. Dora awoke early. She could not stop thinking about the night before, about Randy. Over and over, she berated herself. *I let it happen. I let him do it.* She caught herself and remembered *he loved me. That's what he said.* She considered that for a moment. *Maybe he had, for a few seconds anyway. What did it matter?* He did not love her now. She was pretty sure of that.

She wanted to speak to someone, but who? She certainly was not going to discuss it with either of her parents. She was sure they would be disappointed or angry. She didn't want that. It was bad enough feeling her own disappointment. She felt a sense of shame, that it was her fault. She felt dirty. She wanted to bury those feelings, wanted them gone, out of her mind forever. But they persisted. Well, she could try to talk to Katie. Katie might understand. Maybe something similar had happened to her. Dora didn't know, but Katie was more experienced. It was possible.

She dialed Katie's number. A sleepy Katie answered. "H'lo"

"Where were you last night?" Dora felt her anger surface.

"I looked for you when I got back," Katie answered slowly, waking up, "but nobody had seen you. I went to Compo Beach for an hour with Bill, that guy I was talking to."

"Well, I looked for you. I couldn't find your car in the parking lot or anywhere. I had to walk home," she added sadly.

"I looked for you before I left," said Katie, a

little irritated at Dora. "I couldn't find you. Nobody knew where you were."

"I was...it's all right. Don't worry about it."

"What happened to you?"

"Nothing. I just left early."

"Are you okay?"

"Yeah, I'm fine. I just left early."

"Well, bummer that you walked home. Sorry."

"It's okay. Really."

"All right... See you later?"

"Yeah. Bye."

Dora hung up, feeling more dejected and lonely than before. Her mind was a jumble of thoughts. It was hard to sit still, hard to sort out. Suddenly a new thought occurred to her. She might be pregnant. She might be pregnant now. The thought panicked her. She didn't know what to do. *Does it happen the first time? Can it happen then? Of course it can,* she thought. *Oh God, please don't let me be pregnant. Please...*

****

Over the following weeks, Dora kept it all secret. She could barely sleep. She went through the motions, going to class, seeing Katie, Dick, Jared. But she had changed. To her friends, she seemed quieter, but at times, irritable and opinionated. To her, it felt like a performance. It was all she could do to get herself to school. Feeling ashamed, she avoided her family as much as possible. She began wearing dark clothes, looking for anything in her closet that was black. And all the time, she worried about whether she'd get her period. She was terrified. He hadn't used anything. She was sure of that. Her period wasn't due yet, but still she watched anxiously for it. Alone, scared and guilty, she waited.

Katie wondered about her friend. She'd already forgotten about the night at Pete's Tavern, just one adventure in a life full of adventures for her. She did notice Dora seemed different. But Dora didn't explain and Katie didn't ask.

Finally, three weeks later, Dora got her period. Her relief was enormous. She didn't have to think any more about having a baby or getting an abortion... awful prospects. Despite her relief, she still felt a dark sense of guilt and confusion. What was she? Why had she given herself to Randy? What kind of girl does that? She could say he raped her. But that really wasn't true. She was as guilty as he, she thought. She wanted to hide, disguise who she was. She had no desire to see him. She doubted he'd want to see her anyway. She thought of herself as impure, inferior and condemned.

That had been a year ago. The memory faded, but the feelings never really left.

CHAPTER 8

9/14/71 – Tuesday

Norma blinked awake in a quiet house. She had fallen asleep on the couch and sometime during the night had climbed the stairs to her bedroom. Now it was after 9 am. She had slept poorly. The bed sheets were knotted and twisted around her. She untangled herself. Hank was gone. The air felt damp and chilly. It seemed like a wet wind had come straight off the Long Island Sound and wound its way into her house, dampening her sheets and her clothes. It was only mid-September, but Norma felt cold. *Why hasn't Hank turned on the furnace yet?*

She got out of bed and found her robe and put on her slippers. Standing by her dresser, she stared down at her little collection of glass animals. She picked up a yellow spotted giraffe. No more than three inches high, its little face seemed to stare at her curiously. She put it back down carefully, her hand shaking slightly. She did not want to break him or his delicate companions.

She felt she needed a drink, to warm herself up. Her whole family was scattered, she thought. She felt it was her duty to somehow hold them all together, but it seemed like an impossible task. Dora went one way,

Hank another. Amy withdrew from her. It was as though everyone went in opposite directions, all of them away from her. *None of them think about me. They're selfish. They just think about themselves. Hank should pay more attention to me. What about my needs? I'm cold. Where is he to turn on the heat? Is that so difficult? What about me? I need warmth.*

She walked shivering down the stairs and through the big empty house. Entering the kitchen, she headed for the cabinet containing the vodka. *Maybe a small glass with my orange juice for breakfast...just one, to warm me up...but first I have to clean up.* Last night's dishes were in the sink. An empty glass with milk residue sat on the counter. She groaned and started to collect the dishes. She rinsed out the dirty glass and added it to the contents of the sink. She looked around for the dish detergent. The bottle was kept under the sink. She bent down and thought *I can't do this now*.

Instead she poured her drink and, carrying it with her, she hauled herself shakily back up the stairs to her bedroom to get dressed. If she could get warm enough, she would feel better, she hoped. She glanced at the mirror over her dresser. Her hair was a mess. She should shower and wash it, but she felt too cold to get wet. She gulped her drink and went to the bathroom where she found a brush and tried to tame her unruly hair. At 37, there was no grey. She was still good looking, she believed. She washed her face and applied some makeup. *There, that's better*. She returned to the bedroom, put on yesterday's stretch pants, a bra and a tee shirt, over which she pulled a heavy brown woolen sweater. She thought for a moment about heels, but instead opted for a pair of tan flats.

Norma went back downstairs. She finished her drink and put the glass on the kitchen counter, staring down at the sink. The house felt hateful, as if it did not want her there, and she did not want to be in it. She quickly threw on a blue windbreaker she found in the closet, grabbed her purse and headed out through the kitchen to the garage. Her green Volvo station wagon was not there. She felt confused and then realized Dora must have taken it as she sometimes did lately, without asking. *She probably drove herself to school,* Norma concluded. *Selfish. Did it even occur to her that I might need it?*

Norma suddenly felt a powerful need for another drink and simultaneously realized she had nowhere she wanted to go anyway. She turned around, walked back inside and refilled the empty glass that still sat on the counter. She drank the vodka eagerly and felt better, less shaky. She decided to tackle the dishes.

She was standing at the sink when she heard a car pull into the driveway and then into the garage. She heard the kitchen door open quietly and there was Dora. She looked disheveled. Norma stared at her older daughter. *She must have been out all night.. And this is a school day. She should be in school. Now I'm going to have to take her.*

"You look like you slept in those clothes."

"I was at Katie's."

Norma felt angry and put-upon. *She took my car. She didn't ask. She should be in school. I'll have to drive her.*

"Jesus Christ. I'll drive you," she said. Dora seemed indifferent and agreed to go after she changed her clothes. She handed Norma the car keys.

Norma grumpily took Dora to school, dropping her in the parking lot. She turned and drove out of the lot, down the exit road and stopped where it intersected North Avenue. She felt shaky again. The vodka she always carried with her seemed to be calling out to her. Holding the steering wheel with one hand, she fished in her purse and extracted the small plastic bottle containing her emergency supply. She placed it between her legs and untwisted the cap. She quickly brought it to her mouth and poured the warm liquid down her throat. She instantly felt calmer, as though she had been restored to normal.

It was almost eleven o'clock. She realized she was hungry and decided she'd go to Lily's Diner. At this late morning hour, the restaurant probably would not be busy, she thought. Commuters, local business people, students, all would have come and gone by now.

Set in the middle of a small shopping center on the Post Road, Lily's consisted of a long counter with a dozen red swivel stools arrayed before it. A dozen tables filled in the remaining area of the restaurant. Half of these lined the front windows. The other tables flanked the left and right sides of the counter. Norma walked in and sat at the counter, at the left end, near the cash register. Without being asked, Lily served her coffee. The diner was quiet. Other than a waitress sitting idly smoking at the other end of the counter, only a cook in the back and Lily were working. There were no other customers.

If not exactly her friend, Lily was always friendly and happy to discuss whatever Norma brought up. Lilis "Lily" Apostolos had wavy white-blonde hair, tied up in a ponytail. She wore a white, stained apron around her compact figure. In her late 40s, she had the energy of someone half her age. She was Greek by birth and still retained the accent. Her bright blue eyes looked directly at Norma. She was interested in everyone.

Norma was talking about her girls. "Dora. I don't even know her anymore. She barely talks to me. Does whatever she wants… doesn't even come home half the time."

"Teenagers," said Lily.

"I guess. Maybe… Amy's a different story. She's so good. Just the opposite. Never gets in trouble. Just works on her schoolwork or walks around the woods. She's weird. Never has friends over. She's 14 now. You'd think…" Norma trailed off.

"I haven't seen Amy in a while. Is she as pretty as ever?"

"Well, she's a beanpole these days, but yes, she has that pretty face."

"She could be a model," observed Lily.

That moment the door to the diner opened as a man in a light blue jacket walked in. Norma felt a breeze on her back. "Sit anywhere," said Lily cheerily as she picked up a menu and walked around the counter toward him. He took off his jacket and sat down at a window table. Lily reached him and handed him the menu. "Coffee?" she asked.

"Yeah, please."

Norma was lost in thought. Lily's comment intrigued her. The idea of Amy being a fashion model had never occurred to Norma. She took a sip of her coffee and imagined Amy on the cover of Vogue. *That would be incredible*, she thought. *Could it happen? How did girls really become those models? Some did it. It was possible. When I was a teenager, I could have been one. I was pretty enough. And not as skinny as Amy. I could have been on the cover of Vogue or Cosmo. But nobody helped me. Nobody thought about me that way or told me what to do. I might not have listened anyway. I wanted to be an actress. I didn't think of modeling. But Amy...*

Lily called in the man's order for scrambled eggs, hash browns and crisp bacon. She poured a small orange juice and delivered that to his table. She walked back to face Norma again, across the counter.

"You really think Amy could be a model, like a cover girl?"

"Sure," said Lily. "She's pretty enough and they want them skinny nowadays. How tall is she, do you think?"

"Oh I don't know. She's almost as tall as me. Probably 5' 7" or so.

"That's good And she's probably still growing. They want 'em tall and skinny." Lily herself barely reached five feet.

"Well, that's Amy all right. But she's such a perfectionist, such a goody-goody. I don't know. Maybe that's good for a model. They have to stand still for a long time."

"Yeah, I'll bet she'd be good at it."

"I don't know," said Norma, finishing her coffee and fishing a dollar out of her purse. "Maybe I'll talk to her. Anyway, I gotta go." She handed the dollar to Lily. Her hand shook.

"Okay. See you later."

Driving home, Norma continued to think about a modeling career for Amy. She could not let go of the idea. It took hold of her and she wondered what the next steps should be. She resolved to speak with Amy.

CHAPTER 9

With her mother out of sight, Dora walked out of the school parking lot and headed in the direction of town. It would be a long walk and she wasn't sure she'd find anyone when she got there. So she changed her mind and decided instead to walk to Katie's house. It was equally far, but at least she could sit in the living room. And maybe Katie would be around. Even if Katie weren't home, Dora knew how to get in the house, via the back.

Impulsively, she turned and stuck out her thumb. She would hitch to Katie's. Within minutes, a man in an old green Ford Fairlane stopped and opened the passenger door. Dora looked at the car, with its big rusted fins and worn fabric on the front seat. It smelled musty. She looked at the man. He seemed impatient, patting the seat next to him. She got in and closed the door. "Where to?" he asked.

"The other side of the Post Road, near Compo Beach."

"Okay, I'm going that way." He looked her over and resumed driving.

Dora studied the man. He was older, maybe 50, she thought. He wore a black woolen cap and a heavy brown coat, which seemed odd to her, given the weather. It wasn't *that* cold. She noticed a dark stain on his right sleeve. One hand sat in his lap. Suddenly that hand reached for her. He placed it on her chest and quickly slid it down into her crotch. Dora recoiled in terror. She pushed herself back against the car door, swatting at his hand. They came to a stop sign. "I'm getting out here," she shouted, flinging open the door and leaping out of the car. She slammed the door and he drove away.

Breathing heavily, she stood at the side of the road. *What a jerk. God. Gross!* She wasn't harmed, but she was shaken. Slowly, she began again walking toward Katie's.

Nearly an hour later, she arrived at Katie's house. It seemed deserted. She went around back. The sliding door to the kitchen was not locked and she let herself in. It was quiet. She looked in the refrigerator and found orange juice. She poured herself a glass and sat at the table. *I probably should have stayed in school,* she thought.

The quiet was broken by a noise from the living room. Katie appeared, bleary-eyed. "What are you doing here?" she asked.

"I let myself in," Dora said gesturing toward the sliding door. "I didn't want to stay at school, so I came here."

"Me neither." said Katie. "School's a drag."

"Anybody else here?" Dora was thinking about Hibbard.

"Nah, just me. Ya wanna get high?" Katie asked, after a moment. "I got an ounce from Jared last night."

"Sure, okay."

Katie got up from the table and left the room. A few minutes later she returned with a plastic bag of pot and a small glass water pipe. She walked to the sink, carefully cleaned the pipe and filled it with fresh water. She put a pinch of marijuana in the bowl and held a match over it. As it caught, she breathed the smoke in deeply, holding it in her lungs. She passed the pipe to Dora who did the same.

After exhaling, Dora said "I had a weird thing happen a little while ago. I was hitching here from school and some creep in an old car picked me up and tried to grab me. I was scared shitless. I jumped out as soon as he got to a stop sign. It was gross."

"What'd he look like?" asked Katie, excitedly.

"Oh, he was just an old guy, with dirty clothes, in a dirty car. I should never have gotten in, but I like needed a ride. I ended up walking here, just about all the way from school."

"I wonder if he was from around here... what he was doing there. Cruising for girls, do you think?"

"I don't know. Who cares? He was just some creep. I don't think I'll hitch anymore."

"Yeah, it can be dangerous, I guess."

They continued smoking. It was good pot and they were both feeling pretty high.

"Got anything to eat?"

"I don't think so. Well, let's see." Katie got up and looked in the refrigerator. The juice was there as well as milk and some American cheese, but not much else. Katie opened a cabinet and pulled out a box of Rice Krispies. "How 'bout this?" she asked.

"Oh yeah!" Rice Krispies looked great to Dora.

Katie found two bowls and brought them to the table along with the cereal and the bottle of milk. She found a bowl of sugar and two spoons. They each made a big bowl of cereal with milk and a considerable amount of sugar. Dora thought it tasted delicious.

"I guess you never saw Jared again, after I left?" Dora asked after a moment.

"Nah, I haven't seen him since he was here last night."

"I went to sleep and he went somewhere, tripping. He didn't have a car. He took one of those blotter acid things."

"I wonder where he went... I mean... what

happened to him?"

"Well, I don't know..." Dora found herself feeling a little concerned.

"Wanna look for him?" Katie asked.

"Nah. I guess maybe he's home. I'll try him there."

Dora got up and picked up the wall phone in the kitchen. She knew the number by heart.

"Hello." It was Jared's mother, Betty Appleton.

"This is Dora. Is Jared there?"

"No. He isn't. He wasn't here all night. Did you see him last night? I'm worried."

"Yeah, we were together, but I fell asleep at Katie's. He left but I don't know where he went." Dora saw no reason to mention that Jared was tripping.

"Well his father and I are going to go look for him. We called the school and they said he wasn't there. You said you were at Katie's. That's on Minute Man, right?"

"Yeah, but he isn't here. I'm at Katie's now. Maybe see if he's at the beach. Compo. We were there earlier. He likes it there."

Jared Appleton was the only child of Betty and Vince Appleton and they doted on him. Although he was now almost 18, they were overly protective. Jared was a good student and they had hoped he would go to an Ivy League school. He was supposed to apply to several, though lately he was seeming a lot less focused. "All right, we'll check out the beach. If you see him, please call me. Keep trying if I'm not here."

"Okay," said Dora, hanging up. "Man, my parents hardly notice if I don't come home. His, you'd think it was a national emergency."

"You wanna go down to the beach? We can look for him." suggested Katie. They had both finished their cereal.

"Okay. Let me have another hit first."

Katie fired up the water pipe again and they both had another hit. Stoned and happy, they headed out the front door.

As they made the short walk to Compo Beach, Katie again speculated about the hitchhiking incident. "I wonder what that creep would have done if you hadn't gotten out of the car?"

"Jesus, forget it! Who cares? I'm just glad nothing more happened."

"Well, I just wondered."

When they arrived at the Beach, Dora spotted the back of Jared's head. He was sitting on a bench, facing the water. They walked up to him.

He didn't seem surprised to see them. "What a great night," he said smiling. "I watched the sun come up. It was like the beginning of the world."

"Um, your parents are worried about you," said Dora.

"Oh, figures. Of course." Jared stared out at the waves, kicking the sand at his feet.

"I think they're coming here, looking for you."

"Well, here I am." He laughed.

They sat down on either side of him. It was a bright, clear morning, if a bit chilly. Jared didn't seem at all cold, wearing only jeans and a tee shirt. Dora shivered slightly and wondered if acid warmed you from the inside, like whiskey. They heard a car horn honk behind them and all three turned to see Jared's parents drive up. They watched as Vince and Betty got out. Betty was overweight, but she ran toward them, leaving her slim husband behind.

"There you are," she shouted. "We were worried sick about you."

"Hi mom," Jared said. "I'm fine. Just hanging out."

Jared's father arrived, looking annoyed.

"Well come home," Betty said. "You're supposed to be in school. You want some breakfast first?"

The girls looked at Jared.

"Yeah, okay." he said. He got up and joined his parents.

"Can we give you girls a lift? Aren't you supposed to be in school too?" Jared's father asked them.

"We're taking the day off," said Katie. "But we'll take a ride to town if you're going that way."

"Alright. C'mon," said Vince. They all climbed in his car, Betty in front, the kids in back.

"What are you doing out all night anyway?" Betty asked her son, as they started moving.

"Nothing. I just wanted to watch the sunrise. That's all. It was beautiful."

"I'll bet," his father said. "You have school. You're trying to get into college, remember."

"I'm not worried. It's all cool."

"Whatever that means," said his father. "You have SATs, applications. You have a lot to do. You haven't graduated yet."

"I don't think senior year matters much," said Jared.

"You better believe it does," said his father.

They arrived at the center of town. "We'll get off here," said Katie, not wanting to listen to any more.

"Okay."

Katie and Dora got out and watched as the Appletons drove away. "I wouldn't want to be Jared," said Katie. "His parents are really on him.'

"Well, he's the light of her life, you know. Her only child... Her fair-haired boy," Dora added.

An hour later, they were no longer high. Dora wanted to go home. She decided to catch the bus before it got any later. She waved goodbye to Katie and headed to the bus stop.

CHAPTER 10

When they met, Norma was 19 and Hank was two years older. He was in his junior year at Stanford, majoring in Finance and playing second string wide receiver on the football team. He was a good player, though not an NFL prospect like some of his teammates. Nonetheless, football had earned him a partial scholarship and he was glad for it.

After high school, Norma had moved from Naperville, Illinois to Los Angeles, hoping to become an actress. She expected instant stardom. In Naperville, she had been special. She had been lauded in high school productions. She was considered the most beautiful girl in her class and was elected Homecoming Queen. She was a star there, but the movie industry did not see her that way. Time after time, she read for parts and was not called back. After a year of rejections, she had moved to San Francisco where she had heard there might be theater work. Again, no acting jobs materialized. Instead, she was waitressing. She still believed fame was right around the corner, at the next audition.

She met Hank in a San Francisco coffee house. Norma and her roommate Carol had gone to hear a folk singer. She immediately noticed Hank when he walked in with two friends. Tall, dark-haired and good-looking, she watched him as he surveyed the room. Hank and his friends took a table near Norma and Carol and, when the singer took a break, they engaged the girls in conversation. When the singing resumed, Hank had moved a little closer so he could talk with Norma. She could barely hear him in the smoky club, but when the singer finally left the stage, he had asked her for her phone number, and as she knew he would, he called her two days later. Theirs quickly became a feverish romance. They danced, drank beer and fell into bed together.

Hank was proud to be seen with a beautiful girl on his arm. They made a striking couple. Norma spent what money she had on jewelry and clothes and knew she looked glamorous. She had always had her pick of the best looking boys in high school. She turned heads and she was used to it. Walking across the campus, hand in hand, Hank swelled with pride. Throughout that summer and into his senior year, their life was a whirlwind of parties, drinking and sex.

But that Fall, two nearly simultaneous events abruptly changed their lives. Hank was injured on the field and Norma discovered she was pregnant. Somehow she had managed to ignore her missing periods and other symptoms for months, until finally she could deny it no longer. In 1954, pregnancy was not a small problem. Abortions were illegal and very dangerous. And Hank and Norma were both Catholic. Actually they were lapsed Catholics. Hank never went to church and Norma only attended Mass on Christmas and occasionally, Easter. But they never really considered abortion an option. They could have given the child up for adoption, but Hank disliked that idea. And neither thought to share the problem with their distant parents.

Saturday, a few weeks after he learned of Norma's pregnancy, Hank was playing in the big game against the University of Southern California. They were winning and Hank was called in off the bench late in the second half. He caught a pass from Bobby Garrett over the middle in full stride. Unfortunately, he never saw the outside linebacker who hit him like a freight train from the opposite direction. All-American Luther "The Hunter" Hunt had driven his body into Hank's shoulder dislocating it instantly. The ball had shot up in the air landing harmlessly, while Hank crashed to the ground, all his weight landing on the opposite shoulder. An instant later, Hunt had landed on top of him, driving him further into the hard turf. Hank never played again and neither shoulder was ever quite the same. For the rest of his life, Hank would walk with a peculiar lopsided gait. His right arm swung widely and actively away from his body while his left hung close to his side, barely moving.

As he recovered, Hank realized he would not miss football very much and he found himself thinking about Norma and his future. Marriage seemed the best solution. Although it all happened very fast, Hank was happy about the prospect of marrying her right away. It seemed like the right thing to do, the honorable thing, and a promising next step in his life. Norma, then five months pregnant, though less sure, accepted his proposal. She could not think of a better alternative. They were married October 8th by a Justice of the Peace in Palo Alto. Only Carol and two of Hank's friends attended the event. They did not tell their parents.

They moved to a tiny apartment across the bay in Hayward. Hank commuted to school for the balance of his senior year. Two and one-half months after their marriage, Dora was born. She was several weeks premature. Norma's plans for an acting career were stymied. Not that she was making progress in that area, but her life had shifted. She found herself alone with a new baby, no friends nearby, and no chance to go out, let alone audition. She felt her hopes draining away and she looked at Dora with a mixture of love and resentment.

Immediately upon graduation, Hank began training as a mortgage broker in a small, growing mortgage company. They had little money, but with his new family, Hank felt he was on his way.

Norma struggled. She was 20 years old. Raising a child was not what she was prepared for. Her handsome husband was often late coming home. She felt alone and frustrated. If she drank a glass of wine occasionally, who could blame her? When Hank did come home, enthused about his work, Norma only pretended to be interested. She had nothing to contribute and felt her life had reached a dead end. As the days went by, she grew further apart from Hank. Fueled by alcohol, they could still have sex together, but they rarely talked. She no longer shared her thoughts and aspirations with him. When Amy arrived a little more than two years after Dora, the most exciting event for Norma was the acquisition of a new RCA television. Norma discovered she could lose herself for hours watching it. Competing with the new TV, Amy received even less attention than Dora had. As they grew older, Norma would sometimes take the girls to the movies where she could immerse herself in the fantasy of film. But more often, she drank and gave little thought to her children.

The years accumulated. The family moved around the country as Hank obtained what he thought would be better positions. He was impatient and perhaps could have given some of these jobs more time, but instead, he sought new opportunities. He loved watching his daughters grow but Norma had faded to a shadow in his life. She would prepare meals, do some desultory cleaning and the minimum necessary to raise Dora and Amy. She usually waited until the afternoon for her first drink. She felt life had betrayed her. She had been promised so much, deserved it, she thought, and instead, she seemed to have become invisible.

After eight years of marriage, Norma felt she could not tolerate the emptiness, the sense of failure and frustration, any longer. A few days shy of her 28th birthday, she made a half-hearted suicide attempt. She swallowed a handful of sleeping pills and the better part of a quart of vodka. She climbed into bed, hoping she would not wake up. An hour later, her older daughter came home from school and tried to wake her. Failing to do so, Dora called her father who rushed home from his office. He found Norma breathing shallowly. He could not rouse her. He dragged her into the bathroom and splashed cold water on her face, which woke her up. She claimed she had only wanted to rest. She was not trying to kill herself. Hank had let it go, hoping this was a one-time occurrence. Little Amy had watched it all from the corner of the bathroom. None of them ever spoke of it again.

At last, in an effort to end their nomadic lifestyle, they had settled in Westport, Connecticut. An affluent upscale town, that some celebrities called home, Hank wanted to belong there. Also he hoped that a good town with good schools and an active artistic community might be what Norma needed to start to care about life again. Although it was a lovely growing town, it made little difference to Norma. She no longer took any interest in where they lived. Her drinking had become the most important thing in her life. A foggy cloud seemed to surround her and it was only rarely penetrated by the people around her. She wanted everything to appear normal, but she went through much of her days in an alcoholic haze, sporadically tackling the chores of shopping, cooking and cleaning, and sometimes disregarding these altogether. She vaguely wondered about her family, but felt disconnected from them and angry. They lived their own lives apart from her. It seemed to her that her existence was irrelevant to them.

CHAPTER 11

9/15/71 – Wednesday

And then one day, it all changed. For the first time in many years, Norma felt the stirrings of hope. Maybe she could help her younger daughter become a famous cover girl. It was exciting. She thought she would stop drinking, clean herself up and manage Amy's career. Amy had no idea that her mother was thinking this way, so it came as a complete shock one morning when Norma turned to her younger daughter and said "What would you think about being a model?"

Amy, Norma and Dora were seated at the kitchen table. It was one of those rare days when Norma awoke early and prepared breakfast. They each had a plate of scrambled eggs and toast before them. Amy put down her fork and looked at her mother. "What?"

"You could be a model. You could be a cover girl. Wouldn't that be wonderful?"

Dora looked at her mother and rolled her eyes.

Amy seemed dazed. *She doesn't get it*, thought Norma. "I've been talking to people. They say you have what it takes. You could be on the cover of Vogue."

"I don't want to be on the cover of anything."

"What? Of course you do. Who wouldn't want to be famous… and beautiful."

"Well, I'm not beautiful," said Amy.

"Oh Christ," Dora said, pushing away from the table. "I gotta get going." She got up and walked upstairs to her room. Amy watched her go.

"Yes, you are. Or you could be. We just have to work at it."

"I don't think so. I mean I have school and everything."

"Well, we'll see. We'll talk more about it."

"I have to go out to the bus stop."

"Okay. We'll talk more about it."

Amy picked at her eggs a moment longer. Then she got up. "I'll see you later," she said walking out. She went to the front hall and put on her coat. *I don't want to be a model. I couldn't be a model.* She went out the door and walked quickly to the bus stop.

A few minutes later, Dora joined her. They stood side by side, waiting for their respective buses. They didn't say anything, both lost in their own thoughts. Dora's bus came first. Boarding it, she turned to her younger sister and laughingly said "See you later, Twiggy."

A few more minutes passed and Amy's bus arrived. On her way to school, Amy sat by herself and stared out the window. *That was weird. I'm no model. That's for sure. Where did mom get that idea? She probably won't even remember it tomorrow.* Amy arrived at school and all thoughts of modeling were forgotten. She had to face more teasing, she knew. And she had English class with Miss Olsen. She'd get her Huckleberry Finn paper back. The thought made her tremble.

****

Dora had her own problems at school that day. In the hallway, she encountered Mr. Dinsdale, her Government teacher. "Hi Dora. Haven't seen you much recently," he said with a smile.

"Oh yeah. Mr. Dinsdale."

"Call me Windy."

"Uh, Windy… sorry. I was out sick. But I'm back now. I'll see you fifth period." She spotted Jared out of the corner of her eye. He was leaning against a locker watching them. She made a face for his benefit and he laughed. She turned to walk toward him.

"Just a sec." Windy said. "You wanna stay after class? I can catch you up." He was still smiling. He was staring at her. They were about the same height.

Dora knew she was behind in her classwork. But there was something a little uncomfortable about his offer of help, his eager stare. He was a new teacher, not much older than Dora. He had long pale blond hair and wore rimless glasses. He had on a tan corduroy sport jacket, a madras shirt, blue jeans and sneakers. *It's like he wants to be one of the kids*, she thought. "Well, maybe. Thanks." It was all she could think to say.

"Cool. See you later." He gave her another broad smile and walked off.

Jared pushed himself off the locker and came up to her. "What was that about?" he asked, raising his eyebrows.

"Oh he wants me to make up for the classes I missed. Wants me to stay after class. It was kinda weird."

"Probably wants to get in your pants."

"Gross. He's my teacher."

"Wouldn't be the first teacher to get it on with a student.'

"I know, but it's not gonna happen. He's not my type, anyway." She smiled shyly, thinking *you're more my type, Jared.*

"Where you going now?" he asked.

"Ugh. Gym. The worst."

"Yeah, I got French. I'd rather get high." He laughed.

"I know. But let's just do the school thing today."

"Yeah. All right. Catch you later."

They parted. Dora thought momentarily about Jared. His smile was infectious. She was daydreaming and suddenly realized that if she didn't hurry, she'd be late for gym. She disliked gym even more than most of her classes. Climbing ropes or playing volleyball held no appeal for her. She would much rather have been with her friends, particularly Jared. The thought warmed her. But she was in school today and she would make the best of it.

Dora survived gym and avoided further personal contact with Windy Dinsdale. After Government, her last class, she walked outside where she encountered Jared. She didn't think he had planned it, but there he was in front of her building, at the end of the school day. She happily joined him as they both left school. They watched the buses load up and pull out. It was an unusually warm day. Neither of them had a car, so they walked together. Jared took a joint from his shirt pocket and lit it. They headed down North Avenue, a busy road, with cars whizzing by. He smoked openly. He seemed to have no fear of getting caught. After two hits, he handed the joint to Dora. She inhaled it, filling her lungs, enjoying the day.

They had no particular plans. It was a bright September afternoon, full of possibilities. They finished their joint.

"Let's go to the beach,' Jared said, turning at the same time and sticking out his thumb. "Let's hitch."

"Oh man. I don't know. I don't really want to."

At that moment, a car stopped for them. A middle-aged woman was driving. She rolled down the window. "Where to?" she asked.

"Compo Beach," Jared answered, without further consulting Dora.

"Sure. Get in,"

Dora and Jared got in her car, both in the back seat.

"You kids go to Staples?" the woman asked. "My daughter Connie Raisford's a junior there. You know her?"

"No. We're seniors." Jared replied.

"Well, that's next year for her," the woman said brightly.

"You know, let's go to Katie's instead of the beach." Dora was thinking she would rather be indoors with Jared. She had no desire to walk out on the jetty again, if that was what Jared had in mind.

"Okay, sure," he said amiably.

"Don't turn at the statue. Just leave us up there, at Minute Man Hill." Dora told the driver, as she pointed to the foot of Katie's street, up ahead.

The woman pulled over and they got out. "You kids take care," she said.

"Yuh. Thanks." Jared said as he opened the door and they both climbed out.

The road to Katie's house wound its way up a steep hill. They walked up it together. Nobody was home and they let themselves in through the back door. They entered the kitchen. There were old food containers on the counter, an empty Coke can, and dishes, glasses and silverware scattered about. They hurried through the kitchen to an equally messy scene in the living room. A lampshade was askew; greasy paper bags and a pizza box lay on the floor. They stepped over these things and sat on the couch. Almost without thinking about it, they began making out. Dora was as eager as Jared, pulling at his clothes, his body. The pot gave their passion a dreamy quality. Dora wanted him, wanted to get lost in him, feel his strength. She wanted to be carried away.

"Do you have a rubber?" Dora asked, her voice husky.

"No, but I could pull out just before I come."

"Okay, just don't forget to do it."

Her panties were on the floor. She knelt between his legs and took his cock in her mouth, lavishing it. Suddenly he pushed her down on the rug. He slid down her, licking her between her legs and quickly bringing her to a climax. He climbed on top of her and clumsily shoved his penis in her. Breathing heavily he stroked in and out of her. She looked up at him. His eyes were closed. There was an awkward moment as he shifted his weight, but then, she felt her passion returning, her excitement. She pulled him closer. A few minutes later he slid out of her and spurted against her stomach.

"I wanted to stay inside you so badly," he grinned, catching his breath.

"Yeah, well, good thing you didn't," she whispered, her breath returning as he rolled off of her. She lay on her back, resting next to him. She turned and looked at him. His eyes were closed and he seemed peaceful. His head lay on a corner of the pizza box. She smiled, stood up and walked to the bathroom to clean herself up.

When she returned, he had moved to the couch. She joined him, nestling in the crook of his arm. They were content to be together, not talking. They felt settled in each other's company.

CHAPTER 12

Amy received an A minus on her paper. Miss Olsen had written at the top, in red ink "Good job. I was hoping to see a bit more of Huck's personality and how it intersected with the river theme." Amy wasn't sure exactly what that meant, but she felt she could have dug deeper and written a better paper. She would try harder next time. Cringing slightly, she placed the paper in her notebook and gathered up her books. School was over for the day.

She boarded the school bus, and staring out the window, as it pulled out of the parking lot, she again wondered *could I become a model?*

Everything was confusing to Amy, and frightening. She tried so hard. She knew she was growing up. Life would not stand still. She wished it would. Her changing body made her anxious. She had grown almost four inches this year alone, and she felt she was widening in unwanted directions, as her hips and breasts developed. Caught midway between being a tomboy and a young woman, she wished she could stop this fattening expansion. And just as troubling, her outside world was disappearing. Her precious ponds and fields and forests seemed to be under assault. It seemed to be all about men and destruction. She didn't like it. Even school held no real comfort for her anymore. Where she had once enjoyed her teachers and some friends, now she felt disappointment from the teachers and indifference from her peers. She felt alone. *Why doesn't anybody like me? Well, that's simple,* she thought. *I don't even like me, so why would anyone else? Maybe if I can look just right, act just right, be the best student... that's what I have to do or no one will ever like me.*

The future was especially frightening for Amy. It seemed to her there were only two paths she could take, only two types of person she could become. There was Dora's world, full of danger and drugs, and a boyfriend, it seemed. "Sympathy for the Devil" and "Gimme Shelter" were the theme songs of that world. It was a dangerous one, full of selfishness, violence and temptation. The war in Viet Nam still raged. Important people were assassinated. *Who wanted to step out into a world like that? I'd rather stay alone in the woods...*

On the other hand, she thought, *amazing things did happen. That guy walked on the moon. Neil Armstrong. And people were trying to make a difference, make our world better.* She had seen a photo in Time Magazine where a girl with flowers in her hair was placing a single flower in the barrel of a soldier's gun. It was true. Young people everywhere were trying to create peace and love, or so they said. The Beatles sang about love. The world could be better. It could be a world where people cared for each other and protected one another. Somehow though, she could not imagine herself in that world either. It seemed a distant, foreign place, not a part of her life in any way.

All she believed was that she must try extremely hard to control herself, to be the best that she could be, a perfect girl. She ate little and worked hard. Perfection was her goal. It was endlessly difficult and there were moments when she felt rage welling up inside her. She stifled that with rigid control. She was growing breasts and her periods had started, though they came only erratically. She seemed to grow taller and fatter by the day. She knew that she overate.

****

At home that day, Norma was captivated by the idea that Amy could become a model. *What did it take? How did it happen? Could a skinny flat-chested girl become a cover girl? Yes, it could happen,* she thought. Cosmopolitan, Vogue, Seventeen… all these magazines featured a slender cover girl, but… *Who knew about this world? Not Hank, certainly, but… there must be someone…someone who knew…maybe Lily?*

That night, Norma mentioned Amy's modeling to Hank, who dismissed the idea with a guffaw. "I mean it!" shouted Norma, with surprising intensity. "Who should I talk to about it?"

Realizing his wife was serious, Hank thought for a moment. The idea sounded preposterous but he would humor her. "Well, let me think." He paused. Then, after a moment, he said "I guess you could ask Maddie Hixon. She's pretty sharp. Maybe she knows somebody in New York." Maddie, he suddenly thought, seemed to be his answer to everything.

Norma recognized Maddie's name from the local paper, The Westport News. "She's the one in the real estate ads?" she asked. He nodded and gave the subject no further thought, though Maddie herself lingered in his mind for a moment. He unconsciously shook his head.

Norma, thinking he was being negative about Amy, asked "Why? Don't you think it's possible?"

Hank was confused for a moment, then realized she was asking about Amy's modeling chances. "Oh I don't know. I guess anything's possible. But she seems so shy. Models have to be pretty fearless, I would think. Amy's kind of the opposite. Plus, she's so skinny… Maybe she'll develop," he added, doubtfully.

"Well, skinny's not a problem. That's how they want 'em these days."

"I don't know. I really can't see it. Not with Amy."

"I don't care. I'll see what this Maddie person can tell me. I'm gonna look into it."

"Yeah, go ahead. Better than you sitting around watching TV all day."

Hank thought seriously about Amy for a moment. *It's a pipe dream. Amy's not going to want that. Plus she has her schoolwork. And what good would Norma be? Norma has all she can handle getting up and dressed in the morning. Well, it's something for her to do, to concentrate on... but what she really needs to do is quit drinking and get her life together. She's a mess.*

Hank was often oblivious to Norma. Their separate worlds barely touched one another most of the time. When he did interact with her, like this night, he knew their life together must change, but he could not imagine exactly how. It had a certain predictable pattern, painful, but strangely stable. Once in a while, there would be a blow-up. Hank would come home, find the house a mess, no food to eat, and he would yell at Norma. "What kind of a mother are you? Look at this place! Your kids are a mess. You're a mess." His right arm would flail wildly.

Norma would cringe, expecting to be hit, like her father used to hit her mother, but the blow never came. Instead, Hank would stomp out of the house, slamming the door as he left. Norma would dissolve in tears on the couch. She'd have another drink and gradually she would care less as the alcohol blunted her anxious edges. The next day she would get up and resolve to do better. She would postpone her first drink. She would clean the house, throwing dirty clothes and shoes haphazardly in closets, or drawers, whatever was nearest. To the casual observer, her home would look neat and organized. Underneath, behind the closet doors and in the drawers, all would be chaotic. But it looked presentable.

After an hour or two of this cleaning frenzy, Norma would begin to shake. And she would reward herself with a tall glass of vodka. She had earned it, she would tell herself. The liquor would make her feel better and she'd return to the couch to watch her soap operas. It was a pattern she would repeat many times.

The truth was Hank never realized that what he hated in Norma, he hated in himself…the disappointment with a life of mind-numbing mediocrity. They had both been promised so much and expected so much. Their early lives had been filled with recognition and glory. Hank saw Norma's failure and despised it, but in the dark corners of his mind, what he despised even more was his own mediocre life. Maybe Newport Lane would change that.

And now Norma thought she was at last back on her way. She could glimpse a bright future. This was a new Norma or a return to the Norma she was meant to be. She was going to be special again and successful this time. She would be Amy's manager. Together, they would achieve fame. Amy would be a world-famous cover girl, like Lauren Hutton or Twiggy. And Norma would be right there, alongside the runway, soaking up the glory, people photographing her almost as much as they photographed the beautiful Amy. Yes, it would happen. She would make it happen.

CHAPTER 13

9/16/71 – Thursday

Values everywhere were crumbling, but Dora still felt the press of the moral axioms from her childhood. And she ignored them, just as resolutely. Somewhere, in the back of her mind, she sensed long-standing feelings of guilt and shame, but it was 1971. Freedom was in the air. You could have sex if you wanted to. You could get high if you wanted to. The prevailing credo was "If it feels good, do it." Dora was determined to be liberated, to enjoy herself without constraint. So she did as she thought she wanted...*as long as you weren't hurting anyone else*, she told herself.

This morning, she awakened on Katie's couch, with Jared. She sat up smiling. She liked Jared a lot and wondered what he really thought of her. He was waking up. He blinked and looked up at her. She stroked his cheek. He smiled, feeling good. Without a word, they got up and put on their clothes, content with silence. The house was peaceful. Apparently Katie had not come home. Together, they wandered into the kitchen.

Dora spoke first. "I think there's some Rice

Krispies here. Want some?"

"Yeah. Sounds good."

She rinsed two dirty bowls that were in the sink. She found two spoons and washed them as well. She located the half-full box of Rice Krispies in the cabinet and put that on the table. She put the sugar bowl out as well. Opening the refrigerator, she was glad to see there was still some milk left, at least enough for their two bowls of cereal. They sat at Katie's table and ate their cereal. "When are Katie's parents coming back, anyway?" Jared asked.

"I think next week sometime."

"Cool."

They continued eating. Jared looked thoughtful. "What do you think about tripping today?"

There it is, thought Dora. *There's the question. Well if I'm gonna do it with anyone, it might as well be Jared.* "Okay, yeah, I'm up for it." She suspected she would have done anything he suggested.

Putting aside his cereal, Jared took a plastic bag from his pocket and removed two small pieces of paper. He handed one to Dora and put the other on his tongue. Dora imitated him, sticking out her tongue and placing the blotter on it. They looked at each other and waited, finishing their cereal. "Let's go to my house. I want to hear some Zeppelin."

Not yet tripping, they walked out of the house and back down the hill to the main road, where Jared again stuck out his thumb. And once again, a local citizen stopped and gave them a ride, this time to his doorstep. By now they were tripping. Dora was stunned by the magical change and found Jared more fascinating than ever. To her, he was amazing, exciting, and she loved looking at him. She felt like she was floating, not quite on the ground. It was a very peculiar sensation and she grabbed Jared's hand to keep from drifting off into space. He was in a world of his own, but she felt connected to him. Suddenly, she wanted him to touch her again, to touch her breasts again. She wanted him on her and in her. They walked into his house. Jared's mother was in the kitchen. They heard her say in a cheery voice "Hi kids."

They went upstairs to Jared's bedroom and shut the door. Jared put a Led Zeppelin album on the turntable, looking forward to getting lost in the music. He could barely wait for those extraordinary, rapid-fire Jimmy Page guitar solos. Dora went along with that, but she was overwhelmed by the drug, feeling the disorientation of space and perspective, as if she were outside her own body and seeing the world for the first time. Everything looked magnificent and wondrous. She reached out to touch Jared's chest. He had turned on the record player and put on headphones. He was swaying his head to the music. "Here, you gotta hear this," he said, handing her the headphones.

She put them on, but it was too loud and the

music hurt her ears. She quickly handed the headphones back to him and said "Intense." Everything was intense. Jared was intense. She reached out to touch him with her fingertips, to make contact again.

Jared felt her hand on his chest. She slid her hand under his shirt, wanting to feel his skin. He smiled and welcomed her exploration of his body. The music faded to the background in his mind as he became sexually aroused. He took off the headphones and turned up the music. He reached for Dora. The drums were pounding insistently; the bass and guitar were competing for dominance. Soaring guitar riffs filled the air.

The room was dimly lit. They lay on his carpet and felt each other with an intensity neither had known before. Their clothes fell off, as if by themselves. Side by side, they stroked each other's bodies, examining every part they touched. They rolled together on the carpet, entangled in each other. Dora had never felt such elation. She desired him more than she had ever wanted anything. She rolled him on his back and mounted him. The feeling of having him inside her was perfect.

Jared looked up at her face. Her eyes were closed. She was swaying to the music. He was inside her. She writhed from side to side, savoring the sensuality. He grasped her hips and pulled her down. The feeling was exquisite. They both had orgasms. This time he didn't pull out of her. They were overwhelmed by the intensity of the moment, by each other. It had all seemed utterly mystical to Dora. She thought she had seen the face of God.

DEVELOPMENT

*********.

Amy worried about Dora. Her sister had not come home again last night. Amy guessed she was somewhere with Jared. *He was handsome, it was true, but that was no reason to stay out all night with him. Where did they stay? It couldn't be his house. Surely his parents would object to that. So where?* She wasn't privy to the secrets her older sister kept. *And shouldn't our parents be worried about her? Isn't that what parents are supposed to do? But they didn't even notice she was gone.*

CHAPTER 14

It was late Thursday afternoon and Hank was in a difficult meeting with his boss. In the large paneled corner office of County Savings and Loan, he sat before Walsh's desk with his paperwork arrayed before him. He sat quietly, but inside he was fuming. Walsh wasn't going for it.

"How reliable are these sales projections?" Walsh asked.

Hank heard the skepticism in his boss's voice. He could see the doubt in his face. "As solid as they can be, at this point. It's early, but the market is strong. Westport is a destination location. Of course buyers need to at least see a model home before they sign," he added nervously.

"Holden can't fund a model house?" Walsh asked.

"No, he's stretched pretty thin."

"Well, he should have more skin in the game."

Well maybe he should, but he doesn't, thought Hank. *I'm the one with all the skin in the game. Anyway, is that reason enough to derail the whole thing? Why am*

I even having to present this? Hank was annoyed. As a senior executive for commercial lending, he felt he should be able to approve the loan without checking with the bank president. But at an eventual $300,000, it was a big bite for their small bank. It was beyond Hank's approval level. He knew that. He just didn't like it.

So he persisted. "Look at the growth in the town. Population is increasing, incomes are rising. If we don't do this, someone else will. This is the kind of thing we need to be doing."

"Mmmm, hmmm," said Walsh, shaking his head from side to side. Hank felt his stomach clench. He had to have this financing. It wasn't only the $20,000 Holden promised him off the books if he secured this loan. He was a significant investor here. If he could pull it off, he was on his way. But if not, he stood to lose everything. *Walsh is too conservative,* he thought. *The whole Board is like that. All of them, Walsh, Clemons, Rubin the lawyer, even Raposa, my friend. Christ!*

"Bring me some real commitments," said Walsh. "Then we'll talk."

"You got it," said Hank. The meeting was over. He gathered his papers and walked out of the room. He felt he was going nowhere. He suspected Walsh was only paying lip service to the whole idea. Walsh didn't like Holden and he didn't like the prospect of these big new homes on little one acre lots. *He is never going to go for it*, thought Hank, *no matter what "commitments" I bring him.* Still, Hank had to try something. As long as there was a grain of hope, he had to try. He felt desperate to succeed with his investment. Newport Lane had to be a success.

CHAPTER 15

9/17/71 – Friday

Dora spent the night with Jared in his room. They talked, listened to music and continued to trip. Sometime in the pre-dawn hours, Jared fell asleep, but Dora never did. By sun-up, she felt the urge to leave. She quietly dressed. Rather than wake him, she decided to leave a note. She rummaged through his desk and found a pen and a piece of paper. She wrote "I had to go. See you, babe. D." She resisted saying she loved him, but she wanted him to know it was special. She added "You were amazing." With that, she slipped out of the house unheard by anyone.

She felt stiff and rather sticky. Her clothes clung to her uncomfortably. But the LSD was still in her system and it animated her. She was not ready to go home and certainly not inclined to go to school.

She realized she was hungry and decided to walk over to Lily's. It was a half hour walk. She made her way along the winding road until she reached the Post Road. Cars whizzed past her, bathing her in wind. It was other-worldly for her, an ordinary day that felt remarkable. She felt free. Looking a little bedraggled, she entered Lily's and sat at the counter,

"What'll you have honey?" Lily asked.

Dora looked up with bloodshot eyes and suddenly smiled and said "pancakes."

"Orange juice?"

"Sure"

While waiting for her order, Dora looked around the diner. Other customers sat at tables talking quietly or reading the paper by themselves. *They don't understand how incredible the world is, how life is.* She felt the breeze as the door opened, and to her surprise, her father walked in. He saw her and came up to her. In one sweeping motion of his head, he took in her disheveled state, smudged eye makeup, black clothes, and said "Where have you been?"

"I was with my friends," she muttered and looked back at her pancakes which had arrived. She took a tentative bite. They tasted good.

"Well, you look like a bum. Go home, get cleaned up and get to school." She nodded and focused on eating. Her mood had dropped like a stone.

"I mean it," he said.

"Yeah, okay." He did not offer to drive her. He just seemed angry. She returned to her pancakes, no longer enjoying them.

Hank turned to Lily and demanded a regular coffee and a fried egg sandwich on a roll, to go. He was in a rush. He had nothing more to say to Dora, nor she to him, it seemed. He walked to the take-out section of the counter, to Dora's left, received his order, paid for it and stomped out.

"What an asshole," Dora muttered to no one in particular.

She had lost her appetite and her good mood. Dropping her fork on the pancakes she had barely touched, she fished two dollars and some change from her pocket and placed the money on the counter. She stood up and considered going home, but instead she walked to town, where she entered the park and lay down on her back, in the damp grass. It was cool, but she barely noticed it, staring at the trees and sky. She fell asleep.

Late that afternoon, she woke up and discovered she was lying on the ground. She shivered in her wrinkled clammy clothes. Standing up, she brushed herself off and walked to a nearby bench wondering why she hadn't fallen asleep there, rather than on the grass. She remembered her father yelling at her and before that, a long night with Jared. No longer tripping, she couldn't quite think what she wanted to do next. So she sat there on the bench, feeling a bit down, with nothing she wanted to do.

It was getting dark. She thought she should go home. Her mother might actually miss her. It had been some time since she'd been home. Days and nights blurred together. She was pretty sure her father would report having seen her. Her mother might yell for a moment, but Dora realized she didn't much care. She recalled the night with Jared. It had been magical. She wanted more of that feeling, the excitement, the newness of everything… and especially, she wanted more of Jared. The thought nagged at her that maybe he didn't feel the same way.

But in the growing dark, sitting on the bench, another boy she knew came up and joined her. She had known Jim Newton for years. He'd been called "Fig" since the second grade. His family lived near hers. He was two years older than she. Always slight, now he was so skinny and high-strung, she was sure he was using a lot of speed. "Hey D,' he said, sitting down. He seemed to bounce on the bench.

"Hi Figgy." Dora looked up at him, with a smile. As children, they had often played together. He had a little redheaded sister named Susie who would usually join them, along with Amy. Dora remembered the four of them running through the hallways of the Newton home, a big white Victorian house, which sat perched at the crest of the hill five minutes' walk from Dora's. Dora had an image of Figgy's mother seated at her desk in a darkened study. Cora Ann Newton was a tall, bony woman, who always seemed preoccupied, reading or writing, with only a desk lamp for light.

Dora and Figgy had lost contact during her junior high school years, but they had reconnected when she entered high school. Not much of a student, Figgy was a popular, out-going boy. When Dora would see him, he always seemed to be surrounded by a group of noisy friends. He was known for his sense of humor. Occasionally, Dora would encounter him at parties. These were big, unstructured events, where someone's parents would be away, and a son or daughter would throw open their house to any and all guests. Dozens of teenagers would come and go, drink, smoke, and swim in the pool, if there was one. Dora would bump into Figgy at these loose, rambling affairs, and once in a while, she found herself making out with him and sometimes it went a little further. She liked him, but not in a serious way. He had finished school and remained in the area, working at a small record store in town.

On an impulse, Dora asked him if he had any acid. He did not, but he did have speed which he suggested they take instead. "I have some really good pot, too. Blow you away," he added. Hoping these drugs might lift her sagging spirits and rejuvenate her, Dora agreed. Figgy explained the speed and pot were at his apartment, which was in Norwalk. He had a car and they made the 15 minute drive with him doing virtually all the talking. He seemed so keyed up, Dora wondered how he could even consider taking more speed, but she thought *I guess he's used to it.*

Inside, Figgy's apartment was a mess. It was one cramped dark room, with two small windows. The bed was unmade and his clothes were strewn about on the floor. Opposite the bed stood a small round table containing assorted drug paraphernalia. Figgy stepped nimbly around his fallen clothes and walked up to the table. He sat down and picked up a half-smoked joint which he relit. He took a hit and handed it to Dora. She inhaled deeply and handed it back. He had one more hit and put it out in an ashtray. Then he opened a plastic bag containing some small white pills and handed one to Dora who was standing alongside his chair. "Good speed," he said.

She walked to the sink where she poured a glass of water and swallowed the pill. She turned and handed the glass to Figgy and he did the same. She felt the speed hit her within minutes. It was powerful and it lacked the jangly, jittery feeling she had experienced with other speed. She felt exquisitely clear and energetic. "This is good speed," she said.

"Pure crystal meth. The best. Even better when you smoke it or shoot it."

"No thanks, not that, man. Not me." Dora had an instinctual fear of needles.

"Yeah, I know."

"But man, this feels great."

He looked at her and said "Yeah, this is cool." Then he stood up and bouncing on the balls of his feet, he reached for her. She initially recoiled and then said to herself *oh what the hell*. She looked up at him, his lank red hair falling around his smiling face. She expected to be kissed. Instead, he squeezed her breast through her shirt. She was surprised, but she allowed it.

"I've really got the hots for you, D," he said, pulling her to him and kissing her hungrily. She was startled but the speed and pot made her feel sensual and responsive. She gave in to the feelings and kissed him back. They were still standing. He ran his hands down the sides of her body, feeling the curve of her hips. His hands were at her waist. Without preamble, he unzipped her jeans and pulled them down to the floor, along with her panties. Although energized by the speed, she stood stock still. He quickly stood up and kissed her again. Then unexpectedly, he turned her around and slapped her on the rear end, pushing her forward on to the bed at the same time. She landed face first. "Ouch" she shouted.

Figgy laughed and spanked her again, his open hand leaving a red outline on her bare bottom. To her surprise, she found it pleased her. "Why does that feel so good?" she wondered aloud.

He laughed again and sat down alongside her. She lay sprawled across the bed, on her stomach. He began spanking her repeatedly with his open hand until her bottom was red. Then he stood up and pulled down his pants to his knees. Holding her hips in both hands, he fucked her from behind. It was all over quickly.

It was the second time in two days Dora had had unprotected sex.

CHAPTER 16

Norma was nervous. She'd found the address in the paper for Hixon Realty. The office was downtown on Imperial Avenue. Since getting up this morning, she had been able to think of little other than Amy's future career. Before leaving her house, Norma had fortified herself with her usual tall glass of vodka, but instead of struggling through her chores and watching her shows on television, she'd gathered her purse and coat and gone off in search of Maddie. She did not know Maddie. She had never met her, but in her mind, Maddie was the key to Amy's future. She didn't think to call first. It did not occur to her that Maddie might be busy or out of the office.

Maddie's office building had once been a private home. Now it contained a small group of professional offices. It was a large white Victorian house. A wraparound porch guarded the front and sides of the building and a small parking lot was to the left. Norma pulled her car in to the lot. She parked, walked around to the front and climbed up the steps. She studied the buzzers to the right of the doorway. One said Hixon Realty and she pressed that button. A voice said "Come in. Second floor."

DEVELOPMENT

As the buzzer sounded, Norma turned the knob and pushed open the heavy oak door. She entered a small carpeted foyer. It was a tastefully appointed waiting area. Against the right wall was a round table with several issues of Time magazine and two chairs on either side of it. A floor lamp behind one of the chairs emitted a bright light that illuminated the surface of the table, but not much else. Norma thought briefly of sitting down to get her bearings but she continued on instead. Peering ahead through the shadows, she could see a hallway and closed doors. A stairway with a dark curved railing was directly ahead of her. Pausing for a moment, she opened her purse and quickly drank from her emergency supply.

She climbed the stairs, holding the railing for balance. The landing at the top was similar to the first floor with another table and lamp, though no chairs. A door on her immediate left had "Hixon Realty" lettered on it. She knocked quickly and walked in.

Maddie's office was small, but comfortable. There were two desks in the room. Maddie sat at the one on the left. The right one was unoccupied. Maddie was talking on the phone and held up a finger to indicate she'd be a moment. She pointed to a chair in front of her desk and Norma sat down. She heard Maddie say to her caller "All right. We'll talk later." With that, she hung up and turned to Norma. "Hi."

"I think you know my husband," said Norma.

Maddie was immediately on guard. This would

not be the first time she had been accused of tampering with a marriage.

"Your husband?"

"Yes. Hank Latour."

"Oh Hank. Yes, we work together." Maddie studied Norma. She looked to be about Hank's age. Her hair needed a good cut. Her clothes were rumpled. She seemed nervous and her face was flushed.

"Well, he said he thought you might be able to help me."

"Uh huh." Maddie had no clue where this conversation was headed. It no longer felt like she was being accused of anything, but it didn't seem to be related to real estate, as far as she could tell.

"Yes, he thought you might know someone… or know someone who knew someone…" Norma trailed off, vaguely.

"What's this about?" Maddie decided to be blunt.

"Well, my younger daughter, Amy… Maybe Hank told you about her…"

"No, he never mentioned her."

"Well, we, or I anyway, think she could be a model. You know, a cover girl."

"A what?"

"You know, a fashion model, like in Vogue..." *This was not going well,* Norma thought. But she hurried on. "Hank thought, you know, maybe you knew someone, like back in New York... You're from New York, right?"

"Well, yeah, but big deal. That doesn't mean I know anyone in that industry. I'm in real estate."

"Yeah, I know. I just thought... Hank thought... you might have some contacts or something."

"For what, exactly?"

"Um, I mean someone I could talk to, in that, uh, industry... someone who could tell me what to do, what the steps are...what I should do." Norma looked helplessly at Maddie.

"Well, lemme think about it." Maddie considered this whole inquiry was a little odd, but she paused to consider the question. "Yeah, actually I might know someone you could call. He's a photographer and I'm pretty sure he shoots fashion. His name is Peter Duer. I got him his apartment a few years ago. He would know my name."

"That would be great. I really... thanks a lot."

"All right. Let me see if I still have a number for him." She pulled her Rolodex in front of her and started thumbing through cards. "D, D, D... yeah, here it is.

Peter Duer. Not sure the number is still good, but it was a nice apartment on 53rd. He might still be there." She tore a sheet from a notepad on her desk and wrote down the name and number. She handed it to Norma. "Here you go."

"Okay, thanks. I'll call him. I'll call him right away. Thanks again. Thanks for everything."

"No problem. Good luck."

Norma put the note in her purse and stood up. The phone rang and Maddie answered it, saying "Hixon Realty" and waving goodbye to Norma at the same time.

Norma smiled as she left. She was excited. *This is how it starts*, she thought. *We're on our way.* Driving home quickly, she planned to call Peter Duer the moment she was back in her house.

It was mid-morning, about 10:30, when she arrived at her home. She ran to the living room and picked up the phone at the same time rummaging through her purse for the number. Balancing the phone with her shoulder, pushing it against her ear, she managed to extract the slip of paper and dial the photographer's number.

"This is Peter Duer. You are speaking to my answering machine. You can leave a message and I will call you back. Please speak now."

Norma was confused. It was the man's voice, but it was a machine, a tape recording. But she thought excitedly, *it is the right number!* So, she went ahead. "Uh, my name is Norma Latour." She paused, as if waiting for a response. When there was none, she continued. "My daughter Amy, uh my daughter Amy, is going to be a model. I uh, Maddie Hixon gave me your number. She said you knew her. A real estate agent." Norma waited a moment. Again, there was only silence at the other end. "I uh, I um, want to talk to you about how to get Amy started modeling. Can you call me back, please? My number is 203 555-3076. That's in Westport, Connecticut. That's how I know Maddie. She works here now. So, uh, please call me. Please."

She hung up. She hoped this odd tape recording system worked. After all the excitement, all she could do now was wait for a call back. *I have to be patient*, she told herself. She hoped he'd call her soon. She poured herself a drink and sat down on the couch. She could hardly sit still. She got up and turned on the television. She sat back down again. *Just have to wait.*

****

That afternoon, when Amy came home from school, she did not go right into her house. Instead, she got off the bus at her stop and walked around the house to the fields in back. She needed to look again at the construction. She did not want to believe what she had seen, how devastated her meadow had seemed. But after passing through the field and woods, she heard and then saw the work taking place. If anything, it seemed worse than before. There was a big hole in the ground where doubtless a house would go. Enormous piles of dirt rose alongside it. A backhoe was busily removing shovelfuls of soil. A bulldozer was pushing mounds of dirt in all directions, spreading it out and covering whatever plant life remained. There were more men than before, in hardhats and overalls. None seemed to notice her. She felt invisible there at the edge of the woods. She was heartbroken. They were destroying her field. *This is dad's development, Newport Lane. What about the animals that lived here? They are doomed*, she thought.

Amy turned back into the woods and walked home. As she approached the back door, she could hear yelling in the kitchen. "I can't work. I have school." Dora was shouting.

"Well, you're not getting any more money from me this week. I don't have it to give you anyway."

"That's bullshit, mom." Dora said, just as Amy walked in. Norma looked up at her from the kitchen table.

"Amy, you won't believe what I did today!" The fight with Dora seemed to have been instantly forgotten.

"What?'

"I talked to Maddie Hixon, that realtor from New York. She told me about a fashion photographer she knows. I called him, but he wasn't home," she added.

"Oh Christ," said Dora, rolling her eyes. "I'm outta here." She got up from the table and left the kitchen, slamming her chair. Amy watched her sister go and then turned toward her mother.

Norma was animated and seemed very happy. Amy had rarely seen her mother like this. Usually when her mother got keyed up, it was in anger, like moments before. This was new. Norma was excited and she focused on Amy.

"What? What photographer?"

"He shoots fashion models. I called him. His name is Peter Duer."

"You called him?"

"Yes, that's what I'm telling you. I left a message that you're going to be a model and we want his help."

"Oh mom. Not that again. I can't be a model. I'm not pretty. I never look good in pictures. Why do you keep thinking that?"

"Oh Amy, Amy. Yes you can. I'm going to help you. I know you can do it. We can do it."

"I can't. I mean I don't really want…I just can't imagine that."

"It's okay. You leave it to me. Once this Peter guy calls back, we'll find out what to do next."

"Okay, mom. I guess." She paused, not wanting to dampen her mother's enthusiasm. "But I've got homework." She turned and went upstairs and for the balance of the afternoon, she tried to concentrate on her school assignments.

****

At 7:30 that evening, the phone rang. Norma answered it on the first ring.

"Hello" she said.

"Mrs. Latour? This is Peter Duer. You left a message on my answering machine this morning?"

"Yes." She wondered for an instant about his mysterious telephone tape recorder. "Yes. Thanks for calling back. I really appreciate it. Maddie Hixon said you knew her."

"Well, yeah, I do. What was it you wanted?"

"Um… Uh, my daughter Amy. She's a model. She's 14. She's tall and skinny, like models are supposed to be. She's very pretty."

"You need photos?"

"Uh, no. Well maybe. I mean, what are our next steps? What do we do?"

"Oh, so she can *become* a model. Right. You gotta send photos to the agencies. That's how it's done. See if one picks her up."

"Oh. So we'll need a photographer for head

shots and stuff?"

"No, not yet. Really, just send some snapshots. In color. Color is better. You know, let 'em know what she looks like. But just snapshots. That's all they need to see. Plus her stats. You know age, height, measurements…"

"Oh, just snapshots? Pictures we take?"

"Yeah, that's it. That's what they'll look at. If they're interested, they'll call her in."

"Wow, okay. We can do that. Who do we send them to? What agencies? Or does she need an agent?"

"Look I don't have time for this right now. Just send them to a few agencies."

"All right. Sorry to take up your time. I really appreciate it."

"I know. It's okay, but I gotta go."

"Okay, but which agencies?" Norma persisted. "Just tell me that."

"Oh, just send to Elite, Wilhelmena, Ford. Might as well start at the top."

"Okay, terrific. You've been terrific."

"All right. Glad I could help. If you need head shots at some point, let me know. And say hi to Maddie for me."

"Of course, of course. Right. Thank you again."

Norma hung up. She was ready to go. "Amy, Amy, come down here," she shouted.

Amy heard her mother. She had heard her on the phone. It had to do with this modeling stuff. "Okay. Be right down."

She closed her Biology text book and with a shake of her head, walked downstairs. Her mother was standing by the phone. She had a gleam in her eye. "Oh Amy, we have to get some pictures of you."

"Pictures?"

"Yeah. That was Peter Duer, the photographer, I was speaking to. He said we need pictures that we send around to the agencies. It's like an audition." Norma winced, thinking of her own auditions years ago. *But this is different. This is modeling.*

"What kinda pictures?"

"Oh, just pictures that show what you look like. Peter said just plain old snapshots, color ones. I can take those. Hank has a camera. We need color film. I'll do it. I'll take the pictures. We'll have to work on your hair and makeup. And what will you wear?" Norma was lost in the details.

"Oh mom. This is so ridiculous. Why do you want to do this?"

"Amy you have to believe in yourself. I do. I

believe in you. I know this can happen. It will be great. You'll see."

"It would take a miracle." Amy felt a flicker of possibility. She suddenly imagined herself on a runway, flashbulbs going off, everyone looking at her. She dismissed the thought immediately. It was more frightening than exciting.

"Don't worry. I'll take care of everything," her mother said.

At that moment, the kitchen door opened and Hank came in. Norma had not heard his car.

"Hank," she said the moment he entered the room, "Amy is going to be a model. We're going to make it happen. I spoke with a fashion photographer, a high-end guy, who knows the business. He told me what to do. Maddie knows him."

"Maddie? Oh yeah, she mentioned you saw her."

"Well, yeah, you told me about Maddie, remember? So I went and saw her today. She gave me this photographer's number and he just called me back."

"Moving a little fast here, aren't you?" Hank looked from his wife to Amy who was standing next to Norma. "A model? Is that what you want, Amy?"

"Of course she does," interjected Norma. "Who wouldn't want to be a model? A cover girl. Fame, beauty, money. Why in the world not?"

"Amy?" her dad asked again.

Amy seemed to shake herself out of a reverie. "Well, yes. I guess. I mean, why not?" she repeated her mother's rhetorical question.

Hank shrugged. "Whatever you both want. But we can't afford new clothes, jewelry, anything like that, right now."

"That's not necessary. I mean she has to look good, but they really just want simple pictures, snapshots really, right now. I have to take pictures. That's what we have to send to the agencies."

"All right. Good luck to you both." Hank shrugged dismissively. "How 'bout some dinner?" he asked as he walked toward the refrigerator, with Norma trailing behind him.

"I need to borrow your camera," she said.

CHAPTER 17

Earlier that afternoon Hank had a desperate meeting with Maddie. After his talk with Walsh the day before, he asked her to come to his office to talk over the loan. He hoped she might furnish him with some arguments he could use to sway his boss. Before she arrived, he found himself picturing her in his mind and again he felt powerfully attracted to her. He wondered momentarily if it was because his love life with Norma had become so desolate or perhaps it was that he viewed Maddie as a lifeboat in the storm that was his life. Or maybe he simply liked her. He was not sure, but his longing for her was difficult to ignore. He could not tell if she had any special feelings for him.

At any rate, *this was not the time to think about a romance*. He needed Maddie to find a committed buyer. He believed it was their only chance to persuade Walsh, unless she had some other ideas. Maybe there was some other way to get the loan, but in his heart, he believed they needed to get a buyer or they were in trouble.

Maddie walked into his office and took a seat. She looked at him expectantly. He felt his stomach tighten. *Okay, here goes.* He explained to her that if they could get a committed buyer for one home, it would help greatly in getting financing for the entire project.

Maddie nodded her understanding, but inside she was dismayed by this small town banker. He did not understand how things worked. Well, she might find interested buyers, but nobody would sign a binding contract or pay a deposit until they had at least seen a model home in the development. She explained patiently, "We need the money to get the model built. That's $50,000. We told you that. Once we have the model, I will find buyers."

Hank squirmed. This was an impossible situation. They needed money for the model home, but could not get a loan to build it until they had a committed buyer, and there would be no buyer without the model. Hank confessed "I'm getting some push back from the president here, that he wants to see buyer commitments *before* he agrees to loan anything, even the $50,000."

"It has to go through him? You can't approve that amount?"

"No," Hank said sheepishly. "Not when the eventual total is three hundred."

"Well, he has to take a risk some time. That's his business. And yours."

"But if he won't do it…"

"Then you have a big problem." She softened a

little. "Hank, we're only talking $50,000 right now."

"I know," he said glumly, "but is there anything else you can think of that I can tell him?"

"He probably knows it, but you can tell him the market is tight. People are buying four and five bedroom houses like these. Westport is a family town. There actually is not enough inventory. Newport Lane will be priced competitively. There is a market and it is growing. The town is getting richer." She leaned forward aggressively. "Tell him this is the time to get on board, man!"

Hank swayed back in his chair. The force of her words literally pushed him backwards. *She's tough*, he thought. *She won't take no for an answer*. That was a good thing, he supposed, a good quality in a realtor. "Well, all right. I'll talk to him again. But I need your application before I do. That will help."

"We'll have it to you this afternoon. Hennessy, our lawyer, gave us a thumbs up this morning."

"All right." Hank smiled. He felt buoyed a little by her optimism.

As she put her coat on, Maddie said "Your wife stopped by my office, you know?"

"She did?"

"Yeah. Something about your daughter becoming a fashion model.'

"Oh, that. Yeah." Hank shook his head.

"You gave her my name?"

"Yeah, I hope that was okay."

"Yeah, it was fine. I don't know if I helped her much. Just one photographer I knew a little. Gave her his name."

"Oh, thanks. It's… I don't know. My wife…" his voice trailed off.

"All right. Well, I'll get you that application."

He watched Maddie leave. He wanted her so much, it hurt. He longed to touch that thick, red-brown hair. It seemed rich beyond imagining. At the same time, he thought miserably *this loan is not going to happen. I'll make the strongest case I can to Walsh. That's all I can do.*

Later that afternoon, Holden stopped by with the loan application. He had only put in for the $50,000 at this point. Hank nonetheless had to pass it on to Walsh, because it was ultimately $300,000 they were seeking. Before giving it to his boss, he appended a note urging approval. Maybe they stood a chance.

CHAPTER 18

9/20/71 – Monday

Amy gave little further thought to the modeling idea. Although her mother babbled incessantly throughout the weekend about photos, clothes, hair and shoes, the topic barely reached Amy's consciousness. She was focused on school, on her homework. She was thinking about working hard to improve her grades, avoiding the boys at school and controlling her eating. Coming home from another stressful school day that Monday afternoon, she was preoccupied with these issues and so it was a jolt when her mother pointedly stopped her as she walked through the front door of her home.

Norma had heard the school bus arrive. She was in the front hall the moment Amy came through the door. She did not give her time to remove her coat. She had to make Amy understand. This was Amy's big chance. It felt like Norma's last chance. She grabbed Amy's hand and pulled her to the couch in the living room. "Dora has no future. But you could have one."

Amy was puzzled for a moment. "Oh right. The modeling."

"Yes, the modeling. We need to get started. Are you with me on this?"

"Alright, okay."

"Well good. So the first thing we need to do is get some pictures of you. I have your dad's camera. We'll do some head shots, some in casual clothes, maybe a bathing suit."

"A bathing suit? Please, mom. I don't want to. I look awful."

"Well, all right. Maybe not a bathing suit. But we have to think about what you will wear. And your makeup and hair. We have to fix all that."

"Okay mom."

This is so strange, thought Amy. Her mother barely seemed to notice she was alive for fourteen years. Now she was suddenly the center of her mother's universe. In a odd way, it felt good to Amy.

Norma was looking around the living room. "We'll shoot in here. I'll hang up a white sheet on that wall. We'll take the pictures there. I have to check how the flash works on the camera."

It was all a whirlwind to Amy. "Okay mom," she said again.

"Let's go upstairs and see what you have to wear." Norma took Amy's hand and pulled her up off the couch. "C'mon."

They walked upstairs, holding hands. Amy still had her coat on. Her mother did not seem to notice. When they got to Amy's room, Norma let go of her hand and opened the closet. "Let's see," she said. "Maybe this yellow top… and you have these white Capri pants. I think that would work, with your coloring. Your coloring is a lot like mine, and these are good colors for me. Put these on."

Amy took off her coat. She stood by her bed for a moment.

"C'mon," her mother urged.

Amy took the items from her mother, stripped out of her day's clothes and changed into the shirt and pants her mother had handed her.

"There. That's better," said Norma. "Now your hair, and then, makeup."

Amy's hair was reddish blonde. It was cut short, ending just above her shoulders. "Not much we can do there. It looks as good as it's going to look, I think. Well, let's pin back one side with a barrette. Sit on the bed. Let me go get one." Norma left the room and a few minutes later returned with a simple rhinestone clip which she inserted into Amy's hair. "Yes, that's better, I think."

The makeup took a bit longer. Norma wanted to accentuate Amy's eyes and her high cheekbones. She was careful not to overdo it. She wanted Amy's natural beauty to show. So she worked carefully with rouge and mascara. Her hands shook a little, but she did her best to hold them steady. She used a bright red lipstick so Amy's lips would not look pale. She felt it would give her more life. Finally, she was satisfied with the end result. Amy said nothing, although she thought she had too much makeup on her face.

"All right, come on downstairs. I'll get the camera. I bought film today."

Downstairs, Amy sat obediently on the couch. She watched her mother use duct tape to attach a white bed sheet to the living room wall. The sheet gathered on the floor at the bottom and Norma stretched that out and placed a kitchen chair on it. She opened the camera and loaded the roll of color film. All the lights in the room were turned on. "All right. Sit there and look at me. We'll try some without the flash."

Amy moved to the chair and stared out at her mother.

"Try to smile. Try to look natural."

Norma took three shots of Amy in the chair. Then she moved closer and shot her from the neck up, head shots. "All right. Let's try some of you standing."

Amy stood up and Norma removed the chair. "Try one hand on your hip. Now just leave them at your sides." Norma snapped away. The roll was finished. "I want to shoot another roll," she said, as she emptied the camera. Her hands shook slightly but she successfully inserted the second roll. She had Amy repeat the poses.

DEVELOPMENT

Amy found she grew more relaxed as the shooting went on. *Maybe this isn't so hard after all,* she thought.

When Norma was finished, she was breathless. "I think those came out great. We'll see, but I think I did a good job."

Amy thought she herself had done a good job as well, but she said nothing.

"I'm going to take these to the drug store now, to get them developed."

"Okay. You're going right now?"

"Yeah, why not? The sooner, the better."

"Okay. I'll stay here. I want to start my homework."

Norma put on her coat, took the two rolls of film and left.

Amy returned to her room. She found it hard to concentrate on her schoolwork. She wondered about the world of modeling. She could only imagine that she would sit on a chair or stand and a photographer would take a lot of pictures. It was nice to get that attention, she decided. And it was kind of nice having her mother seem so interested in her. She resolved to always look her best. She would work on her makeup and hair, she thought, just as hard as she worked on her schoolwork. Nervously, she wondered how the pictures would turn out. She believed she had never looked good in photos, but maybe this time would be different. She hoped so.

She heard a car in the driveway. It seemed too soon for her mother to be returning already.

The door slammed and her mother yelled "Amy, come downstairs."

Amy got up from her desk and went down to see her mother who said "The pictures should be back in a week. Meanwhile, we need to get your vital statistics."

"My what?"

"You know, height, weight, measurements."

"My measurements? Great. I'm too fat."

"No you're not. Come here." Norma had a tape measure in her hand. "First how tall are you?"

"Five seven, I think."

"Well, let's check. Take off your shoes. Stand there, against the kitchen doorway."

Amy stood in the doorframe and her mother, who was about the same height, placed a pencil on the top of Amy's head and marked the spot on the wood. Amy stepped away and Norma measured the line from the floor. "Yup, five seven and a half. That's good."

"Now, your weight." They walked upstairs to her parent's bathroom. "Stand on the scale... Okay,

112."

Norma wrote both figures down on a piece of paper. "All right, we have to get your measurements. Take off your shirt and bra."

Amy felt very uncomfortable about the request, but she complied meekly. Her mother measured her carefully. "32....24...32"

Amy quickly put her clothes back on. This had been the hardest part and she was glad it was over. "Is that it?" she asked.

"I think so. They know you'll fill out. I'll tell them you're only fourteen."

"All right." Amy realized she had already been thinking of herself as a model, but now, after taking her measurements, she again had doubts. *Who's going to want a fat girl with too much makeup? It's not going to happen. Forget it.*

But Norma was totally positive. She knew Amy would be a great model. Once they saw her pictures, agencies would want her. Norma was sure. She had to be patient. Get the pictures developed. Make copies of the best ones. She had more work to do. She needed to get the addresses of the agencies that photographer had mentioned. She might need to call them, she thought.

"I gotta get back to my homework," Amy said, as she turned and walked back to her bedroom.

"Okay, honey. We're on our way."

****

That same afternoon, Hank had another meeting with Walsh. He was as persuasive as he knew how to be. He made all of Maddie's arguments about the market, the town's growth, the interest in larger homes for growing families, the competitive pricing... None of it swayed Walsh who had not even reviewed the application yet. It seemed to Hank that Walsh would never part with any money, not without at least one buyer and almost certainly not to Holden.

Hank was devastated. His life was on a downward course. He did not think raising the money would be so difficult. *Damn that Walsh.* There must be a way out, another source of money, but he could not think of one. He could not mortgage his house further. He had no more savings. Going to another bank was out of the question. They would need to know where the initial funds came from. He might have to own up to his investment. It was too risky. He could lose his job if Walsh got wind of that. Maybe he could find someone to agree to say they loaned the initial money. But they would expect a big cut for that lie. And if a bank needed documentation of the investment, there was no canceled check to show them. There was only the check for Hank's investment and he could not show that to any bank. He felt that in his own bank, he could obscure this detail, but for any other bank, his own investment would likely surface.

Like it or not, it seemed he would have to find another investor. He and Holden would have to give up another piece of the pie, if they could even find someone. Hank thought about friends and the only possibility he could think of with was Frank Raposa who owned a popular Italian restaurant in town. In years past, they had been friendly, though less so recently. More to the point, Raposa was on the bank's Board. It could get sticky for him to invest in something the bank had turned down. If it came to light, it could be awkward for him to explain. It wouldn't look right, Hank decided. He realized his friend would not make the investment and might resent being asked.

Thinking further, Hank considered his distant family and drew a blank. His father had died of lung cancer eight years ago and his mother lived now on a meager pension. They rarely spoke. There were no relatives with money, on either his or Norma's sides of the family. Hank pressed his fingers against the sides of his head. He must know someone else who would come in as an investor. But he could think of no one. So he fretted and had no answer.

****

Norma spent her waking hours the rest of the week researching agencies and getting everything ready to contact them. She picked out those agencies she thought were the best, really the same ones Peter Duer had mentioned: Elite, Wilhelmena and Ford. She found their addresses. She called each to ask if there was a contact person she should send the photos to. She was told no in every case. "Just send them to us here," she was told.

She pored over fashion magazines. What were girls wearing today? What did the models look like? How was their hair done? What hair color seemed to be favored? She kept picturing Amy in the ads and on the covers. She noticed sometimes they showed only the models' faces. Other times the whole body was visible. Where would Amy fit in? How should she be prepared?

Monday morning, seven days after the photos were shot, Norma stood anxiously in line at Westfair Pharmacy. As soon as it was her turn, she asked the clerk "Are my pictures ready yet? Latour. The name's Latour."

"Let's see. Just a sec. Yes. Yes, here they are. Two rolls. That'll be $9.70 with tax."

"Okay. Here." Norma handed over a ten dollar bill. She could barely contain her eagerness. She forgot to get her change. As soon as she received the envelopes, she opened them in the store. She ignored the clerk who was saying "Your change." She pulled the photos out of the first envelope. Amy stared out at her, in various poses. Though a bit dark, they seemed to show Amy reasonably well. Norma quickly stuffed them back in the envelope and found pretty much the same images in the second one. *They'll do fine,* she thought. *Amy looks beautiful. And there are plenty here. I don't even need to make copies.* She hurried home.

DEVELOPMENT

    Back at her house, Norma sat down at the kitchen table and fanned out all the photos. She removed several where Amy was either frowning or vacant looking. The rest she arranged in three piles, being sure to put some head shots, some seated and some standing full body shots in each pile. Then she went upstairs and found the three envelopes she had created for this purpose. Each was addressed to a New York agency. Each envelope contained a fact sheet with Amy's age, height, weight and measurements, as well as a cover letter introducing Amy. She carefully placed each set along with its photos in each of the envelopes. She licked the flaps, closed the clasps through the holes and then further sealed them with Scotch Tape. She set them on the table in front of her and admired her work for a moment. Then she gathered them up and rushed out to her car to deliver them to the Greens Farms Post Office.

CHAPTER 19

10/11/71 – Monday

It was Columbus Day, a holiday for some, but after a restless night with little sleep, Hank was seated at his desk in his office. Two weeks ago, Walsh had finally looked at their application for $50,000. As soon as he saw Holden's name on it, he had denied it categorically. The denial had left Hank in a state of panic. When he told Maddie and Holden they had been turned down, they simply looked at him expecting another solution, but he had none.

Now as Hank tried to review someone else's loan application, the papers scattered before him looked like a blur. He jumped slightly as the phone rang. It was Maddie.

"Hank, can you come to my office now? I have a possible way out for us."

"Really?" Hank was instantly awake. "What is it?"

"I can't tell you over the phone. You need to come by."

"Not over the phone… okay. Okay, I'll be right there. Give me fifteen minutes."

Hank shoved aside the papers on his desk, picked up his briefcase and dashed out the door, rushing past Dorothy Barnes, his middle-aged secretary. He said nothing to her and she noticed he seemed to be in a terrible hurry. At his car, he fumbled with his keys and finally got the door opened and his car started. Whatever Maddie had for him could be a lifesaver. He needed something to go right.

Arriving at Maddie's building, he impatiently rang her buzzer. She buzzed him in and he bolted up the steps to her little office. He sat down breathlessly in the chair in front of her desk.

"Okay," she said. "Here's the story. I can bring us a silent partner who will put up the entire $300,000 as a loan to you personally. But he wants a thousand dollars every month from you as a good faith payment and he wants the whole loan plus a hundred thousand back in two years. His name is Rick. Rick Generoso."

Hank tried to take it in. He was rapidly doing the math in his head. "So, let's see… He would want a $1,000 a month. That's $24,000 plus $400,000 at the end of two years? That would be $424,000. That's more than… more than forty per cent over the principal!"

"Yeah, well it's not a conventional loan, if you know what I mean."

It was an outrageous amount. And not only that,

Hank was scared. In fact, he was terrified. He had never dealt with a loan shark, which he felt sure this lender must be. What if they couldn't repay it? What if they couldn't sell the houses? He tried to focus on the figures. A conventional bank loan with a 7.5 per cent interest rate would have cost them about $45,000. Basically, they were increasing their costs by $80,000. "This uh, expense comes off the top? I'm not paying for it myself, right?"

"Yeah, it comes out of the pot after my commission. So it's on you and Mike. It comes out of your shares."

"And Mike is good with this?"

"Yes, he agreed but he..."

"Those terms are outrageous, triple normal rates," Hank interjected. "I'd be screwing myself."

"Well, do you have any other choice?"

"No." Hank looked down. "No, I don't think so, but... can't we negotiate with him?"

"No, we can't. It's take it or leave it. He made that pretty clear. Of course, you'll still get your twenty thousand from Mike," Maddie told him. "Mike understands there's no other way."

Hank thought to himself *at least with that twenty thousand, I could make those monthly payments to this guy.* But then he asked "Why doesn't Mike borrow the money himself?"

"No. It has to come from you. But don't worry, Mike is at risk too. He has to give you the money plus the interest that you give to Rick in two years or you and Mike are both in trouble."

"Well two years feels really tight to me. Can we get them all built and sold in that time?"

"Of course. You get the money. We'll make it happen."

Feeling desperate and fearful, he told Maddie he had to think about it.

"Don't think too long,"

****

Norma could not stand not knowing. It had been two weeks since she'd sent Amy's pictures out and none of the agencies had called her back. She calmed herself with a tall tumbler of vodka as she sat down in front of the phone. She dialed the first agency, Elite.

"Hello. Elite Models."

"Yes, this is Norma Latour. I mailed you pictures of my daughter Amy two weeks ago. I was wondering... I just wanted to be sure you got them.. and if... well... what happens next?"

"Yes. I think we got those."

"You think? Can I talk to someone about her?

"Yes, of course. Just a minute."

There was a pause of several minutes. Norma took a deep swallow of her drink.

"This is Gretchen Seibel. Can I help you?"

"Yes. This is Norma Latour. I sent you photos of my daughter Amy two weeks ago. Did you get them?"

"Just a minute… Oh yes, we did. Thank you. We need to review them, of course. We've been pretty busy. We'll get back to you. You have your number with them, right?"

"Well, yes. Yes, okay. I was just wondering what you thought.." Norma's voice sounded thick to her. She was afraid she might be slurring her words.

"We'll get back to you as soon as we've looked them over."

"Okay. I'll wait then."

"We'll be in touch."

She had virtually the same conversation with the other two agencies. They hadn't looked at the pictures, hadn't thought about Amy at all. They all promised they would. *But would they?* Norma felt her confidence crumble. It was like auditioning all over again. She shuddered at the memory. She decided the agencies had in fact looked at the pictures and dismissed Amy. *That's why they hadn't called back.* It was heartbreaking. Norma refilled her glass. She didn't care how she behaved or what her family would find when they got home.

CHAPTER 20

11/1/71 – Monday

Dora had not had her period. She was at least a month late. For the past three weeks, her tension worsened daily. And this last weekend, she had spent every minute worrying she was pregnant. So this morning, she finally decided she would see Dr. Sheinberg, who had been their family doctor for years. She had to know. He had always seemed kind and she hoped she could trust him to see her discreetly. She called his office and made an appointment for 1:30 pm that afternoon. It was the earliest time he had open. She did not tell his receptionist the reason for the visit.

It was a little cool and drizzly out and she found a hooded sweatshirt belonging to her father in the hall closet. It was red with Stanford emblazoned on the front. She pulled it over her head as she walked through the kitchen and out to the garage. Her mother had gone back to bed so Dora decided she would not miss her car. Dora had several anxious hours before her appointment and she spent them driving, first to the beach and then to the park in the center of town. She stopped at each place for a while until she grew too restless and moved on.

She arrived at the Doctor's office fifteen minutes early and sat tensely in the waiting area. Numerous "Highlights" magazines and children's coloring books lay on a table before her and more were stacked haphazardly in a bookcase. Most of Dr. Sheinberg's patients were children. He was running late. After thirty minutes, the receptionist called her name. Dora walked into the office. Dr. Sheinberg was a middle-aged man, with a receding hairline, wearing round spectacles which mirrored his round face. He smiled at her. He had a kind, concerned expression. He had known Dora since she was a little girl and he was fond of her.

"How are you, Dora?" he asked pleasantly, looking up at her from his desk.

"I'm afraid I'm pregnant… or I'm really late," Dora blurted out. "Please don't tell my parents." She steadied herself with one hand on his desk. She could barely stand still.

"Oh." He frowned for a moment. "Well, let's first find out." Again, he had a kindly tone, and she felt a bit reassured. Maybe she was just late, after all.

"Yeah, right. I need to know. I'm three, four weeks late."

"Okay, Dora. We'll do a Wampole's Test," he said. "It's fast and accurate. We'll know today. I'll need a urine sample." He turned to a shelf behind him and picked up a small jar with a plastic lid which he handed to her. "Use the bathroom there." He pointed to a door in the hallway. She took the jar and stood there immobile, staring at it. He saw her fear. "We'll find out first, Dora. Then you'll see if you have to make decisions. Let's not get ahead of ourselves." She spun around and left the room.

Dora was so tense, she was barely able to urinate, but finally she managed it. She shakily secured the lid and left the bathroom. She handed the jar back to the doctor.

"Okay. It will take two hours. You can come back or you can wait out there." He pointed toward the hallway.

"No, I'll come back. It's like two o'clock now, so I'll come back at four. Okay?"

"Sure. Try not to worry too much. A lot of times it's a false alarm."

"Yeah, maybe. All right. Thanks. I'll be back at four."

Dora pulled up her hood and walked back out to her mother's car. She sat there without moving for a few minutes. *God, I hope it's negative. Oh God, please.* She started up the car. She had no destination, but she needed to move. She drove through town. She found herself heading north on Wilton Road. She saw Glendenning Pond on her left and impulsively stopped. There was a small gravel parking area in front of the water. She pulled in. Hers was the only car. She could do nothing but wait. Staring at the dark pond, she chain-smoked three cigarettes. The car filled with smoke, stinging her eyes. She opened the window and let the cool, damp air in. A spattering of raindrops struck her shoulder. *Oh God, what if I really am pregnant? What will I do? I don't even know who the father is. It could be Jared, but it could be Figgy. Jesus, I can't stand it.*

She allowed herself a moment to contemplate marriage to Jared. *Would that be so bad? Would he even be interested? His parents would think he was ruining his life. They'd probably blame her.* And her own parents... what would they say? She could picture her father. Disappointed and angry. He'd have nothing good to say. And her mother? Dora could not really imagine her mother's reaction. It was hard to know with her. But it wouldn't be good.

Dora had heard about a girl in school who had an abortion. Denise somebody. She had to fly to Puerto Rico. It had sounded crazy, but she had come back to school and seemed to be okay. So, maybe... But no. That wasn't Dora. The idea of an abortion made her cringe. *Is it cause I'm Catholic?* she wondered. No, she didn't think so. Abortion felt wrong, not to mention dangerous.

What am I thinking? I'm probably not even pregnant. This is ridiculous.

She started the car. It had been over an hour, and she decided to head back, even if she was early. She arrived at Dr. Sheinberg's office and parked. She walked in and nodded to the receptionist. "Dr. Sheinberg said I could wait here. He said he'd see me again at four."

"Okay, I'll let him know you're here."

Dora sat down to wait. There was nothing to do and she sat there alone with her thoughts and worries. She kept feeling her stomach as if it might give her a clue about what lay within. She looked at the magazines but they did not interest her. They were for children.

Some forty minutes later, at five minutes past four, the receptionist announced "the doctor will see you now."

Well, this is it, thought Dora, *one way or the other*. She stood up and walked into the inner office. Dr. Sheinberg was sitting at his desk. A group of test tubes stood in a rack in front of him.

"I'm sorry Dora. I won't beat around the bush. You are pregnant."

Dora felt her knees weaken. "Oh God. I knew it. What do I do?"

"Well, sit down. You're what, sixteen?

"I'll be seventeen next month."

"Well, what you do is really up to you and your family. If you want to have the baby, I can recommend a good Obstetrician."

"I don't know. I don't know."

"Well, since just last year, abortion is legal in New York state, though not in Connecticut. So, that's an option I guess. You could go to New York for an abortion. And if you want help with birth control, we can discuss that too. Of course, that's not the issue right now."

"I don't know… Man, I have time, right?

"Well yes, some time. You're not very far along at all. How long do you think?"

"It hasn't even been two months since.. you know."

"Yes, I know. And yes, you have some time, but I wouldn't take too long making decisions. The law in New York allows abortion up to the 24th week, in most cases, but generally, early abortions are safer."

"Oh God. Are you going to tell my parents?"

"No. I'll leave that to you. But you need to involve them. This is too big a decision for you to make alone."

"Yeah, okay. I guess. All right. Thank you. Uh, do I owe you any money?"

"We can worry about that later. Come back and tell me what you decide. In fact, make an appointment with Joanne to come back in three weeks and we'll see where we go."

"Uh, three weeks? Okay."

"Take care of yourself. Remember there's a life growing inside you now."

"Oh Jesus. Yeah, I know that."

"All right. We'll see you again in a few weeks."

Dora left his office and stood at the front counter. She made an appointment to return three weeks later.

She drove home in a state of confusion and fear.

CHAPTER 21

11/3/71 – Wednesday

Hank could see no way out. It had been three weeks since Maddie had suggested the loan from Generoso. Hank could not delay it any longer. He had tried to think of any other source of money. Friends, relatives, other banks, selling his possessions…he had considered and dismissed them all. He had even tentatively approached his sister and several college friends, none of whom he'd spoken with in years. They had all declined, some with more than a hint of annoyance. He had to accept the loan Maddie had found. They had to move forward. It was the only way. And if all went well, he'd still make money on his investment. So he would tell Maddie yes. He was sitting in his office. He picked up the phone and dialed her number. His door was closed and nobody could hear him, but he cupped his hand over the phone anyway as she answered.

"Hixon Realty."

"Maddie, it's Hank." He was whispering.

"Yes Hank."

"Well, I've decided to do it. I'll take the loan."

"It's about time. Okay, I'll let Rick know and get back to you."

"Uh, okay. Okay, thanks."

"You're welcome. Stay there. I'll get back to you soon."

She hung up. Hank stared at the receiver in his hand. It was shaking. He hung up the phone. He looked at the pile of papers on his desk. He stood up and immediately sat back down. He had to wait. This was it. This was a big step. He was betting everything, betting his life, he thought.

He couldn't work. He couldn't concentrate. He couldn't leave, so he sat there drumming a pencil on his desk, tapping his foot. *I just have to meet this guy. He'll give me the money. That will be it. I wonder if he'll want me to sign anything...*

The phone rang and Hank sat up straight. "Hello" he said.

"It's Maddie. I just spoke with Rick. He can meet you Monday, November 15th at 10 am. I suggested Lily's and he said that's good."

"The fifteenth? That's almost two weeks. Why so long?" Now that he had decided to do it, he was in a hurry to get it done.

"Well, I don't know. Maybe he needs time to get

the cash. Maybe he's busy. Whatever. That's the date."

"Uh, okay. I just wish it could be sooner. But, okay."

"All right. I'll let Mike know. I'm sure he'll want to see you right afterward."

"Oh yeah. Of course. All right. I'll be there."

"Good. It's the only way Hank. It'll be all right."

"Yeah, I know." Hank tried to sound more confident than he felt. He wanted to seem as strong and sure of himself as Maddie always seemed to be.

"All right. You take care. And for God's sake, don't mention this to anyone."

"No. Of course not. I won't."

"All right. The fifteenth. 10:00 am. At Lily's. I'll see you later. Try to take it easy."

She hung up and so did he. He was too keyed up to stay in his office any longer. *Try to take it easy. Yeah, right.* He got up from his desk and told Dorothy he was going home, that he didn't feel well. She looked at him curiously as he rushed out, not taking the time to button his raincoat.

Hank drove home. He was early. It was only 4:00 pm. He found Norma sitting on the couch, watching television. She was still in her bathrobe. Hank ignored her and walked into the kitchen. He sat at the table, clenching and unclenching his fists. He felt angry with Norma, angry with Maddie, angry with Walsh, angry with himself. The thought crossed his mind that he could get in his car and simply leave. He could just go. Leave Norma and leave his job. He could walk away from his investment in Newport Lane. He could do it. He could escape all this. It was tempting. *What really is keeping me here, after all?* He rubbed his forehead. *That's always been your way. When the going got tough, you got going.* He smiled. *You got going all right.* He suspected he had always left jobs when the challenges became difficult. No, this time he would stick it out. He was not going to run any more. For better or worse, he'd see this through.

He walked back to the living room and sat next to Norma on the couch. He really looked at her this time. She looked utterly forlorn. "You okay?" he asked.

"Yeah, I'm fine," she slurred. She remained focused on her television show. She was watching "One Life to Live."

Hank patted her leg. She turned and looked at him, as though she just realized he was there. "It's early. You're home early."

"I left work. Wanted to come home. I needed to get away. How come you're not dressed?" His tone was kindly. His anger had subsided. Norma looked so sad.

"I don't know. I just didn't feel like it. I'm kinda down, I guess."

"Why? What's going on?"

Norma could not remember the last time Hank had actually paid attention to her, the last time he seemed to care about her feelings. It warmed her. "Well, you know… Amy's modeling. I really hoped… but now…" Her eyes filled with tears.

Hank moved closer and pulled her to him. For the moment, he wasn't thinking about his own worries. He realized he still felt some vestige of love for Norma. "It's okay. It's okay," he said, stroking her hair.

"Oh Hank." She pushed herself into his sheltering arms. They stayed that way for several minutes. Then she turned her face up toward his and kissed him. "Let's go upstairs," he said. Moments later, they were passionately making love in their bed. Just as he climaxed, Hank closed his eyes and Maddie's face appeared in his mind.

CHAPTER 22

11/5/71 – Friday

Two days later in the late afternoon, Hank was at work when his phone rang.

"Mr. Latour?"

Hank cradled the phone against his shoulder, still reading the loan application on his desk. "Yes?"

"This is Sergeant Gargiulo at the police station. We have your daughter here. Dora. And her friend, Katie Price. You need to get down here."

"What? Why? What happened?"

"They were caught smoking marijuana this afternoon. In town, on the steps of the Y, in fact. We just picked them up."

"Oh Christ! Okay. Are they in jail or what?"

"No, they're with me, out front. Just come to the front desk."

"Uh, okay. I'll be right there."

The Sergeant hung up. Hank sat for a moment, staring at the phone in his hand. *Jesus Christ. Goddammit. Just what I need. I could kill her.*

Hank drove into the parking lot at the police station fifteen minutes later. He was angry. And he was worried that Dora might be in real trouble. *In broad daylight! Did she want to get caught?*

He parked and slammed the car door shut. He raced up the front steps, arriving red-faced, nearly out of breath. A cop sat at a high desk directly in front of him.

"I'm Dora Latour's father."

The cop gestured to a door to his right. "In there."

Hank walked through the door. Dora and Katie were seated on a long wooden bench. He expected his daughter to be defiant and surly. Instead, she looked up at him and her eyes filled with tears. "Daddy," she said.

His heart went out to her. She was frightened. She was his little girl again. He opened his arms and she ran to him. He held her as she sobbed. "It's all right," he said.

Sergeant Gargiulo appeared. "You can take them. They've had a warning. We searched 'em. Nothing on them. Nothing in their purses. It was just the one joint they were smoking. But they know we don't want to see anything like this again."

"Right. Absolutely not," said Hank. He looked at Katie. "C'mon, both of you."

Katie gathered her coat and her purse. She picked up the shoes that she had removed. She balanced on one foot and then the other to put them on. "Yeah, we're outta here," she said defiantly.

Dora looked up at her father. "I'm sorry."

"It's okay. Let's go." Hank gave a solemn nod to Gargiulo. Then, he and the two girls walked out together to the parking lot. At the car, Katie said "Those pigs, man. Can't believe they hassled us."

"Of course they did." Hank felt his anger return. "You broke the law. What'd you think they'd do? Smoking pot, in the middle of town. Jesus Christ. Of course they picked you up."

"They're pigs" announced Katie.

"Well, get in. We'll take you home."

Dora sat silently in the front seat. Katie was in the back. They arrived at Katie's house. As they came to a stop, Katie repeated "fucking pigs." Then she laughed and tapped Dora on the shoulder. "Call you later," she said, as she got out of the car.

Dora and Hank watched Katie enter the big empty house. They drove home. Dora was quiet and Hank said "We'll have a talk when we get home. Your mother needs to hear this."

But when they arrived, Norma was not home. They sat in the kitchen. "Okay," Hank said, "What were you thinking? You weren't thinking."

"No, I guess not."

Hank shook his head. "You got lucky this time. This kind of thing can't happen again. What is going on with you anyway? You stay out all night, you skip school. I see you in the diner. You look like crap…"

Dora started to get angry, but instead, her voice cracked. "Oh daddy. I have to tell you something. It's hard. I don't know what to do…"

"What? What are you talking about?"

"I'm pregnant. There, I've said it."

"You're pregnant? You're *pregnant!* How long? I mean, how… or who?"

"Yes, I am. It's been a couple of months. I had a test. I know it's true."

"Well, who did this to you? Was it, was it Jared? Was it him? Is he the father?"

"Yeah, it's Jared." Dora tried to say this with conviction. She hoped Jared was the father.

"Well, what does he plan to do about it?"

"Who? Oh Jared. Well, he doesn't even know. I mean, not yet."

"You haven't told him?

"I haven't told anybody. You're the first."

"Well Jesus Dora, this is serious. Something's gotta be done. You can't have a baby on your own. That's for sure. And you're too young to get married."

"Why? Mom got pregnant with me and she wasn't married…"

"What? Well, that was different. Those were different times. And she was older than you are."

"Yeah, I guess. So what am I supposed to do now?"

"I don't know. This has taken me by surprise. Maybe you could give it up for adoption. Or maybe get an abortion. Christ, I don't know. How did this happen, anyway?"

"How do you think?"

"Well, I know that, but didn't you use birth control? I mean you should have been careful."

"We tried. It just went wrong."

"Did the rubber break? Or… never mind. I don't want to know. When are you going to tell Jared? Do I need to talk to his parents? I'm going to have to talk to his parents."

"I don't know. I don't know what to do. I'm not

sure I want him to know."

"This will put your mother right over the edge, you know."

"Well, I'm sorry about that. But it's not her problem."

"Oh no? It's all our problem."

"Never mind. I'll figure it out." Dora pushed herself away from the table. "I'm going upstairs."

Hank sat there, stunned and angry. *What next? I can't believe this. Fuck. Things could not possibly be worse. We have to deal with the Appletons about this.*

****

That night, at dinner, Dora announced her pregnancy to Norma and Amy. They were at the kitchen table. Her father sat stone-faced. They all looked at Norma. She was shaking her head. "Pregnant," she said, "pregnant."

"Yes, mom. Just like you were with me 17 years ago."

Norma shook her head. "That was different. I wasn't living at home. And your father and I got married. We made a mistake. But we handled it. We handled it then."

Dora felt a surge of anger. "And I'll handle it now!"

"Oh sure. Hank, did you know about this?"

"She told me this afternoon. Jared's the father. We'll have to talk with the Appletons."

"No. Wait." Dora protested. She wanted to be the one to talk to Jared. She did not want him to hear about it from his parents. That would only lead to more trouble, she thought. "I'll talk to Jared. Let me talk to him first."

Amy watched the scene before her. She felt like a bird staring in the window. *This is what can happen. Serves Dora right. Now everyone's mad at her. She deserves it.* Amy stayed silent.

"You'll talk to him?" said Norma. "And say what?"

"What? I'll tell you what," Dora shouted. "I'll tell him it's our baby. He'll want to keep it. I know him. He will."

"Well, his parents may have something to say about it," said her father. "Anyway, there is no way you can have this child. You have no way to support it and I won't."

Her mother announced. "You'll get an abortion. That's what we'll do."

"No way. I'm having this baby," Dora was surprised to hear herself say this aloud. In that rebellious instant, she had made her decision.

"We'll see about that," said her father.

Before that moment, Dora had not made up her mind to have the baby but somehow she felt forced into that position during the conversation. Her parents wanted to do whatever caused them the least trouble. At least that's how it felt to Dora. They never asked her what she might have wanted. Thinking about it, she felt a smug sense of satisfaction. She would have this baby. She'd show them. But she found herself wondering how Jared would react. She had to tell him, and soon, before all the parents jumped on him one way or the other. She had to know what he thought. She resolved to call him that night, before anything further happened.

Dinner was over. "I'm going to my room," Dora said. "I need to be away from everybody, everything."

"Are you planning to smoke more pot? I had to go to the Police Station to get her today," her father stated to the table.

"What?" Norma was confused. "What happened today?"

"Dora was caught smoking pot in the middle of town, right out in the open."

"She was? By the police? What happened?

"They let her off with a warning."

That does it, thought Amy. *I don't ever want to be anything like Dora.*

"Well that must have made you happy," said her mother.

"It was no big deal. Jesus, mom. It was just pot."

"Just pot. I guess we should be grateful it wasn't heroin. Maybe next time you can shoot heroin in front of the Police Station."

Dora got up and ran out of the room.

"What has happened to her?" her father wondered out loud.

****

Up in her room, Dora held the phone in her hand. She had wanted to call Jared right away, but she hesitated. *How would he react? Did it matter? Should I even tell him? Yes, I have to, or else his parents will.* She dialed the phone.

"Appleton residence," his mother answered brightly.

"Uh, hi Mrs. Appleton. It's Dora. Is Jared there?"

"Yes, he's upstairs. Hold on." Dora listened as she heard Betty Appleton shout "Sweetie, if's for you."

"Hello" Jared said after a few minutes.

"Hi. I think I need to see you." Her voice shook.

"Wow, you sound serious. Is everything cool? I heard you got busted today."

"Oh that, yeah. I'm fine. They let me go. No, this is something else. Let's meet at the park? At the bench. Is that okay?"

"Wow, very mysterious." He laughed. "Sure. What time?"

"Well now, if you can."

"Okay, man. I'll see you in like, fifteen, twenty minutes."

"Thanks," she said, surprised at how relieved she felt.

A short while later, they sat facing each other on a bench in the little park in town.

"So, what's up?" Jared was still smiling. He enjoyed being out, enjoying whatever this mystery might be.

"Well," Dora paused a moment. She looked at his face. It was full in the moonlight, open and expectant. She felt encouraged. He seemed happy to be with her. "Well," she said, "I'm pregnant."

"You are? Really? Wow, that's big. Are you sure?"

"Yes, of course I'm sure." Dora was suddenly annoyed. "I saw Dr. Sheinberg. He did a test. No question about it. I'm pregnant."

"And it's mine?"

"Yes…yes." Dora's voice dropped to a whisper as she said it again sounding less certain than she would have liked.

"I mean, are you sure? Are you sure it was me?"

"Of course." She felt her anger surface. This was not quite the reaction she was hoping for. "Who else would it be?"

"Well, I don't know. I just thought… I don't know what I thought."

"Well, yeah, it's yours. You're the father."

"And you want to have the baby? Is that what you want?"

"I don't know. I mean yes. Yes, I do. You can be with me or not. It's up to you."

"Well, of course. If it's my kid, I'd have to do something. I mean if you're going to go ahead and have it. You don't want to get an abortion, I guess."

"No, I don't want an abortion. We're Catholic. And I don't want to give it up for adoption. I'm going to have a baby. That's what I'm doing." Dora felt her stomach clench. She glared at him.

"I guess you've made up your mind. I don't

know… I have to think about all this."

"Well, yeah. You think about it."

"Uh, how soon? Do you know how soon you're due?"

"Not for like seven months."

Jared did some quick calculations. That would mean two months ago. He tried to remember the times they had sex. He supposed it must be his child. Or maybe not. He felt unsteady and precarious, as if he were in a small rowboat in the middle of the ocean. He tried to imagine the future, but it was a haze at the moment. He felt his life changing course.

"All right. I need to just, you know, process this, you know? I'm not saying no. I mean I want to do the right thing. I just need to think."

"Yeah, well, you think about it." Dora was sullen. She thought *he's not going to help. He's not going to be there for me.*

"I know. I'm just trying to get my head around it. I gotta get home." He reached out and gave her a hug. Dora hugged him back stiffly.

They parted and each drove home.

CHAPTER 23

11/8/71 – Monday

The Wilhelmina agency wanted Amy. It was 9:00 am, the start of a new week. Hank was at work. Amy and Dora were in school. Norma had finally dragged herself out of bed, gotten her morning drink and slumped on the couch when the phone rang. She groggily answered it on the fifth ring.

"Mrs. Latour?

"Yes?"

"This is Ginger Watson at Wilhelmina Models. We would like you to come in with Amy."

"What!" Norma jolted upright.

"We'd like to get a look at her in person."

"Yes, yes of course. When?"

"Well, as soon as you can. We know you're in Connecticut and Amy is probably in school. What would work for you?"

"I don't know. Let me think. Maybe later this

week… No. Could we come in Monday? Next Monday?" Norma knew she needed time to get organized.

"That's good. Shall we say ten that morning?"

"Yes, yes, great. We just come to your office there? I have the address. We'll come there?"

"Yes, please."

"Uh, okay, great. Great. Thanks."

"You're welcome. We look forward to seeing you both on Monday."

"Wait. What will we be doing? I mean what's the plan? What do we need to bring?

"Oh, well, just yourselves really. We really just need to see Amy in person. We'll show you both around, meet some of the staff. We may make plans for a shoot. If we get to that point, there's contracts, legal stuff, we'll need to cover. So, just in case, be prepared to stay in the city overnight."

"Overnight. Okay. We'll need some place to stay. We'll get a hotel. That's not a problem."

"Okay, good. So we're set then? Monday, at 10:00 am.?"

"Yes. Yes, I think so. I got it. Thanks. Thanks so much."

Norma hung up. She was energized. *My God. They do want her! I was right. I knew it.*

It was as though the last six weeks of gnawing discouragement and despair had not happened. Norma was again wildly enthusiastic. She thought about taking Amy out of school for the day, to start getting ready. But that wasn't necessary, she realized. She needed time to think and plan first anyway. They would need a hotel. She had to check the train schedule. She'd need some money. She hoped Amy would come straight home from school. *Maybe I'll go pick her up. Yes, I'll get her right after school. She'll be so excited.*

Norma busied herself around the house happily for the remainder of the morning. She wanted her house to look good. She straightened up the kitchen. She examined herself in the mirror and a grinning woman stared back at her. She was excited and didn't pour another drink until almost noon. That vodka calmed her down. She decided to get her hair done later in the week, when she had time. She wanted to look good as well. *And we'll get Amy's hair done too,* she decided.

At 2:30, Norma left her house and drove to Long Lots Junior High school. She parked in the lot across from the front entrance. *Amy will come out soon*, she thought. *School ends at 3:00 pm.* Norma decided to get out of the car and wait just outside the doors. But she was too restless, so she entered the school just as the bell rang. The halls suddenly teemed with students, talking loudly and bumping into one another. Norma scanned the crowd for Amy, but did not see her. She decided she had better wait by the front. She returned to the entrance, amid the bustling mob. Suddenly she saw Amy's tall head appear. She rushed through the crowd and grabbed Amy's arm.

"Mom! What are you doing here?"

"I came to pick you up. I have the most wonderful news!" She was wide-eyed with energy.

Amy stared at her mother for a moment. "What?"

"The Wilhelmina Modeling Agency wants you. They called this morning."

"They do? They want me? Really? What did they say?"

"Well, they want us there at their office next Monday morning. In a week. To see you. To meet us. We'll go to New York for two days. Isn't that wonderful? I knew this would happen. I knew it!"

"Next Monday? But what about school?"

"Forget school. This is your future. This is what we've been waiting for."

"I know. I know... But I mean I still have school though. What about school?"

"Jesus. Don't worry about school. You'll still have school. But this is big. This is your big chance. It's a lot bigger than school, for God's sake."

"Yeah, okay." Amy was a bit bewildered. She could not imagine how the two, modeling and school, could fit together. "What does dad say?"

"What? He'll be happy for us. C'mon." Her mother took her hand and pulled her along to their car in the parking lot. "Let's go."

They drove home. Norma spoke non-stop throughout the trip. "We'll get our hair done. We'll buy you and me some new clothes. We need to make a good first impression. I mean all they've seen of you is a few photos. So we want to impress them when they see you in person."

Amy did her best to listen and take it in.

"Wait til we tell your father," said Norma. She'd forgotten to call him with the big news.

When they got home, Norma called the bank, but Dorothy informed her that Hank was out. She did not know where he was or if he would be coming back. Norma hung up the phone impatiently.

"Your father isn't there. They don't know where he is. I'm sure he'll be home soon. We'll tell him when he gets here."

"All right. Can I go upstairs?"

"Of course. I have a lot to do."

Amy climbed the stairs and sat down in her room, looking out the window. The fields outside seemed far away to her. She tried to picture New York. She vaguely remembered a noisy, crowded city, with big buildings surrounding her. She squirmed. It was frightening. She really had no idea what to expect.

CHAPTER 24

That afternoon, Hank sat at his desk worrying about his upcoming meeting with the loan shark. It was now a week away. This was a new realm for him. He was worried he was betting his life. He wasn't. At worst, his kneecaps might be in jeopardy. But he didn't know that. As he thought about it, he told himself he still had a choice. He could back out. But then again, he couldn't seem to find the money anywhere else. So if he backed out, he'd lose the $50,000 he'd already put in. *Was that so awful?* He thought it wasn't just the money. It was the feeling that his life would be a failure, that he'd achieved nothing after all this time. No, he had to go through with it.

On a whim, he stood up from his desk and left his office. He thought he might go and speak to Maddie. He wanted to see her in person. Somehow, he thought she would straighten him out, help rid him of his anxieties. He drove in the direction of her office.

As he rounded the corner onto Imperial Avenue and saw her building, he spotted her coming out, walking toward her car. He drove past. He did not want her to see him, embarrassed to be seeking her out to lessen his own worries. He drove on up the hill and made a U-turn in the parking lot of the Women's Club. He started back toward her office, thinking he would see where she went. Maybe he could "accidentally" bump into her in town.

He approached slowly as her blue Ford Mustang emerged from the lot and turned away from him. From a safe distance, he followed her. The stoplight at the Post Road was green and she turned right. He made the light and turned the same direction, hoping he had not been spotted. From several cars behind, he watched her car make its way through the traffic to the top of a large hill, where she turned left onto Roseville Road. Hank made the same turn at the light. He tried to stay with her on the winding hills and just saw her car as it turned right on to Salem Road. He made the same turn. The road bent to the left and he watched as she pulled in to the driveway of a large, modern colonial home. He had been to that house before. The mailbox read "Holden."

So Maddie was visiting Mike Holden. *What did that mean? Why at his home and not his job site?* Hank continued driving until he intersected Colony Road, which he knew would eventually lead to North Avenue. He stopped at that intersection and thought for a moment. He felt more confused than ever. It was none of his business what Maddie did or who she saw. He guessed she might be meeting with Mike to discuss the development. But could she be sleeping with him? He could not imagine it and did not want to. Still, he wondered.

He decided not to return to work. It was late

afternoon anyway. He started driving toward his home. Suddenly he thought of Dora. They had not discussed the pregnancy with the Appletons. He thought that was long overdue. This was his daughter after all. So he headed instead toward the Appleton's house. Ten minutes later, he pulled into their driveway. He parked and walked up the steps to the entrance. Rather than ring the bell, he used the large shiny brass door knocker that sat prominently on their elegant white front door.

He heard Betty Appleton's singsong voice say "I'm coming." Her chubby face greeted him with a smile. "Hank. This is a surprise. Come in."

"Hi Betty. I hope you don't mind my stopping by unannounced."

"Not at all. Would you like some tea? I've just put up a pot. Or something stronger, maybe?" She grinned at the thought.

"No. Thanks. I uh.. I just need to talk to you."

"Uh oh," she smiled. "Well in that case, have a seat," she said, still in bright good humor. She led him to the living room. He sat in one of the big easy chairs and she perched nearby on the end of the couch.

"Well, yes, I guess it's uh, pretty serious," Hank stuttered. "Has uh, Jared spoken to you yet?"

"Spoken to me? About what?" Now she seemed alarmed.

"I guess not… No easy way to say this. Jared has gotten Dora pregnant."

"WHAT? Oh my God! When?"

"Well, as far as we can tell, two or three months ago."

"That's terrible. This could ruin his life. We have to do something."

"Yes. That's why I'm here. That's what we need to talk about."

"I want to call Vince. He needs to be here. I want him here."

"Okay." Hank watched as she bustled out of the room. He could hear the alarm in her voice as she spoke with her husband on the phone. Minutes later, she hung up and returned to the living room.

"He'll be right home. Oh my God. This is terrible. Terrible. I'm so upset. I can't tell you."

"We'll figure it out." Hank did his best to sound reassuring. He did not like dealing with this quivering woman. She sat back down and looked at him, her eyes filling with tears.

They sat that way for some time, Betty quietly crying, Hank, lost in his own thoughts. Instead of Jared and Dora, he found himself thinking about Maddie and Holden and with a start, he remembered his upcoming meeting with the loan shark. He was snapped back to the present by the sound of a car pulling in the driveway.

"Oh, there he is. Thank God," said Betty.

Vince Appleton burst through the front door. He did not sit down. He stood in front of Hank with both hands on his hips. "Tell me what happened."

Hank was a bit disconcerted by the stern demeanor of the usually mild-mannered Vince Appleton. "Well, they must have been together at some point a few months ago. They had sex. She got pregnant. It happens."

"Impossible," said Vince. "Not Jared. He would not make a dumb mistake like that."

"Oh no? How do you know? Are you saying you don't believe he's the father?" Suddenly Hank found himself ready to do battle.

"There are blood tests. I want to know if it is his or not." Betty looked up at her husband. She said nothing, but fidgeted nervously, as her eyes teared up again.

"I understand that can be done after a child is born, I think. But Dora would not lie about this. If she says it's Jared's, then it's Jared's."

"Well, I'm not convinced, Hank. Frankly your daughter is a tramp. I'll bet she's been with other boys."

Hank bristled. "I don't have to listen to this. You talk to Jared. See what he says."

"Oh we will. I think he'll tell a different story."

"I've heard enough." Hank got up abruptly, threw on his coat and stormed out the door.

Betty stared at the space where Hank had been sitting a moment ago. She turned to her husband. "What's going to happen?"

"I don't know. Let's not make any decisions until we talk with Jared. He should be home soon, right?"

"Oh, I'm sure he'll be home for dinner."

"All right. Just calm down. We'll figure this thing out." Vince was not calm himself. He alternated being furious with Hank for accusing his innocent son and being furious with Jared for getting that slut pregnant. Whichever it was, he was angry at someone.

"I guess I'll get started on dinner, then." Betty got up to busy herself in the kitchen.

Vince could not sit down. He paced around the room. Finally, he went to the kitchen and filled a glass with ice. He returned to the living room and poured himself a scotch. He wanted to be alone with his thoughts.

An hour later, Jared came home. He was stoned. He'd been smoking pot in the park. He started to go upstairs to his room, but his father blocked his way. "Come sit down with us. We have something to ask you." Jared was steered to the living room. His mother came running in from the kitchen. She and Vince sat on the couch on either side of him.

Jared turned to his father, his eyes slightly bloodshot. "What's going on?" It occurred to him that his parents did not realize he was high. He had been smoking pot almost continually all weekend and most of this Monday.

"We had a visit today from Hank Latour. He claims you got his daughter pregnant. Dora."

"Oh. I uh, I don't know."

"You don't know? What do you mean you don't know? Did you have sex with that girl?"

"Did you, honey?" His mother covered his hand with hers. He turned and looked at her tear-stained face.

"Well, yes… I did. I guess I could be the father."

"Oh God," his mother wailed.

Jared turned back to look at his father. He saw anger, even rage, there. He shrank back.

"So what do you propose to do?" his father asked him.

"Well, I don't know. I mean I guess I'm the father."

"So you don't know for sure."

"Not really. Not for sure. Dora says I'm the father."

"You two have talked about it?"

"Well, yeah. She told me."

"And what does she want? She probably wants money or she wants you to marry her. Is that what she said?"

"Oh God," Betty wailed.

"No she didn't say any of that. She just told me. That's all. Like a few days ago."

"And were you planning to tell us? Were you thinking about this at all?" Vince's anger was now clearly focused on his son.

"I don't know. I need to process it. I don't know what I was thinking." His mind felt hazy, as if he were adrift in a cloud.

"Well, I know one thing," said his father, "you can't raise a baby. And you're going to college. We're not going to let this ruin your future."

"Yeah. No. I know. You're right." Jared was trying to pay attention.

"As I see it, there are only two choices. Either she gets an abortion or she gives the baby up for adoption. She can't raise a child by herself and no way in the world you marry this girl."

"Okay, dad." Jared felt his usual bravado evaporate completely. He felt powerless and unsure of himself. And being stoned made it all seem rather vague and distant. He tried to think. "I don't know what Dora wants to do," he said.

"Well, we can help with money, if necessary. But that's it. We have to concentrate on your life, your future."

Vince felt calmer. He looked at his son. He saw he was scared and confused. He placed a reassuring hand on the boy's shoulder. "We'll get you through this and get you on with your life. You have a bright future. No reason that should change. We'll get through this."

Betty smiled for the first time. Her hand had never left Jared's. Now she squeezed it fondly.

Vince got up. "Okay. That's that. She'll decide what she's doing, but we know what we're *not* doing. Let's have some dinner."

Jared felt wobbly. He stood up. He really did not know what to think, but he was relieved that his parents seemed calmer.

****

When Hank arrived home, he was still boiling about the Appletons. *That fucking Vince had his nerve calling Dora a tramp. Christ!* Norma had dinner on the table. Her excitement filled the air. She was talking enthusiastically with Amy. Hank had planned to discuss

Dora and Jared with her, but he postponed that since she seemed to be totally focused on Amy. Besides, Dora was not home. The three of them sat around the kitchen table. Hank found it hard to listen to Norma's dreams. His mind was elsewhere. *What about Dora? She's pregnant, for Heaven's sake. The Appletons don't even believe it's Jared's baby. And Christ, I have to deal with this guy, Generoso.* He squirmed. The image of Maddie flashed through his mind again. *And now this. Norma wants to take Amy to New York, to become a model.*

Hank snapped himself back to the present, to the conversation at the table.

Norma was saying "We'll need your credit card. We're going to stay in a hotel. I found a Howard Johnson's there, not too far from Wilhelmina."

"What? How long are you going for?

"Oh, just overnight. We'll go early next Monday morning and stay Monday night. Don't you think this is amazing?" Norma turned to Hank. Her eyes sparkled.

"I guess. I don't know." Hank really could not envision what this modeling business might mean. He just knew it was important for Norma. "What about you, Amy?" he asked. He turned to face her. "How's my little girl with all this? Is this really what you want to do? You're only what, fourteen? Is it what you want?"

"It's okay, I guess. I think I'd like it." She said, turning to look at her mother.

"Well I'm not sure this is the best thing for you."

"What? What are you talking about, Hank?" Norma interjected, practically shouting.

"Well, it's just.. she has school. And we don't have a lot of money right now.

"Jesus, Hank. Money won't be a problem. Do you know what models make? Once you're famous, a cover girl? When Amy gets there, she'll be rich. We'll be rich."

Hank looked doubtfully at Amy. "Rich, huh? I don't even know if it's safe." He turned to Norma. "I'm worried for her."

"I'll be with her," said Norma.

That did not especially reassure Hank. His feelings were jumbled. Soon he would be meeting with Generoso. That worried him. At the same time, he worried about Amy becoming involved in a highly pressured and possibly dangerous business like modeling. On the other hand, she seemed to want to do it. It might make money, and it was clearly important to Norma. He admitted to himself that this would occupy them while he had plenty of other concerns to deal with. In the end, he decided not to intervene.

Filled with doubts, he let himself trust Norma. "You be careful down there, in the city," he told her. "Watch out for her."

"Of course,' said Norma.

Of course, Amy said to herself.

CHAPTER 25

11/15/71 – Monday

Knowing they might spend the night, Amy and her mother had each packed a small bag. It was early on a rainy Monday morning and Hank drove them to the Greens Farms train station before heading to work. He had to admit Norma looked better than she had in years, more animated and less blotchy. He wished them luck and reiterated his concern that they be careful. As he pulled away, he glanced at Amy standing on the sidewalk under an awning, where he had left her. She held her small overnight bag tightly with both hands. She seemed rooted to the damp pavement. He watched in his rear view mirror as Norma ran up the steps to enter the station. Amy followed slowly a moment later. Shaking his head slightly, Hank left them behind.

Finding her mother at the window buying their tickets, Amy watched quietly. Norma turned to her and said breathlessly, "We're on the 7:42. It will be here in ten minutes." Amy merely nodded.

Together, they walked out the trackside door and stood on the platform, under the small overhang, out of the rain. To Amy, it felt like a dream. Her mother squeezed her upper arm and said "Isn't this exciting! I can hardly wait. In a little while, we'll be in New York and you'll be on your way to becoming a model!"

Amy smiled, more at her mother's happiness than for her own. She had been to New York a couple of times and had not liked it.

The train pulled in and they got on board. They sat together. As the train began to move, Norma babbled excitedly. "When we get to the city, we'll go to a bathroom and freshen up. We'll have time. Maybe get a little snack. I don't know. We have to get down to 22nd Street, so we'll have to get a taxi. We should do that first. We need to stay dry. Then maybe eat. I don't know. We'll see when we get there. But we're on our way!" She grinned. Her cheeks were flushed. She had not had a drink today and didn't think she wanted one. But she had her emergency supply, just in case.

Amy gazed out the window of the train, barely listening. She watched the trees fly by. She saw the water carving through the marshy fields as they passed Sherwood Island. A lone white crane posed, its long legs half submerged. They passed through downtown Westport and on through Norwalk. There were fewer trees and more buildings. Amy turned away from the window and folded her hands in her lap. She heard her mother say "I think this is Stamford next. Won't be long now."

To Amy, it did seem long, but finally they arrived at Grand Central Station. The platform was crowded and they moved with the throng into the cavernous station. It was very noisy and everything looked dirty to Amy. She shrank back, but her mother pulled her along. "C'mon. Let's go" she urged.

They walked up a long corridor, out the oversized doors and on to Lexington Avenue. Cars whizzed by. Horns honked. People rushed past them. Amy felt dizzy. The city seemed like an enormous, pulsing creature. It moved furiously around her and seemingly, right through her. People, taxis, buses, all seemed to be going somewhere urgently. They screamed at her. She felt amorphous, as if she had no mass, no solidity. Her mother stepped up to the curb, covering her head with her purse and waved for a cab. One stopped and they climbed in. It was not yet 9:00 am. "22nd Street and Park Avenue. Park Avenue South," Norma said to the driver.

Ten minutes later, they were standing at the corner of 22nd and Park. The rain had let up somewhat. Norma pointed to her left. "The agency is down that way, number 119. We're early. Let's go to a restaurant with a bathroom."

They found a diner one block north. Sitting in a booth, Norma ordered coffee for herself and a glass of orange juice for Amy. "I don't think we should eat anything. I did bring a toothbrush, but let's not chance it," she explained.

"Sure," said Amy.

"We'll use the bathroom here. You'll wash up.

I'll make sure your hair and makeup are good. Then we can go. Use your umbrella. Don't want your hair getting wet."

"Okay."

After going together to the small bathroom, they walked the two blocks to Wilhelmina. They were fifteen minutes early. They entered and approached the receptionist, saying they had an appointment with Ginger Watson. The woman smiled at them and asked them to have a seat. "I'll let Ginger know you're here."

They turned and sat in the brightly lit reception area. A glass coffee table held glossy fashion magazines. Norma fussed with Amy's hair and applied a little more lipstick. She picked up an issue of Vogue and pointed to Lauren Hutton on the cover. The model stared out with a gap-toothed smile. "Well, if she can do it, I know you can."

Amy looked at the photograph and tried to imagine herself in the model's place. It was impossible. Lauren Hutton looked very thin and waif-like. At the same time, she exuded confidence. Amy thought she had none of those traits. "I don't know. Maybe."

"Of course you can." Norma started paging through the magazine. Amy sat still and waited.

About ten minutes later, a young woman walked into the room. She was tall and slender, wearing gold-rimmed glasses and carrying a clipboard. "Amy? Norma?"

"Yes, that's us." Norma answered, dropping the magazine.

"Hi. I'm Ginger Watson." She walked up to them quickly. "And you're Amy." She held out her hand for Amy to take. Norma jumped up. Amy reached up to shake Ginger's hand and was literally pulled up out of her chair.

"So nice to meet you." Ginger smiled at Amy and let go of her hand. She turned to Norma "And you."

Norma shook her hand enthusiastically. "We're so glad to be here. Thank you for calling."

"Oh, certainly. We're very excited about Amy." She turned and looked at Amy. "You are even prettier than your pictures."

Amy blushed and muttered. "Thank you, Miss Watson." Her father had advised her to be polite, an unnecessary instruction for Amy.

"Well, come this way," said Ginger. "We'll go to my office."

They followed Ginger down a long corridor with white walls on which hung photos of famous models. Amy stared at these in wonderment. She could not imagine herself pictured in one of these framed portraits.

"Have a seat," Ginger said as they entered a large brightly lit room. It seemed an unlikely office. Instead of a desk, there were several Eames chairs, another glass coffee table and two potted Ficus trees on either side of a large floor-to-ceiling window. They each sat in a chair. Ginger sat down facing them and glanced at her clipboard.

"So, Amy, why do you want to be a model?"

Amy had been staring at more framed photos on the wall. She reacted with a start and said "I don't really... I..."

Before she could finish the sentence, her mother announced "Amy loves having her picture taken. She can't wait to be on the cover of Vogue. She wants to be a famous model. She's just a little shy about admitting it." Norma beamed.

"Well, one step at a time." Ginger smiled at Norma. "It takes a lot of work to get to that level."

"I know. I'm sure. But Amy has always been a hard worker, haven't you Amy?"

Amy nodded.

"Okay," said Ginger to Amy. "We think you have tremendous potential. A great face. And good stats. And I can see good posture, a natural, fluid walk. Yes, we'd like to sign you."

"That's it? Just like that?" Norma asked.

"Pretty much. I think we can use her in some catalog work. Teen clothing. And maybe her face for cosmetics. Maybe runway. We'll see. But yes, we want her."

"Okay. Okay. I knew it. I just knew it. This is what we wanted, Amy." Norma got out of her chair and leaned over Amy, awkwardly hugging her seated daughter.

Amy sat with her arms at her sides. She felt frozen. Nothing seemed real.

"So, we'll need you to meet with our contracts officer. He and our lawyer will put together a contract for you. It will be an exclusive with us. You'll be a Wilhelmina model, Amy."

Amy nodded mutely and forced herself to smile.

"All right. Good. Can you come back tomorrow, say at nine? We'll have you sign up and get you started."

"Okay, tomorrow. Sure. nine o'clock. We'll be here," said Norma.

"Great."

Back in the reception area, Ginger bid them goodbye. "I hope you liked what you saw," she said to Amy.

"Yes, she did." Norma replied.

"Good. We'll see you both back here tomorrow morning."

"We'll be here," Norma repeated.

With that, Ginger left the room. Norma smiled at the receptionist. "We'll be back tomorrow morning," She said with a big grin. She took Amy's hand and they left. It was not yet 11:00 AM.

They walked to their hotel to check in. It was too early and they were told to return in a couple of hours. Norma, still energized, took this in stride and told Amy they would get some breakfast and then come back. They found a coffee shop on 23rd street. Norma had a Western Omelet. Amy only wanted toast.

Their hotel room turned out to be small, but serviceable. It was clean and contained two twin beds. Glancing around, Norma took her purse and walked into the bathroom, closing the door behind her. By this time, she needed a drink. She pulled the vodka from her purse and took a long swallow. *I need to get more*, she thought. *Don't want to run out.*

The rest of the day passed uneventfully. They walked along the bustling sidewalks. They stopped at a liquor store where Norma bought a pint of vodka which she fit in her purse. "Something for later," she said to Amy.

They walked on and had dinner in the same diner where they had coffee and juice that morning. Amy was hungry, though Norma found she had little interest in dinner. Amy limited herself to a small salad, the dressing on the side. Norma had a bowl of chicken noodle soup with a Coke.

After dinner, they spent a little time walking around Union Square, but Norma was preoccupied and Amy felt a little frightened. They returned to their hotel room.

"We should probably get an early night's sleep. We have a big day tomorrow."

"What's going to happen?" asked Amy.

"Well I guess we'll sign a contract and you'll officially be a model. It's fantastic, really."

"I don't know, Mom. I guess so."

"Of course it is. You'll see. I promise."

Amy looked skeptically at her mother, but said "Okay." She felt ambivalent about what she'd seen. It did seem exciting. She had to admit that, but it made her anxious. The models seemed so beautiful and composed. It was intimidating. She imagined a photo shoot. She pictured hectic frenzied activity. *Maybe for the models, it's calmer*, she thought hopefully, *like they were the quiet center, like the eye of a storm. Was it just a matter of standing still and smiling?* She supposed she could do that.

Norma called down for a 7:00 am wakeup call. They were both in bed by 10:00 pm.

****

Since she told him over a week ago, Dora had not spoken with Jared. He said he had to "process" the fact of her pregnancy, but she had not realized that meant avoiding her. Regardless, she had her own thinking to do. The more she thought about it, the more she liked the idea of having a baby, becoming a mother. It would be hard, she knew, but this was the era of Women's Lib. A woman on her own could make it in the world, she told herself. She tried to shrug off her fears. She wished Jared would come through or at least show some interest, but if not, she told herself she'd be all right.

Dora initially thought that she would not reach out again to Jared. If he wanted to help, he knew where to find her. She dwelled on this for a while, but finally thought, *no, I should talk to him.* It was early morning. He would not have left for school yet. She picked up the phone and quickly dialed his number. His mother answered.

"Is Jared there?" she asked. "It's Dora."

"Well yes, but he's getting ready for school." Betty Appleton told her.

"I just want to talk to him for a minute."

"All right, I suppose. Let me see if he can talk."

Several minutes passed. Jared came on the line. "Hi," he said.

"I haven't heard from you in like two weeks. What's going on?"

"I don't know. I have to think about college you know. I've got to get applications out and everything."

"Uh huh. So you're going to college. Right. Fine."

"No wait. Dora. C'mon. I haven't figured this all out."

"And when are you going to figure it out?"

"Well, like what do you want from me? Are we supposed to get married or something?"

"I'm not saying that. I don't even know if you care. Actually, I don't care if you don't care. You got school. You gotta go. Listen. Goodbye. " Dora was close to tears, but she was not going to let Jared hear her cry. She hung up.

At the other end of the line, Jared shook his head. *What am I supposed to do? Man, I cannot deal with this. I need to get high.*

Dora meanwhile was not sure exactly what she wanted. Jared sounded like he wanted nothing to do with her, so the hell with him. Besides, it still troubled her that she was not certain who the father was. It could be Jared; but it could be Fig. She decided she needed to talk to Fig. Maybe he would want to help, if he thought it might he his child.

Her mother and sister were in New York. Her father was at work. Dora resolved to go find Fig. She would take her mother's car. She went to her mother's bedroom to look for the car keys. She found them on the dresser and was stuffing them in her pocket when she noticed her mother's jewelry box. She placed her hand on it for a moment. Then she quickly opened it and snatched a gold bracelet.

Walking quickly downstairs, feeling almost as if someone were watching her, she hurried out to the car. She knew Fig was probably working at the record store. She headed toward downtown Westport. She thought *I'll just tell him. See what he says.*

She managed to find a parking spot on Main Street and hurried to the store. It was simply called Westport Records. She rushed into the small shop, and there he was, standing behind the counter. He was alone. She walked up to the counter and glanced down. It was covered with decals, logos for Led Zeppelin, T-Rex and Black Sabbath. Looking around, she noticed the walls above the racks of albums were painted black. Then she faced Figgy who seemed as skinny and edgy as ever. He was grinning at her.

"Hey Dor, what's happenin?"

"Hi Fig. I wanted to talk to you."

"Far out. I'm just hangin', you know."

"Yeah. Um, listen. You remember when I went back to your place that other time?"

"Oh yeah, for sure."

"Well, uh, you remember we had sex."

"Definitely." He appraised her with a grin. "Why, you wanna get high and do it again?"

"No. No, man."

"Well, what then?"

"Well, I'm pregnant. And I think it might be yours."

"What! No way, man. That one time? I can't see it. That would be a major bummer."

"A bummer. Yeah, but I don't know. It might be…it might be yours."

"Or someone else's? Is that what you're saying?"

Dora wasn't sure exactly what she was saying. This baby had a father and she really wanted it to be Jared, not Fig. "Yeah, I guess it could be. It could be someone else's." Dora felt her resolve weaken. This was ridiculous to try to expect any help from a speed freak like Fig.

"Well, I don't know, man. That's a bummer." Fig was staring off into space. "What…"

"This was a mistake. Never mind. I'm sure it isn't yours Fig. Look, just forget it."

"Yeah, okay. I…" Before he could finish the

sentence, Dora had wheeled around and bolted out of the store.

On her way back to her car, she thought *what was I thinking? That was a stupid idea. I can't have people thinking I don't even know who the father is. And Fig would be worthless, less than worthless, anyway. What was I thinking?*

She returned to her empty house at noon. She sat in her room fingering her mother's bracelet. She had to think. She wanted to keep the baby. She didn't know how, but she thought she would have to get money. She'd get an apartment. Somehow, she would do it, even if she had to do it alone. Her thoughts turned to Jared. *Maybe he would "process" it and join me. We could raise the baby together. And he could pay some of the expenses. It was possible. Or not. He didn't sound too eager. Either way, this is my decision. It's my life and I'm going to have a baby, no matter what anyone says.*

CHAPTER 26

That same day, Hank sat nervously at a table in Lily's Diner. It was 10:00 am. Across from him was Rick Generoso. The loan shark looked like any other businessman who might have been in Lily's that morning, except for the cold black eyes that locked on to Hank's. Those eyes stayed fixed on Hank as the man slid a leather briefcase across the floor to Hank's feet.

"A thousand a month. Right here, this time, the fifteenth of each month. And the four hundred large, two years from today. Don't make me come looking for you."

Hank nodded as Generoso got up and left. Hank sat for a moment, his mouth dry as sand. He was a jumble of nerves as he picked up the briefcase and left a dollar on the table, though neither had ordered a thing.

The day was overcast and still felt damp from the earlier rain. Hank hurried to his car carrying the briefcase. It felt heavy to him. He half expected to be struck by lightning, but it was a quiet, peaceful morning. Generoso was nowhere in sight. Hank placed the briefcase on the passenger seat and started his car. His next stop was Mike Holden's office.

Holden's office was really only a shed at the construction site. Hank parked in the mud and walked up the two wooden planks that served as steps. He knocked on the door and entered. Holden was sitting in a chair smoking a cigarette and looking at blueprints spread across his desk. He smiled at Hank.

"Well, well. Look what the cat dragged in."

Hank lifted the briefcase in front of his chest and said "I got the money."

"Way to go. I knew you'd come through. You're a trooper."

"You gotta get these houses built and sold. Our asses are on the line."

"Easy as pie." Holden reached up and took the briefcase. "It's all here? Three hundred K?"

"I didn't count it. Maybe we should."

"Okay. Let's. Hey, lock the door behind you."

Hank turned around and slid the dead bolt into place.

Holden opened the briefcase on his desk and admired the banded stacks of bills. He fanned through one group of hundreds. He removed the band and carefully counted the money. There were 100 one hundred dollar bills in the stack. He put it down and counted the other stacks in the briefcase. "Twenty-nine more. All here," he announced.

Hank began to explain the terms of the loan, but Mike held up his hand, silencing him. "Maddie told me. I don't need to hear the details again," he said.

"Well, maybe you do. We don't get this thing built and sold in two years, we are both in deep shit."

"Nothing to worry about." Holden smiled. "Piece of cake. This is the ticket," he said, patting the stacks of bills.

Hank grimaced. *Why did I ever go into business with this guy? Too late now, but...shit.*

"Okay, here's your share," Mike said, shoving two of the stacks across to Hank. "Twenty grand. Don't spend it all in one place." He grinned. "Wait, I'll put it in an envelope for you."

Mike gave Hank a fat manila envelope containing $20,000 in circulated $100 bills.

This is my life, thought Hank. *This is the life I've made.*

Hank drove to his house. It was a little after 11 am. Nobody was home. Norma's car was gone. He decided Dora must have taken it. He went upstairs and found a shoebox of Norma's in their closet. He took the money out of the envelope and put it inside. He replaced the lid on the box and carried it downstairs and out to the garage. Shaking slightly, he put it up on a high shelf in the back of the garage. It looked inconspicuous up there. He turned, got back in his car, and drove tensely back to his office.

CHAPTER 27

11/16/71 – Tuesday

The next morning, Amy and Norma returned to the Wilhelmina Models office. They were sitting at a large glass table in a bright white room. Two men sat opposite them, along with Ginger. She introduced them as the agency's attorney Roger Levesque and the Contracts Officer Andrew Romano.

Mr. Levesque was talking. "These are the contract documents, Mrs. Latour. As a minor, Amy cannot sign, so we need your signature, as her mother."

"Of course," said Norma, "of course."

"Sign at the bottom here, here and here," said Romano, handing her three sheets of paper.

"Well, what do they say?" asked Norma.

"They are our standard terms, that we have for all our girls."

"Terms?"

"Yes, it is a five-year, exclusive agreement. The

agency gets one-third of her earnings. Amy, or you, in this case, get the other 67%, after expenses."

"And that's normal?"

"Absolutely," said Romano.

Norma picked up the pen. 67% sounded pretty good to her. She signed the documents.

Romano gathered up the papers and he and Levesque left.

"Terrific," said Ginger. "Welcome to Wilhelmina. Amy, you're now a Wilhelmina model."

"So, what's next?" asked Norma, brightly.

"We'll take some shots today. We'll need those to shop her around. It can take some time to find work," Ginger explained.

"Okay. I understand."

"Yes. And you'll need to find a place to stay. Once she starts working regularly, it really isn't practical to come in from Connecticut."

"Oh yeah? I hadn't thought of that," Norma said with a note of surprise in her voice.

"Yes, she'll need to move to the city."

Norma was not prepared for that. It was a big step. *What will Hank say?* For the first time, she felt a small twinge of doubt. *Is this really good for Amy?* But she brushed the thought aside quickly. *Of course it is. Whatever it takes, that's what we need to do.*

"Okay. We'll do it." Norma said. She turned to Amy who looked terrified. "Don't worry honey. I'll be here with you. I'll move too."

"But what about school?" Amy asked in a whisper.

"We have schools here, and tutors," Ginger pointed out. "You'll still have school. And we'll help you find a place to live. Don't worry. We won't leave you on your own. Either of you." She turned to Norma, "And if you need money, she can have a draw against future earnings. We're here to help."

Norma smiled reassuringly at Amy. "Everything will work out. You'll see," she said.

"We need to get going. I want to bring you to one of our photographers." Ginger reached to her left and picked up a phone. She dialed a number and said "Jim. Ginger. Can we come by for those portfolio shots now?" She hung up and said. "Okay, let's go."

Together they walked out to the sidewalk. Ginger stepped off the curb and hailed a cab. They all got in. "84 Spring, just east of Broadway," Ginger said to the driver. She turned to Amy and Norma. "Jim Farnsworth. He's great. We're going to his studio. It's a big loft downtown."

The cab wended its way through traffic and left them in an industrial-looking part of the city. They faced a steel door with a panel of buttons to its right. Ginger stepped forward and pushed one. An answering buzz let them into a small hallway. There was a large commercial elevator directly in front of them. It had a cage mesh gate which Ginger slid aside. They entered the cab and Ginger pushed a button on the panel marked "2." They rode the noisy elevator up one floor.

A busy scene greeted them. People seemed to be shouting and scurrying everywhere. It seemed to Amy as busy as Grand Central Station. "Would you like to have a look around?" Ginger asked.

As usual, Norma answered for both of them. "We'd love that."

Ginger took Amy's hand. They walked through several large studio spaces. There was lighting equipment everywhere. Heavy cables snaked across the floor. Some shoots were under way. They watched photographers and models at work. Stylists ran back and forth, fussing with hair and makeup. Other people were arranging props, furniture, fans and in one case, flowers. To Amy, it was eye-opening. She began to understand what models did. They seemed to be the center of the activity. They were so pretty. It started to seem real to her and she was intrigued. Norma, for once, was silent. She stared wide-eyed at everything going on.

Norma loved being in this world. It was what she had been waiting her whole life for. They arrived at their set. Norma and Amy stood transfixed as they gazed out at the big room. Ginger waved to someone. A tall man with long dark hair tied back in a ponytail approached them. He had a camera and a light meter draped around his neck. He was dressed in blue jeans and a tight white tee shirt.

"This is Jim Farnsworth. He's one of our top guys. Jim, this is Amy. And that is her mother, Norma."

Farnsworth ignored Norma. He walked up to Amy and took her chin in his hand. He turned her face one way, then the other. "She has the eyes and the bone structure. It will be better when she fills out a little more. She's small on top. We can use her face. Her body, I don't know. The Twiggy look is over. We'd need to see some development there."

"Well, she's just getting started," Ginger said. She turned to Norma. "I'll leave you for now. I'll be back this afternoon when you finish up." With that she turned and left.

"She's only fourteen," Norma explained to Farnsworth.

"Come with me," he said.

The balance of the afternoon was spent in a whirlwind of photo shoots. Amy had people adjusting her hair, giving her different clothes to wear, and applying makeup. They took close-up photos of her face and eyes, shots from the waist up, and full body shots. She was told where to sit, where to stand, when to smile, and when to gaze off into the distance. She listened closely. If she was going to be a model, she would be the best model she could possibly be. It was puzzling to her when she was asked to "be sexy." She had no idea how to do that, but Farnsworth gave her advice while he shot. He had her dip her head and look up. He told her to slip her shirt slightly off her shoulder. He had her part her skirt slightly and smile. She found she complied easily.

At the end of the day, Ginger was back. She turned to Amy. "Everyone says you did great. Give us a few weeks. We need to work with these shots and speak with some of our clients."

"Okay," Norma said, realizing that once again they had to wait. She frowned for a moment. They had no choice. They'd return to Westport and see what happened next.

Ginger noticed the frown. "It just takes time. I know the ad agencies and catalog houses will want her. We believe in her. We are investing in her. Trust me."

Norma thought about that. She had signed a contract. The agency had invested in Amy, like Ginger said. Of course they'd find work for her. Norma understood the modeling work would be coming. They really were on their way. Her face lit up. She looked at her daughter and felt happy. "Oh yes, everything's okay. We'll wait to hear from you."

"Take care. We'll be in touch soon."

They went back to Westport. Once again, it did

not feel real to Amy. She returned to her school, her woods, and her room. Over the next few weeks, the whole modeling experience receded to the back of her mind. But Norma was animated. She would spend the time planning. She would call Ginger for suggestions about where they might live. And she would wait for whatever came next.

CHAPTER 28

11/22/71 – Monday

Dora returned to Dr. Sheinberg's office. This time there was no wait and she was able to go right in. She looked at his kindly face and said in a quavering voice. "I've decided to keep the baby."

"Well, that's interesting. What did your parents say?"

"They don't like the idea. They think I should get an abortion."

"That is an option, of course. Abortion is legal in New York state now like I said before, so it's pretty safe."

"Yeah, but I don't want one. We're Catholic, or we used to be, not that that makes any difference to my parents."

"Legally, it is your decision. They can't force you to have an abortion. But have you thought about how you would raise a child?"

"I can do it." As usual, Dora was trying to sound

more confident than she felt. "I'll just have to get a job."

"And live at home?"

"I don't know about that. I'm not exactly welcome there these days. My dad's pissed off at me. And my mother... Well, all she thinks about is my sister Amy. She wants Amy to be a model. That's all she talks about these days."

"Well, I can't see you living alone, with a baby, by yourself. What would you do for money?"

"I could work."

"Aren't you still in school."

"Yeah, senior year. I could drop out for a while."

"I don't know, Dora. It all sounds pretty shaky to me. Maybe you should give this all some more thought."

"I have thought about it. I'm doing it. I can do it. Women can do anything nowadays."

"Is that so? I don't know. Why don't you just take some more time and think it through. You're not that far along. You have some time."

"Well, I should get the name of the Obstetrician you said you knew. That's what I'm thinking about."

"Uh, okay. It's Dr. Denison. Nancy Denison.

She's good. She's at Norwalk Hospital. I'll give you her number." He spent a few minutes looking up her name in his address book. "Ah here it is." He wrote the name and number on a piece of paper and handed it to her. "But promise me you'll think about this a little more. A decision you make now will affect the rest of your life. Think about that."

"All right. All right, I'll think about it. Thanks. I gotta go."

"All right Dora. Take care of yourself. Please."

Dora left the office. For some reason, the more people told her to get rid of it, the more determined she was to have this baby. She drove home. She felt stubborn and belligerent. Nobody was going to tell her what to do.

At home, she pulled the car into the garage. Gazing up at the shelves, she thought maybe there were still some baby things there, like toys or baby clothes. She began rummaging through the odds and ends stored on the shelves. There did not seem to be anything useful. She was about to go inside when she noticed a shoebox. Without thinking, she pulled it down and opened it. To her utter disbelief, it contained a lot of money, hundreds, no, thousands of dollars. *Where in the world did this money come from? Whose is it? What's it doing here?* She looked away, pausing a moment. Her heart fluttered. She turned and looked out the garage door. Nobody was around. No one was watching. *Well, I found it and I need it. This is like a gift from God!*

She did not understand why, but she felt as if the money was meant for her. *There must be a reason I found it today. It was left here to help me. I know it. Yes, it's mine. I can live on my own. Now I really can do it!*

Dora quickly put the lid back on the box and slid it under her arm. She rushed inside and up to her room. She hid the shoebox in the back of her closet.

She could barely sleep that night. She was bursting with her secret. She knew she better not tell anyone. All she could think about was the money. She had never seen so much money and she knew it could not stay in her closet. The next morning was a Tuesday. She waited until her sister and her father were gone for the day. Then she snuck into her mother's bedroom, careful not to wake her, and took her mother's car keys.

Dora had heard safety deposit boxes were private and safe, so she decided she would get one. She felt unusually clear and focused. She carried the shoebox to the car, placed it on the seat alongside her. She began driving toward Fairfield, but after a few minutes, she abruptly changed her mind and headed in the other direction, toward Norwalk. She thought a bank there would be far enough away that nobody she knew would see her. She found the Norwalk Savings and Loan and parked in front of the building.

She walked in, the shoebox under her arm. She asked a teller about getting a safety deposit box and was pointed to a desk where a woman sat opposite an empty chair. Dora sat down in the chair. She was trembling visibly but the woman did not seem to notice. They did have safety deposit boxes she was told and they'd be happy to rent her one. They only needed her signature and address on a card and $40 which Dora paid with a hundred dollar bill. She signed the card and was handed two keys. "Come with me," the woman said.

Dora walked downstairs with the woman. She was brought in to a vault area where the boxes were kept. The woman unlocked an inner gate and used one of Dora's keys and another she had on a ring to open a small door and pull out a medium-sized safety deposit box. She handed the grey metal box to Dora and directed her to a little room. When Dora entered the room, the door closed automatically behind her.

Dora sat at the desk, relishing the privacy. She flipped the lid open on the safety deposit box and then opened her shoebox. She again felt the surprise and euphoria that it contained so much money. She picked up the bills with both hands and put the money inside the grey metal box. It felt thrilling. Now she felt the money was really hers, not her mother's or her father's. This was her special secret and it represented her future. For the first time, she felt calm enough to count it. She took it back out and counted $20,000 in hundred dollar bills, minus the hundred she had removed earlier. She put the money back in, carefully closed the lid and placed the empty shoebox in a wastebasket. She walked out of the room and handed the safety deposit box to the attendant. Together, they returned it to the vault. Dora took her keys and left the bank. She was elated.

CHAPTER 29

12/13/71 – Monday

Three weeks later, Hank was in his garage. He thought he would take the first thousand dollars from the shoebox for his meeting with Generoso on Wednesday. But the box was gone. It was not where he thought he had left it, on the top shelf. Initially he was puzzled, thinking he had perhaps used a different shelf, but he did not see it on any shelf. Growing increasingly agitated, he searched the garage shelves again and then the floor, with the impossible hope the money had fallen down there somehow. That made no sense, but he was dumbstruck that it was simply gone. His next thought was of Dora. He suspected her or one of her friends. (Katie? Jared?) But why would any of them even have been here, poking around these shelves? So it could have been Norma. Or perhaps Amy. Or a total stranger. He had no idea. He was baffled, frustrated and very angry. And then he became frightened, as it dawned on him that the loss of the money was going to make those thousand dollar payments to Generoso almost impossible.

He left the garage and went into the house. Norma was sitting on the couch. She nodded to him as he stared at her. She gave no sign that anything was out of the ordinary. He stomped upstairs. Dora was not home. Amy was sitting at her desk. He peered in at her. Her innocent face smiled anxiously at him. "Hi dad."

"Amy. What are you up to?" He noticed the accusatory tone in his own voice.

"Just doing my French homework."

"Uh, okay. Dinner soon."

"Okay." She smiled.

No evidence that she was hiding anything. He thought he would be able to tell if she had just found $20,000. And she would tell him if she had. He felt pretty sure of that.

He went to his bedroom and sat on the bed, putting his head between his hands. *Think. Let's see... God, I need this money back! Well, someone took it... stole it. What about reporting it to the police?* But what would he say? Somebody stole $20,000 in kickback money for a loan from a loan shark? Pretty hard to defend that. Maybe he could say that something else was stolen, like important papers he kept in a shoebox? That didn't sound plausible. If they were so important, why leave them in the garage? He pictured the police laughing at him. *Okay, there must be another way.* He had to handle this on his own. It was a risky thing to accuse anybody of taking money he should not have had in the first place. He was not sure what steps to take. *If it was someone I know, maybe I will spot it. But I can't go off half-cocked. I'll watch everyone, but I better be careful.*

****

When Dora came home, well after dinner, her father was in an angry mood.

"Where have you been?" he asked the moment she came through the door.

She stopped, momentarily flustered. "I was with Katie," she said. "Don't worry. We weren't smoking pot."

"What? I wasn't asking about that. You should be home for dinner on a school night." He was quite angry. That seemed strange to Dora. He had rarely been bothered by her missing dinner before.

In an instant, she realized he must have discovered the money was gone. Obviously it was his money. *Well, he's not getting it back*, she told herself. He was looking at her suspiciously. She put on her most innocent expression. "Okay, daddy. I'll be home earlier from now on." Neither believed it, but she thought she'd deflected his suspicions a little.

She felt him watching her carefully. But she was a good actress and she made sure she gave nothing away. She thought she would just keep doing what she had always done, hanging out with friends, going to school and being home as little as possible. Briefly, she had thought of moving out immediately, but she was smart enough to know that doing so would draw too much attention at this time. She resolved to wait.

****

Norma missed all the drama between Hank and Dora. She was terribly anxious that she had not heard back from the modeling agency. It had been weeks since their trip to New York. Ginger had promised to call, but had not said exactly when. Norma was starting to feel there would be no call. She drank to steady her nerves. It did not help much. *Maybe they really don't want Amy.* That night, she passed out on the couch.

The next morning, Norma awoke right where she had fallen asleep. She was still in her clothes. Her hands trembled and her legs felt shaky when she tried to stand. Whether due to alcohol or anxiety, she did not know. But she could not wait any longer. She poured her morning glass and decided to call Ginger. As she dialed the number, she tapped her foot and pulled at her hair with her other hand. She heard the receptionist's crisp "Hello. Wilhelmina Models."

It turned out there was really no reason not to call. Ginger was fine with it. She reassured Norma. "Soon," she said. "Soon. We'll probably schedule Amy to come back very soon. We have a few things in the works for her. I'm sure we'll have something definite in the next day or two. Or they may want some go-sees. Anyway, we'll get back to you soon."

Norma hung up. She felt better. It was not so bad. They did want Amy. They just needed a little more time and maybe they needed to have some go-sees, whatever they were. She told herself *Just relax. Wait a little longer.* She sipped her vodka and felt better. She decided to go to Lily's for a celebratory breakfast. She looked forward to telling Lily that Amy was becoming a model.

CHAPTER 30

12/14/71 – Tuesday

With the girls in school and Norma out somewhere, Hank decided to come home and search for the missing money. He'd called first and Norma was not home, so Hank thought it was a good time to look around. He did not enjoy the prospect and did not like distrusting his daughters or his wife, but this was serious and he had to know.

He left the bank at 10:00 am and drove home. As expected, the house was empty. He decided if Norma came home, he'd just say he'd forgotten some papers. She was easy to lie to. He walked into Dora's room. It was quite messy so he did not worry too much about disturbing it. He systematically went through her desk, her clothes, her closet. He looked under the mattress, under the bed, in the bathroom. Nothing. Feeling less optimistic he searched Amy's room. No luck. He investigated his and Norma's bedroom. The money was nowhere to be found. *Maybe none of them had taken it. Then who?* He was more frustrated than ever and unsure where to turn next. *It was my money and it was stolen from me*, he thought angrily. *I'll watch everyone. Whoever has it will probably start spending more than normal. That would be a giveaway.* Watching was all he could think to do. Glumly, he drove back to work.

****

Two mornings later, Norma was seated on the couch when the phone rang. It was Ginger calling at last. They had "limited work" for Amy so far. Amy and Norma would need to come to the city for a few days. No need to move there yet. It was a good start, Ginger said.

Norma was thrilled. They were finally on their way. Ginger explained it was a catalog shoot aimed at the early teen market and Amy, she said, was perfect for it. Norma and Amy needed to be in the city the following Monday. Ginger said they would probably need three days. *Amy will be so excited*, Norma thought. *I can't wait to tell her.*

That afternoon, when Amy came home, Norma virtually pounced on her. "They want you. We're going back to New York next Monday!"

Amy had put the modeling into a remote corner of her mind. It had been over a month. But she quickly remembered when hit by her mother's naked enthusiasm. "Uh, okay. That's good, I guess."

"You guess? Of course it's good. This is great. This is how it begins. You start with small jobs and work your way up. You're on your way. This is just the beginning. We'll have to get everything together to go… for three days, Ginger said."

"Well, I have to tell my teachers. I mean I'll be out of school, right?"

"Well, yeah. But you can make it up. It won't be hard for you. They'll understand. Don't worry."

"I wasn't really worrying. I just… I don't know. It all seems strange. That's all."

"That's okay honey. Everything will be fine. This is what we want."

"Okay mom."

Amy turned and walked up to her room. She gazed out her window, longing to be out there. She had little interest in this modeling business. But it made her mother happy.

CHAPTER 31

12/15/71 – Wednesday

Hank had watched Dora and her friends as closely as he could. It was hard as they were always on the go. He wondered about Katie Price who always seemed to have money, as far as he could tell. He asked Dora. "Where does Katie get her money? Does she get a big allowance?" Dora had wondered briefly at the reason for the question, but answered nonetheless. "Oh her father gives her whatever she asks for." That stung Hank a little as he wondered if Dora had wished for the same treatment from him. "And Jared?" he'd asked. "Where does he get money?" "I don't know. Jeez dad. What's your problem?" Hank had to let it go.

And Norma. *Did she have more money lately?* She still asked for his credit card or for cash, when she needed it. It didn't seem likely she had cleverly stashed away $20,000.

****

It had been one month since he'd met with Generoso. It was time for his first payment. Hank had taken the $1,000 from his remaining savings. Now he was at Lily's, seated at a table in front of the windows. He ordered a cup of coffee for himself and then on an impulse, ordered one for Generoso as well. *Might as well be friendly,* he thought. It was a few minutes before 10:00 am. He kept patting the thick envelope in his inside suit pocket.

At precisely ten o'clock, Generoso walked in. He gave Hank a cold grin and sat across from him. He took a sip of coffee and said "Thanks." Hank removed the envelope from his pocket and slid it across the table. Generoso picked it up and quickly pocketed it.

Hank had been troubled about how he could continue to make these payments, with the money gone. He started to say something about the problem, but stopped himself.

"Something wrong?" Generoso asked.

"No. No, nothing's wrong. It's fine," Hank said with a slight stutter.

Generoso took another sip of his coffee, stared at Hank for a moment and then nodded and said "Okay, good. See you next month." He got up and walked out.

Hank sat there drinking his coffee. *How can I come up with $1,000 a month for the next two years?* It was a huge problem. If only he could find the missing money, it would be solved. If not, he wasn't sure what he would do. He abruptly threw two dollars down on the table, got up and left. He'd have to think of something.

CHAPTER 32

12/20/71 – Monday

Early Monday morning Norma was bustling about the house. It was her big day, the start of Amy's career. It was also Christmas season and she had plans. She was anxious to get going. Amy sat on the couch, ready to go, but Hank, their ride to the station, was moving slowly.

"C'mon Hank. Let's go. I want to make the 7:15."

"All right. All right, I'm coming. Just give me a minute." Hank finally seemed to be moving at normal speed. He picked up his keys in the hallway, found his briefcase and said "Okay, let's go."

In the car, Amy sat in back silently. Norma was giddy and talkative. "I can't wait. Our start. Today's our start."

"Yeah. Well, just take it easy. You'll get there. You have the credit card, right?"

"Yes. I have it," said Norma.

"Okay. Try not to spend too much. We're not loaded, you know."

"Yeah, yeah, okay." Norma's mind was already in New York. She was imagining the studio, the photographers and makeup people. She could barely contain her excitement.

They arrived at the station and Hank said "All right. You girls be good."

Norma gave him a perfunctory kiss and bolted out the door. Amy said nothing and quietly got out. As Hank left them there, he again wondered about the wisdom of Amy entering modeling at only fourteen, in New York City, no less. He sighed and headed toward the bank, his worries about money and the real estate development replacing his concerns about his younger daughter.

****

Norma and Amy arrived at Grand Central Station. Norma loved the activity, the sense that everyone was doing something important. She felt they were part of the big city. They belonged there, she thought.

Amy was much less excited. New York was a big, overwhelming place to her. It seemed to be nothing but crowds pushing around her. It was as far from her woods and fields as possible. She did not like being there, but she looked at her mother's bright, smiling face and felt she had no choice but to go along.

They took a taxi down to Spring Street. They were to go directly to Farnsworth's studio. They were half an hour early and they stood on the sidewalk for several minutes. Finally Norma could wait no longer and pushed the buzzer. "Yes?" she heard.

"It's Norma and Amy Latour. We have a nine o'clock shoot this morning."

"C'mon up." They were buzzed in.

Riding up in the elevator, Norma opened her purse, located the bottle she always carried and took a quick drink, all the while chattering away to Amy. "It's a catalog shoot, so they'll probably have you wearing lots of outfits. I'm sure they know your size. But if the fit isn't good, they have people to pin and fix it. Nothing to worry about there."

Amy barely heard her mother. Caged in the elevator she felt like a trapped deer. And suddenly she felt hungry. They had skipped breakfast. But Amy thought that was for the best. She was getting too fat anyway. The elevator opened to the same hum of activity that they had seen previously.

A short, slender man with a closely trimmed beard greeted them. "Amy?" he said, "Ready to go? C'mon. I'm Philip."

"Okay," said Amy.

"Follow me."

The three of them walked single file around the perimeter of the first studio set. They walked quickly, but Norma was practically skipping and it took effort to slow her pace down to match that of the other two. They entered a second studio section. There were bright lights, people, chairs, mirrors, equipment and wiring everywhere. It looked chaotic to Amy.

Philip led her to a tall chair in front a mirror. She climbed up into the chair. Her feet did not reach the floor. "This is Trish, your makeup girl," Philip announced as a pretty blonde woman approached them.

Norma was standing directly behind Amy. "Hi Trish," she said.

"Uh, hi. So this is Amy," Trish said facing Amy. "How are you?"

"Fine." Amy fidgeted a bit with her hands. She felt conspicuous and uncomfortable. The makeup session made her nervous.

Trish saw her discomfort. "It will be fine. We'll just do a little blush, a little work with your eyes. You're beautiful."

Amy chewed her lip. Norma chimed in "She has natural beauty."

"Yes, she does." Trish turned to Philip. "We'll be fine," she said.

"All right. Have fun."

Philip left. Amy sat expectantly. Norma gazed around the room. "Look at this place. This is just amazing," she announced, even though they'd seen it just a few weeks earlier.

Trish said, "All right, let's begin." She expertly brushed on blush, added eye liner, applied mascara to Amy's eyelashes. "Just a light lipstick."

As Trish worked, Amy watched herself transform. Staring at herself in the mirror, when she could see around Trish, she saw she looked older. She did think she looked almost pretty. It was exciting, but unsettling as well.

Trish finished. "We're going to need to do something with your hair. Let me talk to Jim and see what he wants." She hustled off.

Amy looked at her mother. Norma's face was flushed. *Must be the drink,* Amy thought. Norma was beaming proudly. "Isn't this the best? It's like you're a star already. Look at all this attention you're getting."

Amy did not feel much like a star, but the attention did feel nice, in a way. "Yeah, mom," she said. "It is nice."

Norma lapsed into a reverie of her own. She imagined herself being primped and photographed, being fawned over. She wondered momentarily if they ever used older models. With a start she returned to the present, as Trish came back. "Okay, we're going to do your hair. There's a different stylist for that. I need to bring you to Emily. C'mon."

Amy carefully climbed down off the chair and she and her mother followed Trish to a small brightly lit room. There was a tall cushioned stool in the middle of the room, again in front of a mirror. Amy was told to sit there. The mirror was surrounded by lights and Amy squinted at their brightness. "Careful. Don't ruin your makeup," Trish cautioned.

Emily, the hair stylist, was watching from the corner. She was a tall woman with sharp features and spiky blonde hair. She was scowling. "All right. Let me see what we can do," she said.

She brushed Amy's hair back off her face. "Well. We'll pin it back. Trim it here and there. The color's okay for now. We'll clean her up."

Amy saw her hair get snipped and trimmed and pulled back with a clip. It took only ten minutes. They were done.

"All right, let's get her to Jim. Thanks Em," Trish said.

Together, the threesome marched back across the studio.

"You ready for her?" Trish asked Farnsworth.

"Yeah. Get her into these." He gestured toward a bright yellow shirt and matching pants on a small table to his left.

"All right Amy. Go in there and put these on. Careful of your hair and makeup." Trish gestured toward a small curtained section at the back of the set.

Norma hustled over to have a look. "Right. You can change in here Amy. I'll help you. We don't want to mess your hair."

Amy gathered up the shirt and pants. There were no shoes. She guessed the ones she was wearing were okay.

Norma squeezed into the small dressing area with her. "Let me hold those while you get out of your clothes." Amy felt crowded in the small space standing next to her mother. The curtains seemed to flap open of their own accord. Privacy seemed completely out of the question. Nevertheless Amy removed her top and quickly grabbed the yellow blouse from her mother. She put it on, careful not to touch her hair. Then her skirt came off. She exchanged the skirt with her mother for the pants Norma was holding. Putting on the pants was even more awkward in the small, semi-public space. She put them on as quickly as she could, nearly falling over in the process. Relieved to be done, she stepped out from behind the curtain.

Her mother popped out immediately after her, took her arm and brought her back to Trish. "Doesn't she look wonderful," Norma said. It was not a question.

"Yes, she does," said Trisha, turning to hand her over to the photographer.

"Put these on." He handed her a pair of yellow beach flip flops. Amy took off the shoes she was wearing and handed them to her mother. She put on the sandals. "Okay, stand here," Jim said. He pointed to a spot under the lights. "You're going to be holding a watering can. Where is it?" He turned to the room. Philip rushed up with a large yellow watering can. "Okay, good. Now hold this, as if you're about to water something."

He stepped behind his camera. It was mounted on a tripod. "Give me a smile." He fired off a number of shots. The camera had a motor drive. Not quite satisfied, he said "I want to take a few Polaroids, check the color." He picked up a Polaroid camera and moved around Amy, snapping her from several angles. After each shot came out, he set it on a table nearby, not waiting for it to develop. When he finished shooting, he stood by the table. After a few moments, he picked them up and examined them in the bright light. "Okay, not bad. Give me a little more red in her lips." Trisha walked up to Amy and applied a new lipstick. "Yeah, better," said Farnsworth.

He quickly posed Amy with the watering can again. "Another smile," he said. "Just like last time." Amy smiled and another set of shots were taken. "Okay, next I need you to look up, to your right, like you're seeing a bird up there. Give Philip the watering can." The little bearded man reappeared and took it from her.

More shots were taken throughout the morning with different colored clothes and props. They stopped for a quick lunch in the studio and resumed in the afternoon. For Norma, the day flew by. It was over before she knew it. Amy did not enjoy it. She felt confined. It was hard to stay still, hard to smile all the time. She had done her best to do exactly as she was told, applying her usual determined perfectionism. She worried constantly about displeasing Farnsworth and Trish. Neither seemed unhappy with her, however, and Trish told her at the end of the afternoon that she had done a good job.

"Back for more tomorrow,' said Jim.

That was it for their first day. They returned to the same Howard Johnsons Hotel they had stayed in on their last visit. Norma was enthralled by all that had happened. "Wasn't that amazing, Amy?" she asked. She didn't really expect an answer and Amy did not give her one. Amy was tired.

"We'll do it again tomorrow," said Norma. "I can't wait to see you in the catalog when it's done. You'll like that, I'm sure."

"Yes, mom."

The next day was more of the same. Amy was moved about, told to do various simple things, always in clothing that was all one color. Sometimes it was a sky blue outfit, sometimes red or more yellow like the day before.

By the end of the second day, both Amy and Norma were exhausted. It turned out they did not need a third day of shooting. Ginger said everything went very well. Norma would receive a check, less expenses, in about two weeks.

They headed back on a late train. Hank picked them up at the station.

"How'd it go?" he asked.

"Terrific," said Norma, as usual speaking for both of them.

Hank noticed that Amy seemed sullen. "And you? What did you think?"

"Oh, it was okay dad. Like mom said." Hank let it go, but he noticed her lack of enthusiasm. Maybe it will be better for her next time, he hoped.

"So what happens next?" Hank asked.

"Well, we wait for the next call. Oh, and we get a check."

"A check? How much?"

"I don't' know."

"You didn't ask?

"No. I forgot. But I'm sure it will be good, for two days' work. It was a lot of work."

"We can use the money. That's for sure."

Norma looked puzzled for a moment, but then

said brightly "And this is just the beginning. You'll see."

Hank felt a moment of hope. *Could this possibly get me out of this hole? In your dreams,* he scoffed. It seemed highly unlikely. Plus, if he immediately started spending all the money Amy earned, it would be hard to explain. No, that wasn't going to be the answer.

Saying no more, he drove them home.

CHAPTER 33

12/25/71 – Saturday, Christmas Day

It was Dora's seventeenth birthday. Wanting it to seem like a normal Christmas, Hank had bought a tree the day before and this morning Dora saw several wrapped presents beneath it. She wandered into the kitchen. Her father was seated by himself, a cup of coffee in front of him. He stared at her intently as she entered the room.

"Merry Christmas. And happy birthday," he said without a smile.

"Thanks Dad." As she walked to the counter, she felt his eyes on her back. She was determined to reveal nothing about the money. "Mom still sleeping?" she asked, turning to face him.

"Yeah. She's still in bed…recovering from her big trip to New York. I think she's more worn out than Amy. And Amy did all the work." He paused. "How are you?" He looked at her carefully. Her pregnancy was starting to show, he thought. He briefly felt an urge to comfort her, but he stayed seated and said nothing further. Instead, he wondered *does she have my money?*

If she doesn't, who does? He stared hard at her. For the moment, he could only watch. It was impossible to tell if she was avoiding his glance more than usual.

"I'm okay," she said as she turned away and poured herself a glass of juice. All she could think about was the money. It represented a way to become independent and a way to take care of her baby. She wouldn't have to work. She could picture her future. The money made it all possible. Right or wrong, nobody else was going to get that money.

"Dora, did you find a box in the garage, a shoebox? It had some important papers of mine and now I can't find it."

"A box?" Dora thought *be very careful.*

"Yeah, a shoebox. With a lid. It was out there. Now it's gone."

"No, I didn't take any box." She turned and faced him with this statement.

Hank thought to himself. *I didn't say anything about taking the box. Just did she find it.* "So you didn't see a shoebox out there?"

"No, no I didn't. I mean.. what was in the box?"

"Oh just some old papers I need. I shouldn't have left it out there. Has anyone been out rummaging in the garage, do you know?"

"No, not that I know of." Dora did her best to

look concerned and innocent. She gave nothing away, she hoped. Thankfully, she heard her mother and sister coming down the stairs. Hank heard them too and it interrupted their talk.

They all assembled in the living room to open gifts. Norma chatted excitedly about Amy's first modeling job. Amy was quiet, but smiled when asked about it. Although anxious to go out, to be anywhere else, Dora stayed home, intent on keeping up the semblance of normalcy on the holiday. After breakfast, Norma announced they would go to church for the morning Christmas service. This had been an annual tradition in their early years in Westport, attending either Christmas Eve or Christmas Day services. However, everyone but Norma seemed to think that tradition had ended. Nonetheless, they all dressed up and made the short drive to Trinity Episcopal Church in nearby Southport.

Years ago, when Dora was nearly ten and they had just moved to Westport, the family began attending St. Luke's Catholic Church. Back then, Norma would dress the girls, often in identical outfits, and the family would go each Sunday morning for the 10:30 mass. Norma liked to say she was making her "bad little girls" into "good Catholic girls." This had lasted two years, until one Sunday, when Norma surprised everyone by announcing she wished to go instead to Trinity Episcopal in neighboring Southport. Though puzzled, Hank realized he had no objection, and even saw a benefit to it, the chance to connect with a different, and wealthier, congregation. Only Dora was upset. "What about my catechism classes?" she had asked. Norma told her that she could just as easily be confirmed in the Episcopal church. It wasn't really that different, she explained. "Then why are we changing?" Dora had pleaded.

That first Sunday at Trinity Episcopal, they arrived, dressed up and nervous among the self-important crowd. They recognized a few faces and nodded hellos, before slipping into a pew. Something didn't feel quite right to any of them, but for whatever reason, this was now their new church. Over the subsequent weeks, Dora continued to protest and Hank wondered if they shouldn't return to St. Luke's, but Norma was adamant. They stuck it out over the next year, through Dora's confirmation, but after that, their attendance diminished, and now they never went at all. Not much of a believer to begin with, Hank had gone because it seemed "good for the girls." Norma was much more conflicted, but as her drinking continued to increase, her church attendance declined and eventually stopped altogether. At least until today.

The service this Christmas was uneventful and mercifully short. Dora fidgeted throughout the hymns and Hank endured the whole thing stoically. Only Norma seemed to enjoy the occasion. Afterward, returning home, Amy said she had homework to do, but Norma stopped her. "It's your sister's birthday. Sit down." They all gathered around the kitchen table.

Norma had bought a cake for Dora. Lunch was

an awkward birthday celebration. Norma seemed oblivious to the sullen moods that surrounded her. She had had a quick glass of vodka before leaving for church and another secretly in the bathroom when they returned. She was in a good mood. Everyone else seated at the table was nervous, suspicious or detached. They had tuna salad sandwiches. Then Norma roused them for a chorus of Happy Birthday after which she served them each a slice of white frosted cake. Amy left hers untouched on her plate. After lunch, Norma stayed in the kitchen to clean up. The other three retired to separate sections of the house. It was a quiet afternoon in the Latour household.

CHAPTER 34

1/3/72 – Monday

Hank was seated at his desk when his phone rang.

"Hello?"

"Mr. Latour?"

"Yes"

"This is Sergeant Gargiulo, down at the station."

"Oh, yes. Hello Sergeant."

"Mr. Latour, can you come down here? We need to speak with you.

Oh God, thought Hank. *What did Dora do now?* "Uh sure. What's this about?"

"We'd rather not discuss it on the phone. Come down here. Detective Goldschmidt has some questions for you."

"Well, of course. I'll be right there."

"Good. We'll see you soon."

Hank shoved aside the papers on his desk. He was annoyed. *It must be about Dora. Probably caught her smoking pot again. The second time it's bound to be more serious. They can't let her off with a warning this time. I have enough on my mind without this crap.*

It was a short drive to the station. When he got there, Sergeant Gargiulo greeted him. "Thanks for coming in. C'mon in here." He gestured to his right. Hank followed him to a small, windowless room. "Have a seat."

Hank sat at the metal table. The Sergeant sat in a chair across from him.

A second man came in, carrying a manila folder under his arm. He was wearing a grey suit and a silver tie. He had a narrow hawk-like face. "This is Detective Goldschmidt," Gargiulo said. "He has a few questions for you."

Goldschmidt nodded to Hank and sat down in a second chair alongside Gargiulo. "We'd like to know about your activities on Wednesday, December 15th."

"*My* activities?"

"Yes. We know you met with a Richard Generoso that day. What we would like to know is why."

"What? No. No, I didn't..." Hank was taken by

surprise. This had nothing to do with Dora. He was suddenly nervous.

"I'm afraid you did. Maybe this will refresh your memory." Goldschmidt opened the folder he'd been carrying. He removed two large photos and dropped them on the table in front of Hank. Hank saw pictures of himself and Generoso seated at Lily's. The photos were grainy, but there was no question it was them.

"Oh well, right. Yes, of course. I forgot it was that day."

"So what was the purpose of that meeting?"

"We.... we were having coffee... It was nothing."

"We don't think so. We know Generoso. He's trouble. Trouble for you. You have the right to remain silent, but we think you'd prefer to help us."

"Wait. Do I need a lawyer?"

"I don't know. Do you?"

"Well, no."

"All right then. Tell us what you were doing with Generoso."

"He's thinking of buying some property, " Hank improvised. "We were talking about a mortgage." Hank thought he'd stick as close to the truth as possible.

"Are you sure he wasn't laundering money? If there is Mob money moving through your bank…"

"Oh God, no. No, of course not."

"You're saying no money was exchanged?"

How much did they know? Hank felt cornered. *Don't say any more than I have to.* "No, nothing. He was just asking about mortgage rates. I think he may buy a house."

"Did you give him something, an envelope?" Another photo landed in front of Hank. This one showed Hank holding an envelope or small package. It was not clear.

"What was in it?" This came from Gargiulo.

"What? Nothing. I mean.. oh, I think I gave him a mortgage application, maybe."

"Maybe? You're not sure what you gave him?" Goldschmidt asked.

"No, I mean, yes. It was mortgage papers. Look I don't want to answer any more questions."

"Why not Mr. Latour? Is there something you don't want us to know?"

"No. It's just… I don't like where this is heading?"

"Where is it heading?"

"You think I have something to do with the Mafia or money laundering or something."

"Do you?"

"No. No, I don't. And I want to leave now. Unless you have more evidence of something I did wrong. In which case, I would want a lawyer with me."

"No. that's not necessary. This is enough for today. But we're keeping an eye on you. Don't think you can conduct illegal activities in this town."

"No. I know that. I won't."

"All right. You can go. Watch who you do business with."

Hank got up quickly and almost ran to his car. He was flustered. He did not want any of this getting back to Walsh. All he knew was he had to be much more careful. No more meeting at Lily's. As he drove back to his office, he thought they had nothing concrete on him, nothing they could pin on him. He certainly wasn't laundering money for the Mafia. They were wrong about that. Still, he couldn't afford any more suspicion.

As soon as he was back at his desk, he called Maddie. "You have to tell Generoso I can't meet him at Lily's anymore. The police saw us."

"Calm down. What happened?

Hank recounted the conversation at the police station.

"All right," Maddie said. "Let me see what Rick says. I'll get back to you. In the meantime, don't do anything stupid."

"No. I know." He paused. "Uh, something else," he blurted. "I might have some trouble with the payments"

"What? Look, that's your problem. You can't miss payments. You gotta take care of those. Jesus. All right, stay put. I'll check on the next meeting. I'll call you back." She hung up before Hank could say another word.

Hank was a jumble of nerves. *The police. They were watching us. Oh God. What next? And where am I going to get the damn money?* He could not focus on the paperwork in front of him. Instead, he waited for Maddie's call. It came 15 minutes later.

"All right," Maddie said, "Here's what Rick says to do. Your next monthly payment, you go to Bridgeport, the corner of Broad and John Streets. That's near the train station. At 11:00 am on Saturday, January 15th. Put the money in a folded newspaper and leave it on the bench there on the Northeast corner. Leave it there and walk away. Walk away immediately. Don't look back. You got that?"

"Yes. Yes, I think so. 11:00 am. Did you say anything about the payments?"

"No, of course not. You want your legs broken, or worse? You gotta work that out. I can't help you.

What about the money Mike gave you? You didn't spend that already, did you?"

"Uh no. You're right. It's okay. I'll take care of it."

"Good. Jesus Hank, don't make this any harder than it has to be. Just do what I said about the delivery. Rick said that's how it will work from now on. The fifteenth of every month at eleven o'clock. Just be careful you aren't followed. Do other errands that morning and then drive to Bridgeport. Can you do that?"

"Yes. Of course."

"Good. Everything will be fine. You'll see." She hung up.

Hank thought things were anything but fine. Still, he'd have to go along with this and maybe it would work out. Somehow he had to come up with a thousand dollars a month and he hadn't figured out where it would come from. At this point, he was pretty sure he was not going to find his missing money. Maybe he could cut back on expenses. Meanwhile, he'd better be extra careful and do nothing else to arouse the suspicions of the police. They would not see Generoso in town again, he hoped. At least not with him.

****

Tuesday morning brought bitter cold and light snow flurries. Hank drove by the construction site. A foundation hole sat vacant on the lot destined for the model home. A bulldozer and a dump truck sat silently nearby. Nobody was about. Hank knew Holden's little shed would be empty as well. He shivered. *When would the work really be finished?* He worried that nothing would resume until Spring. *Certainly no work would go on in this Arctic tundra.* Hank turned his car around in the frozen mud and drove out.

****

At home that morning, Norma was up. The phone rang and she answered it on the first ring. She listened as Ginger outlined another opportunity for Amy. "This new year is starting off with a bang," Ginger said. "We've been shopping Amy around and now Maybelline wants to see her. So that plus the new catalog work for Sears I told you about. We need her back here soon. As soon as possible. When can you come in? Can you get in tomorrow?"

"Of course," Norma said. "Nine o'clock?"

"Yes. Good. Go right to Farnsworth's studio."

That afternoon a check arrived in the mail from Wilhelmina. It was for $36. Norma thought it was a mistake. It seemed like a pittance for two days' work. This time she had no compunction about calling Ginger.

"That was due to start-up expenses," Ginger explained. She patiently told Norma that Amy had worked twelve hours over the two days. At $40/hour, that came to $480.

Norma had started to protest, but Ginger pressed on. "Our fee, one-third, comes off the top. That's $160. Then there were all the initial expenses. The promo shots, printing the portfolio, sending it around, travel expenses, plus hair and makeup, and other costs. It all adds up."

"Well, I expected a lot more. This doesn't even cover our hotel, train, meals, all that."

"Of course, but most of the initial costs are one-time expenses. After all, we need a good portfolio to sell her. You understand that, right? Next time she'll get more. Okay?"

"Okay. I guess so. I just didn't realize."

"It'll be better next time. Have some patience."

"Yeah, all right."

"See you tomorrow."

"Okay. Bye." Norma hung up. She was disconcerted. She thought they should make more for that much work. Although she had been told expenses came out of Amy's pay, Norma had forgotten. *No one tells you about these things*, she grumbled to herself.

****

Amy would not be in school the next day and would miss a math test. Instead, she went in to New York with her mother on an early train again. The day included a frenzied morning shoot of Amy and two other models seated in chairs, at tables and standing alongside pieces of furniture. Once again, her hair and makeup were urgently fussed with. She was told what to wear. Her clothes were smoothed, straightened and arranged on her body. In the afternoon, she was rushed over to Maybelline where her face was examined in minute detail. She apparently passed scrutiny as Ginger told them it was a tremendous opportunity and they had a good chance of landing it.

Amy and Norma went back to Westport that evening. Ginger told them to return again on Friday, for another half day of shooting. Amy was able to make up the math test on Thursday, but she felt ill-prepared for it and feared she might have failed. She did not want to go back to New York, but she resigned herself to the prospect of another early morning trip on Friday.

Amy had always clung to her schoolwork. She focused on it and depended on it. And now she felt she was losing it. But she was too good a girl to fight with anyone about it. She had been told since before kindergarten by her father that she was a hard worker and that work came before play. He also told her she was a good girl who did not cause trouble. She tried her best, but it was getting extremely hard to do everything she was expected to do.

CHAPTER 35

1/6/72 – Thursday

Hank was seated in his office. Loan documents were spread across his desk. He had phone calls to return. None of it registered with him. The only thing on his mind was his lost money. With the $20,000 gone, Hank had no idea how he could regularly pay Generoso a thousand dollars every month. He only knew he had to do it somehow. He could make the payment for this month, but then he would have exhausted his savings. He finally decided the best option was to talk to Mike Holden. Mike, he thought, would want him to stay out of trouble and Mike definitely would not want to see their project in jeopardy. Plus, if it were anyone else, Hank thought he would have to explain too much. He couldn't share his situation with relatives he never saw or with friends in town. There was Maddie, but he instinctively knew she would not loan him money and also it pained him to have her think less of him for losing it in the first place. So Mike was really his only hope.

With a tight swallow, he picked up his phone and dialed Mike's number. Mike's wife, Ronnie, answered. She put Mike on. "Hey Hank, how's it going?"

"Well, not so good," Hank replied, feeling his stomach clench. "I'm in some trouble. You know I have to pay this guy Generoso a thousand bucks a month every month?" Hank thought he would not mention about the police. That would make it sound too dicey. The money problems were enough to share.

"Yeah. What about it?"

"Well, I'm short on cash. I don't see how I can do it. We have a lot of expenses right now.. the family... you know."

"Yeah?"

"Well, it's just... I don't know where else to turn." *This is degrading*, Hank thought. "I was hoping you could tide me over until our deal gets done."

"Tide you over, huh. How much we talking about here?"

"Well, I guess $20,000 would do it."

"You want me to lend you $20,000? Didn't I just give you $20,000 a month ago?"

"Yeah, but I needed that for the house." Hank had anticipated the question and rehearsed his answer. "We had a lot of problems with the plumbing and all." Hank hoped that sounded plausible.

"Twenty thousand dollars' worth of plumbing? What'd you do, put in an Olympic pool?"

"Well, there was other stuff. Look, I just need the money. Can you help me?" Hank realized he sounded angry. He backed off a little. "I'd pay you back as soon as we sell the houses, out of my share."

"Were you planning to pay me interest?"

"Uh, yeah. Of course. Whatever is fair. Sure."

"I don't know. We'll see. Let me think about it. I'll call you back."

Hank was disappointed. He had hoped this would be easy, but of course it was not. "Okay, call me as soon as you can. ...and thanks."

"I'll get back to you in an hour or so."

"An hour. Great. Okay, thanks."

Holden hung up. Hank gripped the phone tightly for a moment and then put it down. *Maybe*, he thought. It sounded like Holden might do it. *If he doesn't, I'm really screwed.*

So Hank waited. He didn't dare leave his office. He couldn't work. He couldn't concentrate. The hour went by painfully slowly. Finally, the phone rang.

"Sorry Hank. I just can't swing it," Holden said. "Every dime I have is tied up right now."

"Nothing? Even $5000 would help." Hank tried to keep the desperation out of his voice.

"Nah, sorry man. Don't you have family, relatives? What about your bank? Can you get a payroll loan, an advance, something like that?"

"I don't think so." Hank was whispering. His eyes were closed as if it were painful to see anything in front of him.

"Well, there must be something you can do. If I think of anything, I'll tell you. But you gotta work this out. You don't want that guy coming after you."

"No, no I don't," Hank groaned.

"All right, buddy. Best of luck. I mean it."

"Yeah, thanks." *Thanks for nothing.*

Hank felt like smashing something, but he hung up the phone gently. He sat still, straining to think. He could make the January payment. He had some savings left. And he could postpone paying some of his bills so he could perhaps scrape it together for the February payment, but after that, he would need to get some money somewhere. At least he had a little time, he told himself.

CHAPTER 36

1/14/72 – Friday

Alone in the house on a very cold morning, Dora sat shivering in her mother's usual spot on the living room couch. Now that she was rarely going to school, she was not socializing much and generally stayed home. Her mother and sister seemed to move around her as if she were not there. Only her father paid attention, but his attention was hardly solicitous. "How are you feeling?" he would ask or "What are your plans for the day?" all the time eyeing her suspiciously. The missing money was an unspoken obstacle between them. Neither could openly acknowledge it and neither could ignore it.

The phone rang. To her surprise, it was Jared. "Listen," he said, his voice sounding unusually pressured and high strung, "I want to be with you, help you raise the baby. I've decided."

"You have?" Dora felt her heart in her throat. "What about college?"

"Well, yeah, I should hear about that soon. I mean all my applications are in, so I should find out where I get accepted, like in the next month or so."

"So you're going off to college somewhere. How does that help me?"

"I don't know. Maybe you come with me?"

"What? To college? I don't think so. I'll probably stay around here. Maybe not live at home, I don't know, get my own place, but near here." Dora tried to imagine living with Jared, while he was in school, in some distant city. It didn't feel right. "Well, what exactly were you thinking?"

"I haven't gotten in anywhere yet. I mean, who knows? Maybe I'll stay here."

Dora felt the same frustration and annoyance she had felt before with Jared. He had nothing concrete to offer. "Look," she said "I'm going to get an apartment around here. I don't know how that fits in with your plans."

"You're getting your own apartment? When?"

"I don't know. I'm not sure. Maybe after the baby's born. Maybe before. Living with my parents is getting pretty weird. Weirder." She was tempted to tell him about the money she had, but she held back.

"Well, I want to be there for you, you know. I do. I just have to figure out how."

"Sounds like you got a few things to figure out." Dora's irritation came through the phone.

Jared felt the rift growing between them. He

wanted to make amends, to reconnect. "Look, I just want to support you, help you, you know, be there for you."

"Well, pretty hard if you're away at college."

"I know. I just..." Jared trailed off.

"Look, I gotta go" Dora said. She had nowhere to go, but she realized there was no real offer forthcoming from Jared. "I'll see you."

"Okay," Jared said reluctantly. "See you later."

****

Holden only had one foundation dug. Nothing else at all had been done with the lots. The land was not even completely cleared yet. Hank was getting panicky. Six entire houses had to be built and sold by November 15th of next year. That was 22 months away. Hank admitted to himself he knew nothing about construction, but the timeframe seemed awfully tight to him. The builders couldn't work in the dead of winter. So no work was under way now. Nonetheless, Holden did not appear worried nor did Maddie. *How could she know sales would go quickly? Wasn't that unpredictable?* He hoped he was feeling anxious for no reason. Just the same, the schedule worried him. He had a restless night's sleep and was up early the next day.

It was the fifteenth of the month, the day Hank had to make his next payment to Generoso. Hank was dressed and out the door early that morning before anyone else awoke. It was bitterly cold. He drove around

Westport aimlessly for over an hour. It was a quiet Saturday. He bought a newspaper. He kept glancing in his rearview mirror. It did not seem he was being followed. He suddenly thought, *if they tapped my phone, talking to Maddie or Holden, they have me. Christ! Well, nothing I can do about that. What's done is done. Just gotta hope for the best.* At last, he got on the Turnpike and headed to Bridgeport. This was the new arrangement, to avoid the police.

Hank parked his car on John Street, a block from Broad Street. As instructed, he folded the newspaper and placed the money inside. Determined to appear inconspicuous and relaxed, he carried the paper under his arm and strolled down John to where it intersected Broad. There was a bench there on the northeast corner. He sat down. As casually as possible, he placed the folded paper alongside him. He sat still for a moment, thinking it was not a good neighborhood. Anything could happen. Someone could mess this up, easily. Then he looked at his watch abruptly, as though he remembered he had an appointment. He jumped up, leaving the paper where it was and walked back to his car. He did not turn around. It was exactly 11:00 am. He drove back to his office.

He was now sitting at his desk. Despite the cold air he carried in with him, he was sweating slightly. He had not yet begun his work for the day when the phone rang. It was Maddie. "Rick says you did good," she told him. "Just do the same thing every month."

"Okay. I don't think I was followed. I guess the

Police don't go to Bridgeport." Hank laughed stiffly. He was trying to sound light.

"Don't count on it. Just be careful."

"I know. I know. I will"

"All right. Later." She hung up.

Well, that's over, at least for this month, thought Hank.

****

It was a strange weekend in the Latour home, but it was becoming typical. Norma buzzed about with great energy. She was much more active than she had been for many years. Dora sat like a statue in the living room, saying little and rarely moving. She seemed to have lost interest in seeing her friends. Hank glared at everyone. He stalked through the house like a restless bull. Sometimes he would shout at Norma who would blink quizzically. Dora watched her father out of the corner of her eye, but rarely interacted with him. Only Amy seemed to go on as she always had, studying quietly and going out for walks in the woods and fields.

But things did not feel normal to Amy. Despite her outward calm, she felt considerable tension. In the back of her mind was an ever-present sense of her life being altered by the modeling. It was still new and disturbing. She tried her best to ignore her disquiet.

That Monday, Norma and Amy were back on a

train to the city. Hank had again dropped them at the Greens Farms station, before heading to work. He had handed over his credit card admonishing Norma to please go easy on the spending. This was a longer stay for Amy and her mother. They had been told to plan for a week.

On this trip to New York, they had an intensive series of photo shoots. Amy was pushed and prodded, primped and prepped. It seemed endless. Often she felt like a mannequin. She was asked to smile and "look natural." Sometimes she would feel an unfamiliar rage well up inside her and she would surprise everyone by snapping at a stylist who was trimming her hair. She would immediately feel guilty and stifle those feelings with a muttered apology. More often she felt nothing, a kind of listless numbing of all feeling.

At times the work was terribly stressful for her, made worse by her own pressure to be a perfect model. For Norma, it was thrilling. Norma could almost believe that it was she who was up there being photographed, the center of attention. But in truth, she was consigned to the sidelines. The photographers and stylists all seemed pleased with Amy. They complimented her and told her she looked young and beautiful. Amy was not at all sure about the "beautiful" part. She was still uncomfortable about her looks and her growing body, but she nodded and tried to smile. She watched her mother out of the corner of her eye. Her mother was usually smiling.

On Thursday of that week, Amy went to Maybelline headquarters. She was again examined in detail, this time by a different group of people. They sat her in a very bright light and looked carefully at her skin. They studied the shape of her lips, discussed her eyebrows and debated about her eye color. Amy's eyes were blue, but it was not that simple. Apparently, some blues were better than others. Amy hoped her blue was acceptable. On several occasions, she noticed some of the people glancing at her chest. She suspected they were troubled by her lack of development there, but it was not mentioned. She thought *this is Maybelline. It's about makeup, my face, not about my body.*

The next day, they were back in Ginger's office at Wilhelmina. Ginger was explaining that there were a lot of important jobs coming up. Amy would be busy, she said. "Amy's had a good week, but this is just the beginning."

"We can't wait," Norma said.

Amy definitely could wait. She worried again about school. Now she had missed a whole week. *Why doesn't that bother mom?* she wondered. *And it must bother dad… shouldn't it?*

"I'll be in touch about her schedule. You might want to start to think about moving to the city." Ginger announced.

Amy knew this was coming, but she felt unprepared. "Mom…" she pleaded.

Norma ignored her daughter and turned to Ginger. "What do people usually do? I mean, do they get an apartment, or what? Or is there somewhere you have for us to stay?"

"No, we don't, but we can help you find a place. She could live with some of the other girls. That can be pretty cheap. Or you two could get a place. I gather you'll be coming in with her."

"Yeah, that's the idea. So, we would need to find a place together. We can't afford much yet. Not until Amy is making good money."

"Well, the Lower East Side's not far from here. That might be a good option. Pick up the Sunday Times and the Voice. Check out the listings for two bedrooms or a big one bedroom."

"Okay, yeah." Norma was excited, but Amy felt nauseous. She squeezed her eyes tight for a moment and said nothing.

Leaving the office, Norma was bubbly. "What a week!" she said.

"Mom, do we have to move to New York? I really don't want to. I really don't like it here."

"Oh don't be silly. You need to be here, now that you are going to be busier. That's the idea. You live and work here. That's how it's done."

"Yeah, but what if I don't want to live and work here?"

"That's nonsense. Of course you do. This is

where you make it. You're not going to become a famous cover girl staying in Westport, climbing trees." Norma laughed.

"I know, but, well… what about school?"

"There are schools here. We'll talk to Ginger about that."

Amy shuddered. "All right mom," she said.

CHAPTER 37

1/21/72 – Friday

Hank sat at his desk. He was very worried. The next payment to Generoso was still more than three weeks away, but he did not have the money in the bank. His monthly salary was $2,250, before taxes. *How much of that could I use for Generoso?* He tried to sort out the budget… heat, food, insurance, the mortgage, property tax, credit card bills. There were many items he had very little control over. They had to eat. He had already turned down the heat. He could postpone paying some bills, but that could not go on very long. He decided he could put off the oil and electric bills for a month, cut down on any extra driving and cut out all entertainment. It would help, but it would not be enough.

Where else can I get money? He struggled with it. He could ask Walsh for a salary advance. He could make up some excuse about needing money, maybe for college for Dora, something like that. But he thought about how conservative Walsh was and how humiliating it would be to ask him given that he had a good job and a reasonable salary. So he suspected the answer would be no. Holden had suggested friends and family. Thinking about it, Hank realized once again he had no friends he could turn to that were close enough and wealthy enough. His father was dead and he had no contact with his mother or younger sister. There was no one he could think to ask. Longer term, he could sell the house and move the family to a less expensive home, in a less expensive town. But that would not solve the immediate problem and giving up on Westport felt to him like a defeat. No, he would not do that.

Unhappily he decided to ask Walsh for the advance. So, it would be humiliating. He'd live. It was worth a try. Cautiously he stepped out of his office. The corner office belonged to Walsh and the door was closed. He smiled sheepishly at his secretary. "I'm going to talk to the boss," he explained to Dorothy. She regarded him quizzically and returned to reading the newspaper.

Outside the corner office sat Deirdre, Walsh's long-time secretary. "Uh Dee, is the boss in?" Hank asked with a forced smile. She nodded, "but he's on the phone right now."

"Oh that's okay, I'll wait. I'll wait here."

"Suit yourself," she said.

Hank sat down in one of the customer chairs in the waiting area. After about five minutes, Deirdre looked up. "He's off now. I'll buzz him."

Hank heard her speak into her intercom. "Hank's out here. Needs to see you about something." She listened and after a moment, looked up and said

"Okay, you can go in."

Hank approached the door with trepidation. He was having second thoughts. *Walsh isn't going to like this. But what else can I do? Oh what the hell. Might as well go for it. It's like fourth and ten. If I don't try, I've already lost.*

Walsh was seated behind his big desk, chewing on a cigar. Hank could not have been more intimidated if he were meeting the Pope. His boss looked up and said, a bit impatiently, "what is it?"

"Well, uh, I need to talk to you about something, something personal."

"Okay, sit down."

Hank walked between the two over-stuffed armchairs that faced Walsh's desk. As he sat down in one, his right arm hit the edge of the desk painfully. If Walsh noticed, he didn't say anything.

"Um, I muh, might as well get right to the point," Hank stuttered. "I could use an advance on muh, my salary. We, we have uh, a lot of expenses right now and some big ones and it would really, really help me. I mean I'll work it off. I could work extra hours for a while until it's paid off. You know…" Hank realized he was probably talking too much. He was very nervous.

"Well, sure Hank. We could do something like that I think. You've been here a while. We like you. How much we talking about? A few hundred?"

"Uh, no. No, I really need more than that."

"Well, how much?"

"I was thinking twenty thousand. We need money for Dora, for college. And then there's…"

"What!" Walsh cut him off in mid-sentence. "Forget it Hank. We're not going to advance you that kind of money. It doesn't matter how good an employee you are. It's out of the question."

"But.."

"No, and that's final. I'm sorry."

"But.."

"I said no. And I meant it. Get a loan like anybody else. Now get back to work."

There was nothing more to say. It had been a bad idea to ask. *Maybe I could have asked for less, taken less. Anything would have helped. Now I can't even bring it up again. Dammit. And I can't get a loan, for Chrissake. They'd need to know why. Too much paperwork. Too much stuff I can't disclose.*

Disconsolate, Hank returned to his office without another word.

CHAPTER 38

2/10/72 – Thursday

Two weeks later, Hank had scrimped and scraped together every cent he could find. He had amassed a little over six hundred dollars. Tuesday, the fifteenth, loomed ahead ominously. He could not come up with any more cash this month. In an anxious moment, he decided to ask Holden again. He thought *Holden does have the cash. He has all that money Generoso gave us in the first place.* So he dialed Holden's number.

"Listen, Mike. I am in real trouble here. I really need you to let me have some cash. I don't want Generoso on my back, and we can square it away when everything is over. I'll pay whatever interest. You know I'm good for it."

"No Hank, *you* listen. I have commitments for that money. I'm using it to pay electricians, plumbers, suppliers, everything. How do you think I get these places built? People have to be paid. That's how it works. So, no, I can't spare $20,000. You're going to have to get it somewhere else."

"I tried." Hank could hear himself whining, hating it. "Please," he added.

"No, I can't do it, man. I just can't. And I gotta go."

"Even a couple thousand…"

"Forget it."

"All right," Hank said, giving up.

****

Later, as he thought more about it, he started to think of it from Generoso's point of view. Generoso would have to understand that he was a little short this month. *This kind of thing must happen often and he must have to make allowances. He'd get all his money in the end. That was the most important thing, wasn't it?*

Hank turned it over in his mind the next few days. The more he thought about it, the more reasonable it sounded. After all, the bank sometimes had to redefine terms on some of its loans. That wasn't so unusual, as circumstances changed.

By Tuesday morning, Hank had convinced himself that Generoso was a reasonable man who would be willing to wait a bit longer for his money as long as it was eventually paid in full. It was the fifteenth. The next payment was due. Hank decided to write a carefully worded note that would explain his situation and he would include the note with the six hundred dollars he would leave in the folded newspaper. Before leaving his house that day, Hank sat at his kitchen table with pen and paper.

> Dear Mr. Generoso,
>
> I am sincerely sorry but I don't have the full payment this month. Please accept this $600 and I will plan to get on track with the remainder in the coming months. Due to some circumstances beyond my control, money has become a little tight for me, but you have my word that I will pay you in full by the time we complete our transaction.
>
> Sincerely,
> Hank

There, Hank thought. *That should do it.* He folded the note in his pocket and left the house. He took his usual winding route to Bridgeport, picking up a newspaper along the way.

He parked up the street from the drop-off point and placed the money and his note inside the folded newspaper. He walked rapidly to the designated bench, sat for a moment, and then got up, leaving the folded paper on the bench.

He returned to Westport, feeling better for the moment. He would still need to come up with money, but now maybe he could work things out with Generoso. And maybe they could wait until the houses were built and sold, before paying the full loan amount, the interest, and whatever he had not been able to manage of the payments along the way. He was actually humming to himself as he walked back through the bank to his office. Dorothy even commented "You seem cheery today." "Yes, I am," he said, with a smile, his first real smile in months.

****

Hank's upbeat mood continued the next morning. He arrived early at the office. Only Dorothy was there. He smiled at her and entered his office. Walsh was out of town all week and Walsh's secretary Deirdre had the week off. Hank was engrossed in the financial records of a loan applicant at about 10:00 am, when Dorothy buzzed him.

"There are two men out here to see you. They don't have an appointment." She sounded a bit anxious to Hank.

"Well, who are they?" he asked.

"Uh, their names are Joe and Tommy. That's all they said" she whispered. "Should I let them in?"

"Sure, go ahead." Hank had no inkling of why they were here. He did not think to connect this visit to yesterday's note.

His door opened and two men entered. They closed the door behind them. One man was small and wiry. "I'm Joe," he said, "and this," pointing to the much larger man on his left, "is Tommy."

"Okay, what can I do for you?" Hank asked innocently.

"You can pay us the money you owe our friend," said the smaller man.

"What? You mean Mr. Generoso?"

"Hey, no need to mention any last names."

"Oh. Okay." Hank squirmed a bit in his chair. Neither man sat down. The smaller one approached Hank's desk. He picked up Hank's Cross Pen, taking it out of its white marble holder.

"Nice pen, don't you think?" the little guy said as he handed the pen to the one named Tommy.

"Yeah," Tommy said, snapping it like a toothpick. "Too bad it broke."

"Hey!" Hank shouted.

"Now, now, calm down, Mr. Latour. Nothing to get upset over. It's only a pen. You got lotsa pens."

The little man came around to Hank's side of the desk. He put his hand gently on Hank's shoulder. "We're not here to hurt anybody. But our friend needs the money you owe him. He's a businessman and he's got, you know, other needs for the money. He can't afford to have you jerking him around." The man gave Hank's shoulder a little squeeze.'

"Well, no. I know," Hank stuttered. "I left him a

note, explaining. He'll guh, get the money, I promise."

"Well, maybe you don't quite understand. Time is money. That's what we say. And now you have a problem with time. There's a little extra interest when you're not on time."

"What? What interest?"

"Mr. G's a patient man. He will wait til next month's payment. That's very reasonable, don't you think? But he wants the $400 you owe him, plus the regular $1,000, and for this trouble you've caused him, let's say another $500. That would make him feel better."

Hank started to stand up, but the little man was surprisingly strong. His hand on Hank's shoulder kept Hank rooted to his chair.

"Do we understand each other?"

"Can't I discuss this with Mr. Gen...with Rick or... I could call someone to talk to him?" Hank was thinking Maddie could intervene on his behalf. He gestured vaguely toward his phone.

With amazing speed for a big man, Tommy lunged at Hank's desk. In one swooping motion, he grabbed Hank's phone with his big hand, yanking the cord out of the wall and raising the phone high above Hank's head. He held it over Hank for a moment and then brought it crashing down against the edge of the desk, shattering it in hundreds of pieces that went flying across the desk and all over the floor.

Hank would have jumped out of his chair, but he found himself held in place. He was terrified, seated between the two men, one at his left shoulder, the other looming above him to his right. His only thought was that he was certain that if he raised any further questions, his arm or some other body part would be next.

Hank felt his shoulder being squeezed again. "Do we understand each other now?" Joe asked him.

Hank could only nod. He would agree to anything if these men would just leave.

There was a loud knock on the door and they all heard Dorothy shout "Is everything all right in there?"

Hank looked anxiously up at Joe, who shook his head slightly, from side to side.

"No, yes I mean, everything's okay Dorothy."

"I heard..."

"It's *okay* Dorothy," Hank said sharply.

Dorothy apparently went back to her desk.

"All right, very good," said Joe, turning back to Hank. "So we have an understanding now, I think."

Hank turned and looked anxiously up at Joe and then at Tommy who grinned. With a gulp, Hank said "Yes, yes, I'll do what you say."

"All right. Good. So 1900 next month. And no more excuses."

"Yes," Hank whispered.

"What? I didn't hear you?"

"Yes. Yes, I understand."

"You understand what?"

"Uh, 1900 next month. No more excuses."

"All right then. You have a good day."

They walked out, shutting the door behind them. Hank stared down at the pieces of his shattered phone.

Moments later, Dorothy came rushing in. "Are you all right?" she asked breathlessly.

"Yes, I'm fine." Hank swallowed hard.

"Oh, I'm so glad. I heard that loud crash and those two strange men... I got really scared. I tried to call you and it didn't work. The phone didn't work. I didn't know what to do. I called the police because I thought you might be in trouble.

"You *what!* You called the *police*? Jesus, Dorothy, you didn't have to do that."

"Well, I was worried about you," she said somewhat indignantly, "the way they barged in without an appointment. And then that crash. And I couldn't reach you. I didn't know what to think."

Dorothy glanced down at Hank's desk and saw parts of his shattered phone. "Oh my God," she exclaimed. "Look at that! What in the world happened? Who were those men?"

"They were… associates… of a client. Jesus, are the police coming?"

"Yes, they said they'd be right over. I didn't know what to do," she repeated.

"All right, leave me alone, til they get here. Shut the door, please."

"All right, Mr. Latour. I was just trying to help. That's all."

"All right. Let me know when they get here."

She looked at him one more time, perplexed, and then she left, shutting the door behind her.

Hank bent over and started gathering up the scattered pieces of his phone. He put everything in his waste basket and shoved that under his desk where it couldn't be seen.

What in the world do I tell the police? If they connect this to Generoso, I'm sunk. Well, I'll keep his name out of it. I'll explain it was just two brothers thinking of buying property or something and I'll tell them things got a little heated, because they didn't like the interest rate, the points we charge, or something.

Hank rubbed his forehead. He felt a headache coming on.

There was a knock on his door. Dorothy stuck her head in. "Officers Finlay and Michaelson to see you, sir," she announced formally.

"Show them in."

Two uniformed patrolmen came in, looking out of place, their hats in their hands. "We had a report of a disturbance here. Is everything okay?" The older one was talking. "I'm Officer Michaelson, by the way. This is Officer Finlay."

"Yes. Uh, good to meet you both. Everything's fine here. We had a little discussion a while ago. I guess it kind of heated up. They didn't like our rates." Hank laughed, hoping the cops would be equally dismissive.

"Your secretary said there was a loud crash."

"Oh yeah, one of the men kicked the chair and it hit the desk. Made a loud noise."

"Did he break anything? Any damage?"

"No, no, really, everything is okay. We uh, came to an understanding. Parted friends. Of course I don't think they'll be doing business with us." Hank laughed again.

This time the cops smiled. "Well, if everything's okay, and no harm done, then I guess we'll be going."

"Yeah, just a false alarm."

"Okay. If they come back and there are further problems, let us know. We can get here quickly."

"All right, thanks. I'm sure we'll be fine. It's a one-time thing, rare. You know, these things happen once in a while. Nothing serious. No harm done."

"Okay. We'll go. You take care."

They walked out and Hank breathed a momentary sigh of relief. They hadn't noticed his missing phone and they evidently knew nothing of his prior visits to the Police Station.

But Hank's relief was short-lived. His thoughts quickly returned to the fact that he needed money, now more than ever.

****

The following morning, Hank was still wrestling with the problem of how to get more money when Dorothy leaned into his office.

"Hank, there's a Detective Goldschmidt here to see you."

"Oh, for God's sake," Hank groaned. "All right, send him in."

Goldschmidt walked into his office. Hank realized the Detective must have been standing right behind Dorothy in the doorway.

"Morning, Mr. Latour. Sounded like you maybe didn't want to see me. I guess you remember me, eh?"

"No sir. I mean I was just surprised. That's all."

Hank tried to present a relaxed smile, but he knew it looked false. He watched as Goldschmidt's sharp eyes examined the room and studied Hank's desk, the empty pen holder, the lack of a phone, before finally settling on Hank's face. Hank felt completely exposed, as though exactly what had happened was apparent to the Detective.

"Tell me about yesterday's incident."

"Incident?"

"Yes, I heard you had a problem here, a problem with two men. It got a little noisy I gather."

"Oh that. Uh, that was nothing."

"Didn't sound like nothing to me. Did it get violent?"

Hank winced, picturing his phone shattering. He'd been terrified, but he couldn't let the Detective know that.

"No, not really. They banged a chair is all."

"A chair, huh? So who were they?"

"Uh, their names were Joe and Tommy. They didn't give me their last names."

"Isn't that a little unusual?"

"Well, I guess maybe. If we had talked longer, of course I would have found out, but it was just a short conversation."

"About what?"

"Uh well, they wanted money. I mean they wanted a loan."

"What for?"

"They said they wanted to start a restaurant in town, a pizza place."

"A pizza place? And what did you say?"

"Well, I said we'd need collateral for a loan and an application with references, a business plan, you know, that kind of thing."

"And they didn't like that?"

"No. That's why they got angry. But we parted friends. No harm done."

"You're sure that's why they were here? That's your story, a pizza restaurant?"

"Well, yeah. That's the truth."

"And nothing to do with Rick Generoso? Nothing to do with that meeting we talked about before?"

"What? No, no, it's not related to that at all. That was a different situation." Hank did his best to seem surprised and puzzled.

Goldschmidt eyed Hank suspiciously. "Well, we're not so sure Mr. Latour."

"No, that's the truth, Detective." Hank could hear the note of pleading in his voice and he hated it.

"Look. I don't know what's going on, but I don't like it and we're gonna keep an eye on you. I think you're bringing trouble to this bank, to this town. We don't know what you're doing but we're gonna find out."

"I told you nothing's going on," Hank insisted.

He could tell Goldschmidt didn't believe that for a minute. The detective leaned across Hank's desk and said "We get any more reports of suspicious activity and we'll turn you and this bank upside down."

"That really won't be necessary, Detective. I assure you I've done nothing wrong. Nothing it all. You won't hear anything further from me. No more trouble. I promise."

"We'll still be watching you. Believe me, we see anything or I hear anything else, anything at all, I'll come down on you so hard you won't know what hit you."

"Yes sir. I understand. I promise. No more uh,

incidents."

"All right. Consider yourself warned."

"Yes. Yes, thank you."

Goldschmidt turned and walked out. Hank sat there visibly trembling. *Money, money, and now the police.* Hank looked across his desk at his empty pen holder. *I have to get a new phone*, he thought. *And Dorothy better keep her mouth shut.*

Hank gathered himself together and walked out of his office. He stood in front of Dorothy. "Please don't say anything to anyone about the meeting I had here yesterday or this one today. I don't need Walsh hearing about the police and all. Oh, and please order me a new phone. Just say the old one broke. I spilled coffee on it or something."

"Okay, Mr. Latour." She looked up at him. She would keep his secrets. She was fond of him and very loyal.

"I'm not feeling well," he said. "I'm going to head home."

"Okay," she nodded.

Hank went home where he poured himself a good-sized glass of scotch. It did little to calm his nerves.

CHAPTER 39

2/26/72 – Saturday

Dawn was finally breaking. Hank had lain awake most of the night. He had drifted off to sleep at around 4:00 am only to awaken an hour later. Now he sat alone in the kitchen of his big house. He was wrestling with how to come up with the money for Generoso. He needed $1,900 on the fifteenth of March and then $1,000 a month thereafter. He tried to think of everything, anything. He could sell some of his furniture, sell a car, rent out a room in his house, get a part-time job. Nothing seemed like an adequate solution. Nothing would produce enough money quickly enough. This time he knew he could not scrape together the money, nor could he come up with another source. And now it was abundantly clear there was no negotiating with Generoso. There were no options there and Hank was terrified of the consequences of missing another payment. *Keep thinking,* he told himself.

He briefly wondered about crime. *Could I rob a bank? Or break into a neighbor's house and steal valuables, like jewelry or a coin collection? Or art?* As quickly as he thought of these things, he dismissed them.

He knew he would make a terrible thief. Someone would hear him or see him. He knew it. Then he would really have trouble with the Police. The prospect of being caught in a robbery was mortifying and going to prison was unthinkable. No, he could not be a thief.

Then he thought of Amy. Was she making any money? Was Norma suddenly living well when she went to New York? No, Hank knew that wasn't the case. Norma still needed his credit card. There was no money there. Not yet anyway. He'd have to get that card back soon, he thought. Hank pushed himself back from the table and went to the cabinet for the scotch. He needed to calm his nerves. He put some ice in a glass. *This is exactly what Norma would do*, he thought irritably, but he poured the drink just the same. He took the glass and the bottle back to the table. He took a long drink and then buried his face in his hands.

Think, he told himself. Once more, Holden came into his mind. Holden had as much to lose, almost, as he did. He couldn't afford to have Generoso's people coming after him for the loan any more than Hank could. And they would come after Holden. Why not? He was the one with their money. *Mike's in as deep as I am. Makes sense for me to go to him. I know he can afford to give me some money right now. Sure, he doesn't want to, but he really doesn't need it all right away. He'll need it all as it gets closer to the end of the construction, but not now. And really, he's just dealing with contractors and suppliers. They can wait a bit to get paid. Yes,* Hank thought, *Holden is the answer. He has to say yes. This time he has to say yes.*

Hank took another long swallow of his drink and once again, he picked up his phone and dialed Mike's number.

"Yeah?" Mike answered sleepily.

"Hey Mike, how are you?"

"Oh. Hank. Yeah. I'm fine. What is it?" Hank thought he detected some suspicion in Mike's voice.

"I hate to call you again about this Mike, and I'm sorry it's so early, but I am really desperate. Things have gotten a lot worse. I was threatened and our whole deal could go to Hell."

"What do you mean threatened? What are you talking about?"

Two men came to my office last week. They smashed my phone. They threatened me with bodily harm. I know they were serious. They were not fooling around. I think my life is in danger. And Hell, you too, if they don't get their money."

"Jesus H. Christ, Hank. What did you do?"

"Oh, well I told you I had a problem coming up with the payments, the $1,000 payments each month…"

"Yeah, and?" Holden was fully awake now.

"Well last month I only had $600, so I gave

them that. But they want it all. They want $1,900 next month." Once again, Hank did not mention the police.

"And you don't have it."

"No man. I don't. I'm sorry. Truth is I lost the $20,000 you gave me."

"Whadda you mean you lost it? How? Christ, Hank, how do you lose twenty thousand dollars?"

"I know. I know. I was an idiot. I left it in the garage and someone stole it."

"You're right. You are an idiot. For a supposedly smart man, that was incredibly stupid."

"Yeah, I know. But that's, you know, that's water under the bridge. The problem is now." Hank felt himself trembling.

"Yeah, I get that." Mike paused. "So you're telling me you still need the twenty grand you asked me for before? Is that it?"

"Yeah, it is. I need it. I tried everything. You're my only hope. I wouldn't be begging you if I had any other choice."

"No, I guess not. Probably not."

"So, what do you think?"

"Well, you're putting me in a hell of a bind here, Hank. You're putting the whole project at risk. Shit, man. I could kill you."

"Yeah, well if you don't lend me the money, you probably have."

"What? Oh yeah, right. All right. Fucking A. Give me a few days to see if I can put the cash together, get you out of this mess. I'll get back to you."

"Okay. Okay. Thanks!"

"Well I haven't done anything yet. But I'll be in touch." Holden hung up.

****

The following Monday afternoon, Hank's new phone at the bank was installed. There were no calls that afternoon, but the next morning, as he sat anxiously at his desk, the phone rang.

"Okay, I'll do it," Holden said. "But here are the conditions. I'll give you $20,000 but I want $25,000 back out of your share at the end of our project."

"$5,000 extra?" Hank paused. "That's 25%. Well, over… what is it? About 20 months? That's like fifteen per cent annually."

"Hey, I want to be fair."

Hank could picture Holden smiling at the other end of the line. He didn't think it was especially fair, but he sensed Holden was not flexible. It was take it or leave it. *It could have been worse*, he thought. *I'm in no position to bargain here.*

"All right. Let's do it."

"Okay. Give me a couple of days to move things around."

"Yeah, right. Of course."

"I'll get back to you once I'm ready to go."

"All right. Thanks again, Mike."

"You're welcome. I know you're good for it. Hey, I know where you live, buddy." Mike laughed.

"Yeah, okay."

"I'll get back to you," said Mike as he hung up.

****

The waiting was difficult for Hank. He barely slept. He could not concentrate at work. He arrived late and left early. And he was drinking, which only added to his misery. He suspected Dorothy, his secretary, could tell. He hoped not. He did not want to jeopardize his job and he lived in fear that Walsh would see what was happening to him.

It wasn't a couple of days. Mike didn't call until the following Tuesday, a week after their last phone call. The fifteenth was only a week away. Hank was in his office.

"Okay, I have the money," Mike said. "Why don't you stop by the house? I'll be in all morning."

"Your house? Okay, okay, I can do that. I'll be right over."

Hank literally ran out of his office, past Dorothy who glanced up as he ran by. "I'll be back later," he shouted.

Hank drove quickly on the curvy hills to Holden's home. He was eager to get the transaction over with. Mike was outside in his yard when Hank drove in the driveway.

"Let's go inside," Hank said nervously.

"Sure, sure," said Holden placing a meaty arm over Hank's shoulders and ushering him up the walk.

Inside, Holden asked if he wanted a drink. Hank declined, eager to get down to business.

Instead, Holden launched into a joke. "You know why scientists, when they do experiments, they use lawyers now instead of rats? Ya know why? Lawyers instead of rats?"

"No," said Hank, with annoyance. "Let's just do this."

"Well," said Holden, ignoring Hank's wishes, "first of all, there are more of 'em." Holden waited for a laugh that didn't come. "More lawyers than rats. Second, you don't get attached to 'em, and third," Holden began chuckling, "There are some things a rat just won't do." Holden gave a loud laugh and Hank smiled tightly.

"There are some things a rat just won't do," Holden tried again.

"All right, c'mon, let's get this over with, Mike."

"Okay, okay. Sit tight. I'll be right back."

Holden left the room and returned a few minutes later with a check. He crossed the room and handed it to Hank. "Okay, here's your birthday present. Try not to lose it."

Hank looked at it. "A personal check?" he asked.

"Yeah, it gives me a record of the loan."

"I was hoping for cash."

Holden merely shrugged.

Hank took the check. "Thanks." He was already puzzling over how to convert it to cash, without drawing attention to what he was doing with the money. "I appreciate it," he added. He also wondered if it would clear in time. He needed the money in a week.

"Glad to be of service," Holden grinned.

"Well, I'll be going," said Hank.

"Be good, and hey, if you can't be good, at least be careful," chuckled Holden as Hank went out the door.

****

Hank decided he had to open a separate checking account for the money. As a banker himself, he knew about the Bank Secrecy Act passed two years before, but he understood that only applied to currency transactions. A check was not subject to special reporting requirements. He thought the deposit of a $20,000 check would be safe. He decided to deposit it in a Bridgeport bank. That would be away from the prying eyes of the police and he could readily withdraw the money there when needed for his payments to Generoso. Driving to Bridgeport, he thought *maybe this can all work out. You just solve one problem at a time. That's what I'm doing. One thing at a time.* He saw a Westport Police car behind him on the Post Road, but he didn't think it followed him on to the Turnpike. *Maybe they weren't following me. They must have better things to do than follow me around all day,* he thought hopefully.

Starting a couple of days after he had opened the account, Hank had called the bank daily to see if the check had cleared. And although it had not fully cleared, the bank at last allowed him to withdraw $1,900 out of the $20,000. And so, the day before he had to have it, Hank drove to the bank and took out $1,900 in cash.

The next morning, the fifteenth of March, was cool and overcast, but by mid-March, it was finally warm enough for construction to resume. According to

Holden, they'd been working for a few days already, but Hank wanted to drive over and see for himself. To his immense relief, the site was abuzz with activity. Two bulldozers were clearing ground for two of the planned lots. The framing of the model home had begun where before only a hole for the foundation had existed. Hank was relieved, at least for the time being. He left, picked up a newspaper, drove around town for fifteen minutes and then headed to Bridgeport. He did not think he was followed.

CHAPTER 40

3/15/72 – Wednesday

Amy and Norma moved to a large one bedroom apartment that Norma found on Avenue A, near East 10th Street. The rent was $165 a month. They had received a $500 advance against Amy's earnings, so there was no need to ask Hank for money. It was a furnished apartment and convenient to Wilhelmina. Norma was glad to get it. It had two twin beds in the bedroom. There was enough space for them. But it was in a dangerous and dirty neighborhood. Abandoned buildings nearby held squatters and drug addicts. Coming out their front door, Amy and Norma sometimes had to step around sleeping homeless or drunken men passed out on the sidewalk. For their safety, when they went out, it was usually together. Amy was enrolled in P.S. 226. She was frightened in school and missed Westport terribly. Norma promised it was only temporary and as soon as they had more money, they would move to a better neighborhood.

****

Meanwhile, Dora formally dropped out of school. Her Guidance Counselor had silently noted her pregnancy and did not ask for her reason. He had seemed relieved. He did not want her staying in school. That was two weeks ago. Now with her mother and sister in New York City all week and her father at work, Dora found herself alone in the silent house. She felt like an outcast there. When he was there, her father seemed suspicious in her presence, watching her closely. She was constantly on guard around him. At six months pregnant, she wished she could move out. She could afford it, but she worried her father might connect a move with his lost money. So it was a quandary. Then she thought of Jared. Maybe he could say he was paying for the apartment. She decided to call him.

She reached him at home that afternoon.

"You said you wanted to help me."

"Yeah... Yeah, I do." Jared said slowly.

"Well," Dora mustered her courage, "I need to move out. I need money to get an apartment. You could move with me," she suggested hopefully. She sensed he would not want to simply spend money to help her move. She had a feeling he would want to be more involved. She was right.

"Yeah. We could like totally do that!" He sounded surprised and pleased.

"You have money right? I have some too," she added.

"Yeah, I've got some. I make some on the pot

and pills."

"I figured."

"Well, when? Like is this... like now?"

"Well, we'd have to find a place. Something we can afford. You know?"

"Sure"

"So we'd need some time for that, but yeah, I'd like to do it soon, before I get any bigger."

"Okay." He paused. "It is my baby, right?"

"Yeah. Of course." Dora felt her stomach tighten and the baby moved inside her.

"Okay. Okay, I'm psyched."

"All right. Good. I'll see you." Dora hung up and clasped her belly protectively. She started thinking about her next steps. They would need to find an apartment. Something small, inexpensive, maybe near the hospital in Norwalk, she thought. She went downstairs to look for the newspaper. She couldn't find one.

That night, she encountered her father in the kitchen. He looked at her curiously. "Do you have the paper?" she asked.

"The Westport News? In my briefcase."

"Can I have it?"

"Why?"

"Well…" she hesitated, then blurted out "I need to find an apartment. I'm moving out."

"You're what! Since when? When did you decide this? And how will you pay for it?" Now he was really suspicious. "Do you have the money? Where'd you get it?"

Dora knew the question would come up, just not so soon. Nevertheless, she had an answer prepared. "Jared's moving with me. He has money."

"Oh, Jared. The father. Jesus Dora, have you thought this through? That's too much responsibility for you kids to take on. You have school. What about Jared's parents? They can't be too pleased with this."

"Well Jared has to tell them. What can they do? It's what he wants…what we want."

"And you? You have school to finish."

"Well, I dropped out."

"You what? You dropped out of school? That's stupid, Dora. You sit down here right now!"

Dora felt like bolting from the room, but she thought it best to comply. "I can finish school later, daddy, after the baby comes," she said. She heard the doubt and fear in her own voice. She felt like she was ten years old again.

"I don't think this is a good idea at all. What's wrong with staying here, in your home, getting a tutor or whatever?"

"I just don't want to. I don't know. It's my baby, my life." She tried to sound forceful.

"Of course it is. But it doesn't sound to me like you know what you're getting into."

"I do dad. We'll be fine."

Hank was about to continue arguing, but he paused. His mind was whirling. This could be an answer to his problems, he thought. With Norma and Amy moving to New York and Dora moving out, he could sell the house. He could move to his own apartment. He'd have money. He liked the idea. Still, he felt he had better challenge Dora further. He did not want to see her hurt.

"So what are Jared's plans in all this? Did he drop out too?"

"No. I think he'll stay in school. He wants to finish and go to college. That's what he plans to do."

"I don't get it. What happens when he goes to college?"

"We'll figure that out. For now, we're just getting a place together."

"Uh huh. Some plan. Are you two getting

married?"

"We haven't talked about that yet, but yeah, probably."

"Well, you might want to discuss it before you make this big leap." Hank was angry. He did not feel Dora's plans were well considered at all. At the same time, a little voice in his head kept telling him *this could be a good thing.*

"We will. One thing at a time. First we need to find an apartment." She thought that sounded reasonable.

"And where is this apartment going to be?"

"I was thinking in Norwalk maybe. Something near the hospital." Dora was pleased she had at least thought out that much.

"Oh yeah, the paper. I don't know if you'll find listings in the Westport News."

"Well, where then?"

Suddenly Hank became helpful. "You might ask Maddie, the realtor."

"Who?"

"Maddie Hixon. She's a real estate agent I'm working with. And she helped your mother. We know her. She's good. She would know about Norwalk rentals or she would know who did."

"Okay. I guess so." Dora was puzzled by this change in her father's attitude, but she was happy to take his advice. "Do you have her number? I'll call her tomorrow."

"Yeah. Here, I'll write it down." Hank knew Maddie's number by heart. He wrote it on a slip of paper. Above it, he began to write "Maddie," then changed and wrote "Hixon Realty."

Dora took the paper from him and looked at it. "Okay. I'm gonna call her in the morning."

Hank let it go. He was not going to argue further. He was worried for Dora, but he would not stop her. *Would Norma care?* Would she have wanted him to put his foot down? He thought not. He wondered how the Appletons would feel. He suspected Vince would be furious. He smiled at the thought.

****

The next morning, Dora called Maddie. She explained that her father told her to call about finding an apartment in Norwalk. Maddie primarily handled sales, she explained, but she agreed to help Dora find a rental. After gently confirming Dora had enough money to rent a one bedroom and pay her fee, she suggested "Why don't you stop by the office this afternoon? Meantime, I'll see what I can find for you in Norwalk."

"Okay, that would be great. Thank you so much."

"You're welcome. Come by around three."

"Okay, I'll see you then."

Dora hung up. She was in the living room. She looked around at the empty house as though she were seeing it for the first time. *I'm leaving here*, she thought. *I'm getting my own place.* She liked the idea.

That afternoon, she sat in Maddie's comfortable office. She felt nervous and excited. Maddie smiled warmly. "So you're Hank's daughter?"

"Yeah, I'm the older one."

"Yes, I met your mother. I think I helped her out with your sister."

"You did?"

"Yeah, she needed to speak with a photographer I know, so I connected them."

"Oh really? Wow. Cool."

"So now I'll help you, if I can. You want your own apartment?"

"Yeah. For me and my boyfriend, Jared. We're moving in together. It's his baby." Dora patted her stomach, smiling nervously.

"Uh huh. Okay." Maddie found she liked this nervous, sweet girl, with her dark hair and eyes.

"We'll be a family," said Dora with a hopeful smile.

"Of course," Maddie reassured her.

"Yes! So did you find anything for us?"

"I did. I found two one-bedrooms on the hill, near Norwalk hospital. They're both in three family homes over there. The top floor in both."

"Okay. That sounds good. Can we see them?"

"Sure. I'll take you over today if you want."

"Yeah, yeah. Great. If I want one, can we show it to Jared?"

"Of course. They've both been on the market for a while, so there's no time pressure here. We can check 'em out, see what you think. If you like, you come back with… what's his name? Jared?"

"Yeah, Jared. Cool. Can we go now?"

"Sure. Give me a moment." Maddie pulled together some papers on her desk. She turned to get her coat. "We'll take my car."

Together they drove into Norwalk. It was a short drive from Maddie's office. Dora could not sit still in the passenger seat. She was excited. She was more talkative than usual. "I am so psyched to get a place. I know how I want to decorate it. I have curtains from my room. And I'll take my bed and dresser, but I'm going to get a nice kitchen table. Well, something second-hand I guess, but I want it to be nice."

Maddie smiled. "I think there's a Goodwill down there. You might find something there. And check the classifieds too."

It occurred to Dora that she liked Maddie, who seemed to accept her and maybe even like her. As she thought about it, since becoming pregnant, Maddie was the first adult Dora had met who did not seem to judge or pity her. She treated her like another person. Dora glanced over at Maddie and smiled.

For her part, Maddie found she liked Dora as well. Whether or not this was a good decision for someone so young, she admired Dora's courage and spunk. It could not have been easy to decide to go out on her own, a pregnant, unwed teenager. It took guts.

They arrived at the first house. Maddie parked in front and they walked to the front door. It was a white three-story, wood-shingled house. It needed a paint job. They climbed the steps to the porch and rang the buzzer for the first floor. The name next to the buzzer said "Hitchcock." A portly man in a dirty white tee shirt answered. "You the people interested in three?"

"Yes" said Maddie. "I'm Madeline Hixon and this is Dora."

Dora stepped out from behind Maddie and offered to shake his hand.

Hitchcock looked directly at her pregnant midsection and then looked up at her face. Then he shook her hand. "Okay, c'mon in."

"We go up here." They followed him up a narrow stairway. At the second floor, there was a door. "That's two," he said. "C'mon."

They continued up. At the third floor, there was another door. He unlocked it and they followed him in. "I cleaned it up a bit, but uh, maybe could use some paint."

Maddie and Dora looked at the living room before them. It was empty save for a worn looking grey couch. "Let's see the kitchen," said Maddie.

Hitchcock led them into a small kitchen. It had a fading yellow Formica counter top, discolored white linoleum squares on the floor and an old white stove and refrigerator. Maddie glanced at Dora who was frowning. "Okay, how 'bout the bedroom?" Maddie asked.

Hitchcock waddled back out of the kitchen and turned to his right. They entered a small, musty room. It had two windows and an open closet. Dora noticed a few coat hangers dangling in there. She turned to Maddie "You have another one to show me?"

"Yeah. This one's $145, right?" Maddie asked Hitchcock.

"Yeah, plus one month security."

"Okay. We'll get back to you. Let's go," she said to Dora.

The three stepped back down the narrow steps. "I'll be in touch," Maddie said to Hitchcock.

"Uh huh," he grunted. He was breathing heavily after climbing up and down three flights.

In the car, Maddie turned to Dora. "What'd you think?"

"Kind of dirty... I don't know. And dark."

"Well you can clean it up. Paint it. Whatever you want. I'll bet you could make it nice."

"Yeah. I guess. Let's see the other one."

The second apartment was three blocks away. It was further down the hill, nearer the stores and a little further from the hospital. It was also a three-family house. They parked in front and got out.

"This one's only $110," said Maddie, as they approached the building.

Dora looked at the dirt yard. It contained a rusted tricycle and several old tires stacked in a pile. A man sat smoking a cigarette on the porch. "You the folks looking to see the third floor?" he asked.

"Yup, that's us," Maddie said with false cheer. The man unfolded his long legs and got up. "I'm Hector Rodriguez. The landlord." He flicked the cigarette into the yard.

"Maddie Hixon. I'm the agent. This is Dora Latour." She looked at Dora who was looking up at the house.

"Well, I'll show it to you," said Rodriguez.

The vertical slats on the porch railing dangled without touching the bottom. They had rotted out where they should have met the porch steps. Dora gingerly climbed up to the porch behind Maddie. There were two entrances.

"That goes to my apartment," the Rodriguez said, pointing to the right one. "We go in here." He opened the left door. It was another narrow stairway. It creaked badly as the three trudged up. They arrived at the top floor where Rodriguez paused, knocked and then unlocked the door. "I don't think they're here," he said.

They entered a small, cluttered room. "They're moving out in two weeks. You can have it starting the first."

They picked their way around toys, piles of magazines and unopened mail. They walked through a maze of ragged easy chairs and floor lamps. The room was a mess. "Guess they weren't expecting company," joked Rodriguez.

"No, I guess not." Maddie smiled grimly.

The kitchen was even worse. There were dirty

dishes in the sink and on the counter. Several roaches scattered when Rodriguez turned on the light.

"I don't like this place at all," Dora whispered to Maddie.

"Okay, we'll let you know," Maddie said to Rodriguez.

"Don't you want to see the bedroom?"

"No, that's okay. I'll be in touch."

Dora felt they could not get out of there fast enough. As soon as they were back in the car, she said "That makes the first place seem like a palace."

"Well this one's $35 a month cheaper."

"You couldn't pay me to live in that dump."

"Okay," laughed Maddie. "What about the first place? Can you afford it?"

Dora thought about her secret stash in her safety deposit box. "Oh yes," she said. "That's no problem."

Maddie wondered about this, but said "Okay. So you liked it?"

"Yeah. Well, let's let Jared see it. Maybe on the weekend? Can he see it then?"

"Probably. I'll have to check."

"All right. Yeah. I liked it."

They drove back to Maddie's office. Dora jumped out happily. "I guess you'll call me, right?"

"Yes," Maddie smiled at her.

"And we could see it with Jared Saturday?"

"I think so. I'll let you know."

"Okay. Far out." Dora climbed in her car and waved goodbye. She could not wait to tell Jared.

****

"You found a place already?" Jared asked that night.

"Yeah. In Norwalk, like we talked about, near the hospital. It's cool. I think you'll like it."

"Yeah, okay. But I haven't even, like, told my parents yet."

"Well, maybe you should see it first. Maybe Saturday? Could you come on Saturday?"

"This Saturday? I guess so."

"Cool. I'm waiting to hear from Maddie. She's the real estate agent helping me. She'll let me know if we can go on Saturday. Anyway, I'm psyched. You'll like it. It's cool."

"Well, yeah. Yeah, okay. I gotta tell my parents I'm doing this," he said, an anxious edge to his voice.

"That's gonna be World War Three."

"Well, it's your life you know. You can do what you want."

"Yeah. That's right. I can."

"And hey, you're going to be a father."

"Shit. That's big. For sure."

"So okay. We'll talk soon."

Jared did not wait to see the apartment before telling his parents. It did not go well with them. Betty Appleton dissolved in tears immediately. His father said "I forbid it. I'm not going to watch you ruin your life." But that only made Jared more determined. He found he enjoyed defying his parents. He was being his own man, he told himself. As Dora said, it was his life. His father predicted he would come "crawling back" soon enough. Jared was determined not to.

That Saturday, Dora, Jared and Maddie returned to the apartment. To everyone's relief, Jared liked the little one-bedroom unit in the white house on the hill.

****

That evening, seated at the dining room table, Jared and his father waited for dinner to be served. His mother was in the kitchen.

"So I'm moving in with Dora, to her place in Norwalk. With our baby," added Jared.

"No. We talked about this. That's a bad idea, Jared. You know your mother and I want you to go to college."

"I know. I can still go, but a year or two now working won't hurt me later. I feel like it's the right thing to do right now."

"Look Jared, there are better ways to handle this thing. Move on. You don't want to stay with that girl."

"Oh gimme a break dad. How do you know what I want to do? This is what I want to do. And I'm doing it!." Jared slammed his fist on the table rattling the glassware. "Jesus Christ, I can make up my own mind about some things!"

"Well, not about this you can't!" his father yelled.

Jared jumped up from the table. "This sucks! I'm outta here." He stormed out the front door, not even bothering to put on his jacket.

Betty Appleton came rushing in from the kitchen. "Where'd he go?"

"Oh he'll calm down. He'll see we're right."

"I don't know. I don't know." Betty was crying.

"Calm down. He'll be back. He'll get hungry soon enough. And cold. He didn't even put on a coat."

Fifteen minutes later, Jared returned, shivering.

"Sit down. Let's eat." His father had resolved to be reasonable and not lose his temper again. "How do you feel about Dora?" he asked.

"I like her. She's cool."

"You love her?"

"I don't know. We have a good time together."

"How long have you two been together?"

"A while. I'd say like two, three years…"

"Well, that's something. But you don't want to screw up your future over this, this baby thing. I mean you don't even know for sure it's yours. Why do you have to raise it?"

"I don't know dad. I just…" Jared's voice trailed off. He fidgeted nervously with his knife and fork. He turned and stared at his mother. Her eyes were still damp from her earlier tears. She smiled reassuringly at him.

"Whatever you do, we love you," she said, her voice quavering. "We just want what's best for you." Her husband shot her an angry glance.

"Well, moving in with Dora is what I think is best," Jared said, sounding a lot more certain than he felt.

"So you're determined to go ahead, no matter what we say? Is that it?" His father, Jared noticed, was gripping his dinner knife fiercely.

"Well yeah, but just for a year. Then I'll go to college, if I get in."

All of a sudden, Vince Appleton seemed to deflate. "Okay, fine. We'll trust your judgment."

Jared squirmed uncomfortably. He wanted desperately to get high on something.

CHAPTER 41

4/15/72 – Saturday

Amy was rising rapidly in the fashion world. She was just what the magazines, the cosmetic industry and the catalog companies were looking for. She was a tall slender girl, 15 years old and fresh-faced, with good cheekbones and beautiful eyes. She was bustled around from shoot to shoot. She was treated like an object. Her arms and head were positioned; she was trained to smile on command, to stay still and look natural. She felt detached from everyone, including herself.

Norma was always there, on the perimeter, where she was permitted to watch, but not get involved. Let the professionals do their job, she was told. She watched Amy happily. While it was frustrating to be kept apart, it was nonetheless tremendously gratifying for Norma. Amy's success was her success. It was what she had dreamed of for both of them.

For Amy, modeling had become an ordeal to be endured. Sometimes she would glance at her mother's flushed, beaming face and that pleased her. But mostly, she wished she were somewhere else, back in Westport, back in school or better yet, out in her woods and fields.

At times, after a shoot or in a makeup session, Amy would find herself among other models. Each was different, had a different story, a different background. But they all seemed comfortable with what they were doing. To Amy, they all appeared very self-assured. Most of them smoked, which Amy considered an awful habit. She watched them as they delicately placed a cigarette between their lips, careful not to muss their lipstick. When offered one, Amy at first refused, but as time went on, she eventually gave in, and smoked without inhaling. Within weeks, she had become a regular smoker. It was easy. There was something comforting about it. She was surrounded by smoke. The girls smoked and at home, back in their apartment, her mother smoked. Occasionally a stylist or photographer would urge Amy to stop, saying it was bad for her skin. Amy listened and wondered, but didn't stop. She was hooked. In her lonely isolation, cigarettes became her only friend.

****

At seven months pregnant, Dora moved with Jared to their one bedroom apartment in Norwalk. Simply climbing the stairs was an effort for her, but she was pleased she had made the move. They would live there as a family. She liked the idea. *Her new family.* Her original family, she thought, seemed to be scattered to the winds. What reason did she have to stay with her father, always watching her, where she was constantly on guard? This was much better, she thought. She was on her own, making her own way. True, Jared was a little unreliable. He had been an hour late coming to get her for their move, but he showed up eventually. He had borrowed a friend's van and they had loaded her dresser and bed into it. That was all they took with them, other than clothes. They would have to buy furniture and kitchen supplies.

Although Dora had dropped out six weeks earlier, Jared had remained in school. Moving in with Dora in April of his senior year, he only had two months left to finish. With help from his mother and pressure from his father, he had applied to a number of colleges the previous winter. He had not been accepted to any in the Ivy League, but he was offered admission to several good schools, including Colgate and Bucknell. Now these schools needed an answer. To the great chagrin of his parents, Jared told the colleges he would not attend that Fall. He told his parents he had deferred admission, though neither school had guaranteed him a later acceptance. He would go in the future, he said, after a year maybe, but not at this time. He wanted a year "to experience life."

Under Dora's direction, their apartment began to take shape. They found kitchen items at Goodwill. They bought curtains and a small table and chairs they found at a yard sale. On the sidewalk, Dora found a little desk that someone had left as trash. She discovered a desk chair the same way. The only new items they acquired were for the baby. She bought a bassinet, a little crib and a colorful mobile to suspend above it. These items were placed in a corner of their bedroom. They formed a cheery little spot in their dark apartment. To lighten the rest of the place, they bought two floor lamps from Goodwill. Using Dora's money, they had also purchased a well-used Honda Civic.

Dora invited her father to visit, but thus far, he had not come.

****

It was Saturday, April 15. Taxes were due and so was Hank's payment. He got on the Turnpike at Exit 19 and headed toward Bridgeport. He glanced at the newspaper on the seat alongside him. He would go first to the bank and withdraw the thousand dollars. Driving in the right lane at the speed limit, he watched his rearview mirror anxiously. It did not appear that he was being followed. *Maybe they're no longer watching me.* In Bridgeport, he withdrew the money from his account and repeated his drop-off pattern as before. It all seemed to go smoothly and as he headed back to Westport, his mind turned to other things. He thought of Norma and Amy taking an apartment in New York. He knew without saying so, that the move was a trial separation for him and Norma. *We'll see how it goes. I was glad to see her move out,* he admitted.

Hank was less worried now about each payment to Generoso, but he continued to worry about the police. He did his best to be extra careful. On the fifteenth of each month, he would first do errands in Westport before going to Bridgeport. He varied his routes. Sometimes he took local streets. Other times, he would take the

Turnpike or the Merritt Parkway. He did not think he was ever followed. Since the police had not seen Generoso back in town, Hank hoped they had lost interest in him, but he doubted that and he remained careful and took precautions each time he went to Bridgeport.

CHAPTER 42

6/15/72 – Thursday

After his high school graduation, instead of college, Jared found a job in a Norwalk warehouse. He began working for a company that sold office equipment. He moved desks and file cabinets around the warehouse floor or loaded them on to trucks and he often had time to sneak off and smoke a joint. It was a lazy, unchallenging life and he settled in contentedly.

At nine months pregnant, Dora found it hard to get comfortable. She had difficulty simply sitting or lying down. This morning she sat heavily in the one easy chair she and Jared owned. She was due any minute, she knew. Jared was not home when the phone rang. It was her father.

"How are you?" he asked.

"Oh God. I can't stand it. I wish it would come already. I am so ready."

"Yeah, that's what I thought. So you all packed and ready to go when the time comes?"

"I guess. I mean Jared's not here. He's at work

and he has the car."

"You want me to come over?"

The offer surprised and pleased Dora. After all that had gone on between them, her father was thinking of her. He cared about her, she thought.

"Oh Daddy," she said, "that's so sweet. But I'm okay, really."

"Well, I don't know. I just thought I could help maybe."

"Nah. I'll be fine. Our landlord can take me if necessary. It's just up the hill. And he's always around here."

"Well, okay. If that's what you want."

"Yeah. I'll be okay.

"All right." He hung up.

Dora smiled to herself. A moment later, she felt a violent contraction. Her baby was very ready to be born.

****

Hank was seated at his desk, lost in thought. He did not agree with Dora's decision to move out, but he had to admit it had freed him up. Now that he and Norma had separated and with Dora living on her own, he thought seriously once again about selling his house and moving to his own apartment. It was an appealing thought. He'd save money and he would be a bachelor, almost. It felt like a chance to be 20 years old again. That was not exactly true, he knew, but the prospect of freedom appealed to him. He wondered briefly if Maddie would go out with him.

Dora had sounded tired and anxious but optimistic as well. He felt reassured by the call. Things were looking up. On an impulse, he called his younger daughter.

"Hi hon. It's your dad."

"Oh, hi."

"How are you?" Hank thought to himself *I have no idea what her life is really like.*

"Okay, I guess."

"Is your mom there?"

"No. She went out. She'll be back soon. We have a meeting, like an appointment, this afternoon."

"Okay. Well, uh, Dora is due any day now. Maybe you want to come out and see her after the baby is born? And your mother too?"

"Uh, yeah. I guess," Amy said vaguely.

"Well, okay. I'll let you know when the baby's born."

"Okay."

"All right. Take care, honey."

He hung up and thought *my family is falling apart. Everyone is moving away from me. And I'm letting it happen.* He wondered about Amy. Amazingly, she was really succeeding at modeling apparently. Norma had not needed any money from him for months. She had returned his credit card and they were evidently living comfortably on Amy's earnings. He wondered briefly if he might be entitled to some of that money and then dismissed the idea. The desperate need he had for money was gone. And besides, wasn't it his role to give his children and wife money, not the other way around?

Hank found he still had trouble imagining Amy being happy as a model. It seemed so unlike her but then he thought again *how well do I really know her?* He wrinkled his brow and thought *maybe I can reconnect a little with her when she comes out to see Dora. We could spend some time together then.*

****

That night Dora's contractions started in earnest and her water broke. As she feared, Jared was nowhere to be found. She staggered downstairs to Hitchcock's door. Her landlord was home and with little more than a grunt of agreement, he loaded her into his car and drove her up the hill to Norwalk Hospital. She had the baby around 4 am, on Friday, June 16. It was a girl. Without consulting Jared, since he was absent anyway, she told the staff her baby's name was Christine Latour. She had not thought of a middle name, but she liked the sound of "Christine."

Dora called her father early that morning and he came to the hospital. Realizing Jared was not there, and had not been there, Hank looked sadly at Dora. He had no idea how she would manage raising this child by herself, but that seemed to him the likely scenario. For her part, Dora was exhausted but very happy. She kept drifting off to sleep. She would awaken and ask to see her baby, and the nurse would bring Christine to her. She was thrilled to be a mother, to have given birth. Whatever happened from now on, she felt happy about what she had done.

Hank called Norma from the hospital. It was mid-morning and Norma's speech was slurred. Hank knew she was drunk. He clenched his fist and asked if Amy was there. She was. As it turned out, Amy did not have work that afternoon, and yes, she would take the train out right away. She wanted to see Dora. Norma did not want to come. So Amy left on her own and met her father that afternoon at the South Norwalk train station. Together they drove up to the hospital.

Hank was struck by the transformation he saw in Amy. Although only fifteen, she no longer seemed to be the timid, thoughtful little girl he had known. In the course of a few months, she had assumed an air of haughty sophistication. At the same time, she was edgy and nervous. Hank watched as she puffed on a cigarette, as though she had been smoking for years. "Are you sure you should be doing that?" he asked.

"Yeah, I know. Ginger says it's bad for my skin, but I don't care. I like smoking. It feels good." She gave a practiced, rather self-conscious exhalation of a cloud of smoke into the car. Hank cringed and pulled back in annoyance. They arrived at the hospital. As Hank parked, Amy stubbed her unfinished cigarette out in the ashtray. "I won't smoke up there, around the baby," she said.

Together, they went to Dora's room. Dora was holding Christine to her chest. The two sisters looked at each other. "Hi Dor," said Amy, twitching slightly.

Dora studied her sister. She seemed different somehow. She could not put her finger on it and didn't try. She was too happy. She held out Christine. "Isn't she amazing," she said.

It wasn't really a question, but Amy nodded.

"Come see her," Dora suggested.

Amy moved closer to the bed. She looked down at the squirming, red–faced infant. She could not bring herself to pick her up. "That is amazing," she said, backing away.

Hank stepped around Amy. "Can I hold her?" he asked.

"Uh, sure."

Hank gently lifted Christine, who promptly

began crying loudly. "It's all right," he cooed as he rocked her slightly. "It's all right." Christine's tears subsided somewhat. He rocked her for a moment longer and then handed her back to Dora. "Where's Jared?" he asked.

"Oh working, I guess. He doesn't even know, unless he came home and ran into Hitchcock."

"Well, you'd think he'd be here."

"Yeah, well. It is what it is. Que sera, sera." Hank glanced at Amy. She certainly didn't seem concerned either. It was hard to tell what she was concerned about.

"Well, what's the plan? When do you go home?"

"Today, if I want."

"Already? Are you ready? Do you want a ride?"

"Yeah. That would be good. Let me speak to the nurse. See if it's okay." She rang the buzzer on a cord at the side of her bed. A few minutes later, the nurse hustled in. "Is it okay for me to go home?" Dora asked.

"Well yes, I think so, if you're feeling alright."

"I'm tired and a little sore, but I'm okay."

"All right. Let me just check with Dr. Denison. I'll be back as soon as I know." With that, she left.

"Okay, I might need that ride." Dora smiled.

"Sure. Whatever you need."

Her father seemed awfully accommodating, which pleased Dora. *I guess he likes the idea of being a grandfather.* Amy had turned and was staring out the window.

"You okay?" Dora asked her.

"What. Oh yes. I'm fine" said Amy. "Just thinking about things, I guess."

"How's mom?" Dora asked.

"Mom? She's okay, I guess. She follows me around everywhere. The photographers have to tell her to shut up sometimes and stand back. It's a pain."

"I hear you're doing good. You're getting rich and famous, right?" Dora asked with a little smile.

Amy didn't seem to notice Dora's tone. "Yeah, I'm doing great. A lot of work for Maybelline. That's big."

Dora noticed Amy didn't seem especially pleased or excited by her success.

"It is. Maybelline! That's far out."

"Yeah…." Amy trailed off and stared back out the window. A parking lot and another tall brick building stared back at her.

The nurse came back in. "Dr. Denison says it's fine for you to be discharged. I have some papers for you, instructions, what to do at home. If you have questions, or problems, anything, our number and Dr. Denison's is on there."

"Okay." Dora took the sheaf of papers.

"I'll carry them" Hank offered.

"Okay, thanks. I have Christine to carry. That's enough." She smiled.

"Can I go home?" Amy asked.

"Yeah, of course, after we get Dora settled."

"Okay."

Hank drove Dora to her apartment. "You gonna be okay? If you need anything, call me."

"Thanks. I'll be fine. We'll be fine."

"Well, let's get you upstairs. You coming Amy?"

"No, I'll wait here."

"All right. I'll be back in a sec," Hank said as Amy lit another cigarette and blew the smoke out her open window.

Dora got out of the car, carrying Christine. Hank carried her discharge papers. Together, they clamored up the steps and up the stairs to the third floor.

When they got inside, Dora said "Thanks, dad. I'm fine now." She was a little out of breath.

"All right. Take care." He looked around the room. "And uh, congratulations."

"Yeah. Thanks. See you. Thanks for coming," she said smiling at her father. She watched him close the apartment door behind him and said to Christine, who she was still holding, "That's your grandpa." She stood and looked out the front window, watching her father get in the car. Amy had moved to the front seat and was still smoking, facing out her window. Dora watched them drive off. She turned and settled Christine in the bassinet and lay down on her bed where she could watch her daughter. She felt some residual pain, but she felt happy. *I'm Christine's mother,* she thought. *Christine Latour. My daughter.*

****

Amy and her father returned to their house. Hank tried to make conversation, but Amy was a million miles away. She stared out the open window and lit another cigarette. At the house, they separated. Hank went into the kitchen to look for a snack. Amy wandered out the back door. Hank watched her through the glass as she walked slowly away from the house, toward the woods. *Now that seems like the old Amy,* he thought, *except for the smoking.*

Amy walked through the woods and came to the

housing development she'd seen months before. It was well along now. Men were working there. Gone was the open meadow with the little stream and the untamed bushes and saplings. Her field was now bisected by a paved road leading to six cleared lots. Even from a distance she could see a dead turtle, crushed on the asphalt. She walked up to it and stared down. It was an Eastern Painted Turtle, a female. *She was probably looking for a place to lay her eggs*, Amy thought sadly. With a sudden rush of anger, she thought *Dora has a baby but this mother gets run over.* Nobody seemed to take notice of Amy as she picked up a stick and gingerly moved the dead turtle off the road.

She looked around. On one lot, a large house with an empty swimming pool was nearly finished. Two more houses on either side of it were under construction. She imagined people living in them, people with cars and barbecues and busy lives, walking on their sidewalks or on their driveways. She felt lost, alone and depressed. She thought briefly of her modeling success but it provided no consolation.

****

Back in New York, Norma sat on the edge of her bed in her apartment. It was a larger apartment than the one she and Amy had started in and it was in a better area, further west, a little north of Gramercy Park. They each had their own bedroom here. With Amy's earnings, Norma had purchased a large color TV.

This morning it was quiet. Amy was in

Connecticut and there was no reason for Norma to dress or go out. She wandered into the living room and turned on her new TV, sipping her vodka. She remembered dimly Hank's call an hour earlier telling her Dora had had a baby girl. Norma did not care. She thought *serves her right for getting pregnant.* She felt no sympathy or concern for Dora and had no wish to see her or the baby.

Some things don't change, Norma thought. *A girl has a baby and her future is finished.*

The news was on television, catching Norma's attention slightly. The story was about the war in Vietnam winding down, a result, at least in part, of protest from people in their teens and twenties, the Hippies. The world was in upheaval and it all felt distant and confusing to Norma. She thought *and now there's Women's Lib, Black Power. And girls like Dora are trying out drugs of all kinds, and listening to rock and roll, and making free love.* The Watergate break-in had just occurred. Richard Nixon was in trouble. Norma felt disoriented. She perceived these events in a blurred way, as if she were watching it all through a curtain. She sipped her drink.

CHAPTER 43

7/15/72 – Saturday

Amy was back in New York, working constantly. She was beginning to be asked to do work calling for a more mature look. Although still only fifteen and one-half, she was already being seen less as a teen model and more of a true adult fashion model. While this was promising for her career, it also resulted in more scrutiny of her body. Jim Farnsworth, the photographer who knew her from the beginning, had pulled her aside and told her she should have breast enhancement surgery as soon as she was old enough. He stared at her chest. "I'm not seeing much development. I don't think you're going to get big enough on your own," he told her.

Norma had jumped in and announced "Oh yes, we're going to have them done."

"No, mom." Amy tried to put her foot down, something she almost never did with her mother.

"You don't understand. It's good for your career. A lot of the girls do it, right?" she asked Farnsworth.

"Oh yeah. It's getting pretty common. No big deal."

"But...isn't it uh, you know, dangerous?" Amy stammered.

"Amy!" her mother shouted, "He said it's no big deal. And he's not the first one who told you. So we'll get it done."

Amy nodded and turned away. She found her purse and pulled out a cigarette.

"She'll be okay," Norma said to Farnsworth.

"Well, she really shouldn't do it til she's 18 anyway, so no hurry, but I guarantee she'll need it."

"Yes," Norma agreed. "As soon as she's 18."

****

Hank returned from Bridgeport, having made his eighth payment to Generoso. He was home and he was feeling better. The payments were working out. At least there, he thought, things were looking up. It was a peaceful Saturday afternoon. He was still concerned about Dora's situation and worried about Amy, but he thought he would let things take their course. He would help where he could, but they were both leading their own lives now. The thought of Norma chewed at him, but he shrugged. She was also living her life as she seemed to want it, without him.

Suddenly, Hank's reverie was interrupted by a

ringing phone.

"Hello."

"Hank, this is Detective Goldschmidt, down at the station. We need to speak with you again. I'd like you to come down here."

"Now? It's Saturday. What is this about?" Hank was immediately on edge.

"We'll explain when you get here. We'll be waiting for you."

"Okay, okay, I'm on my way."

"Good. We'll see you soon."

What now? Just when things seemed to be going better. What do they want? Hank headed out to his car. He would know soon enough.

At the station, Hank was met by Sergeant Gargiulo. "C'mon Hank, let's go in here," he said pointing toward the same room Hank was in on his last visit. Hank sat down and Gargiulo sat opposite him. A moment later, Detective Goldschmidt entered the room. Hank looked nervously back and forth at the two men.

Goldschmidt spoke first. "Let me get right to the point. We know what you've been doing. We know about the bank in Bridgeport and your payments to Generoso."

"You what? You do?" Hank was flustered, and

frightened.

"Yes, we know you borrowed money from Generoso. You know he's connected? He's a dangerous man."

Hank wasn't sure a response was expected, so he remained silent. Goldschmidt went on. "We're not sure how much you borrowed or why. We suspect it has to do with that housing development you're involved with."

Goldschmidt paused. Hank nodded mutely. He looked at Gargiulo who actually gave him an encouraging smile.

Goldschmidt continued. "All right Hank, here's the story. It's not a crime to borrow money from a loan shark… incredibly stupid maybe, but not a crime."

This news surprised Hank and he suddenly thought *then what am I doing here?*

"But it is a crime to *be* a loan shark. We can bust Generoso on this, but we need your help."

"What kind of help?"

"Well for starters, we'd like you to meet with him and wear a wire. Don't worry. We'd be nearby if anything went wrong."

Hank swallowed uncomfortably, wondering how much choice he had. "Uh, that sounds pretty risky."

"It could be, but not if you're careful. And we'd

right nearby, like I said."

"And if I didn't want to do that?"

"We could still get him. As long as you are willing to testify against him."

Hank looked at both men. They were peering at him intently. "I'd have to testify? In court? That sounds dangerous too. I mean leading up to court…"

"We won't lie to you. It is. These guys do not like the law coming after them and they might take steps to prevent you from testifying. We'd do our best to protect you of course, but… we can't you know, one hundred per cent guarantee it."

"Well, I don't know." Hank's mind was whirling. *They know everything!* The thought of testifying was terrifying. The only thing worse would be trying to trap Generoso by wearing a wire. The guy didn't say much, as Hank recalled. Then another thought occurred to him. If they did arrest Generoso, could that mean he possibly wouldn't have to pay off the loan? Could he actually profit from this? No, he doubted that and he might get killed in the process. "I don't think so," he said at last.

"Yeah, that's what we thought you'd say. Truth is you could be compelled to testify, but we'd rather you did it voluntarily."

"It seems pretty risky. I mean, you're right. These guys mean business."

"True. There's not much in it for you, except being a good citizen. You could do some good here."

"And I wouldn't have to repay the loan?" Hank asked hopefully.

Goldschmidt smiled for the first time. "Really, even if we got Generoso, he would just pass the loan on to someone else. Somebody else would take it over. You'd still be on the hook for it from their point of view."

"So?" Now Hank wasn't sure where the conversation was headed. Was there something else they wanted from him, he wondered.

"Listen Hank, we can arrest him anyway. It might not stick, but he'd know we trailed him through you. He's not gonna like that. This is your chance to get out in front of it. You wear a wire when you see him and then testify. In the end that's probably safer than us busting him now and getting him pissed off at you. If you don't go along, the DA could subpoena you anyway. Compel you to testify."

"Jesus guys, I don't even talk to him. We don't meet any more. How can wearing a wire help now?"

"You'll meet him again either for the final payoff or maybe we'll think of a problem you need to see him about, maybe another loan, or something."

"I can't believe this." Hank slumped forward putting his face in his hands.

"It's okay Hank. You can do this. It will be okay."

"Oh Jesus," Hank said.

"Well, think about it. You don't have to decide now."

"Yeah, okay I will. Can I go now?"

"Yeah, you can go. Call Sergeant Gargiulo by Monday and let us know your decision."

"Well, okay."

Gargiulo handed him a card. "There's my number there. Call me."

"Okay. I will."

Hank walked back out into the bright sunshine, feeling terribly anxious. *It could have been worse,* he thought, *but they're trying to force me into it. It's not a crime. I haven't committed a crime.*

****

By the next day, Hank knew what he wanted to tell Gargiulo. He had weighed his options. On the one hand, he would be helping the police, but that was hardly his concern. What would happen if he refused? Would they really arrest Generoso and use his name, say that he was a witness or a victim? His reputation and career would be ruined. *What kind of banker uses a loan shark?* If he did wear a wire and testify, or even just testify, that seemed an even bigger risk. He could be beaten up or worse to prevent his testifying. He remembered his phone being shattered in his office. Could the police really protect him? They couldn't guarantee it. No, he would not do this. He would not wear a wire and he would not agree to testify. Without that, apparently the police didn't have much of a case. Maybe they'd drop the whole thing.

If the DA forced him, well he'd deal with that then. At least Generoso would know it had not been his choice to testify. It was nerve-wracking. He had no wish to antagonize the police and he really did not know what their reaction might be when he refused. They had seemed reasonable, but he could not be sure.

Monday morning, Hank sat at his desk. He had work to do, but he was too keyed up to concentrate. He thought about talking to Maddie, telling her what had happened. She would listen, he knew, but then she would probably tell Generoso. She might feel she had to warn him. And what good would that do? *It would be almost the same as the police telling him. It would piss him off and God, I don't need that.*

Hank felt alone with his anxiety. His head suddenly ached sharply on the left side. He pressed his hand there and got up from his desk. He had to get out of the office. As he walked past Dorothy, he said "I need to go out for a few minutes." She nodded. She was getting used to his unexplained comings and goings.

Hank started his car and pulled out of the

parking lot. This time he noticed a tan Crown Victoria start up and follow him out. He wondered if it was an unmarked police car or merely a coincidence. He didn't know but it added to his nervous state. He started driving with no destination in mind.

Finally, he settled on Lily's. He'd go have a cup of coffee and try to calm down. He pulled in to the parking lot and the tan car seemed to have disappeared. He ordered his coffee and sat staring out the window, sipping it and burning his lip as he did so. He angrily put the cup down, left a dollar on the table and walked back out. He drove back to his office.

Back at his desk, he promptly dialed Gargiulo's number, before he could think any further. He had to get this over with.

"Westport Police. Sergeant Gargiulo speaking."

"It's Hank. Hank Latour" he spoke rapidly. "I'm sorry. I've decided I just can't do it. I'm sorry."

"Yeah, we thought you might say that. You're not helping us."

"Well, I'm scared. I admit it. These guys don't fool around."

"That's why we need to put him in jail. Piece a crap like that belongs behind bars, not driving around in a big fancy car."

Hank pictured the black Lincoln and shuddered.

"I know… but…"

"I'll tell you what. Just tell us how much you borrowed and what you have to pay back. What are the terms, exactly?

Hank hesitated. *They know I'm into this guy, but they don't know for how much.* He felt he should hold something back. He didn't know why, but he didn't feel like providing this additional information. So he said "I don't have to answer that."

"No you don't but it would help us."

"But you can't force me?"

"No, no we can't. Not now, but in court, the DA can. So eventually…"

"Well, I don't know. I'm sorry. Not now."

"You're scared. We get that."

"I just can't. I'm sorry."

"All right Hank, we're not gonna force you."

"Right I don't have to. I'm sorry, I just can't," Hank repeated.

"All right, I said, you don't have to. I don't think we'll arrest him at this point. But we will get him eventually."

"So," Hank paused, a sense of relief flooding

over him for the moment, "I go on as before?"

"Yeah, you just keep making your payments and get this thing taken care of. But keep it in Bridgeport. We don't want to see that guy in Westport again."

"Okay, okay. Yeah, of course. I never want to see him again either, after this is over."

"That's right. Keep your nose clean after this Hank. Don't pull anything like this again."

"I know. I won't, believe me," Hank said gratefully.

"All right, be careful."

They hung up. Hank sat motionless for a while. He was lucky, after all. He hoped he was lucky. He hoped the police would stay out of it. He couldn't be sure. No, they'd arrest Generoso. They said so. He would most likely be forced to testify. *Christ!* His headache had not gone away.

CHAPTER 44

7/31/72 – Monday

Dora awoke to the baby crying. It was still dark. She guessed it was about 3:00 am. Jared snored loudly next to her, oblivious to the baby's cries. The sheets lay tossed aside at the foot of the bed. She pulled herself up and looked at his long bony body in the dim reflected street light. He was still high, she guessed. He'd come home only a few hours before and fallen onto the bed in his clothes. He smelled. She wanted nothing to do with him. And, it occurred to her that he wanted nothing to do with her either, at least nothing sexually.

She got up and began nursing Christine, talking softly to her as she did so. It was a hot sticky night and she blew air on her baby, cooling her a bit as she suckled. Dora looked over at Jared. These days he was using heroin. She had asked him about it and he said he only did it once in a while. He enjoyed it. He didn't even shoot it, he claimed. She had seen what she believed were needle marks on his arms so she thought he was lying. He had offered it to her. "Just snort a little," he suggested. Dora had refused to touch it. She wondered about their future together and didn't like what she imagined. It had been a month or more since they had

had sex. *What is it about heroin that makes him love it more than he loves me?* She was curious about the power of the drug but too frightened to try it. She could not trust herself not to get hooked. She'd seen its effect on Jared and she had responsibilities now.

Christine fell asleep in her arms and they stayed that way in the chair for a long time. Eventually, she put her baby down and climbed back into bed. The rest of the night she drifted in and out of sleep but was nonetheless startled fully awake when Jared stirred the next morning as the sun penetrated the gloom. He groaned and rubbed his eyes. "Hey D," he grunted.

Dora shook her head slightly. "You going to work this morning?"

"Oh Christ. Yeah." He suddenly seemed edgy, scratching himself through his tee shirt.

He staggered out of bed. He looked painfully thin to Dora. "You want something to eat?" she asked.

"Nah, I'm cool. All right, I'm outta here. Supposed to be there at seven." He squinted at the clock on the kitchen wall. It read 7:20.

Dora rolled out of bed and picked up Christine who had started to cry. "All right. See you tonight?" Despite his many lapses, Dora still clung to the idea they were a family. Jared would come home, she hoped. They'd eat together like normal people.

"Yeah, later." He was out the door. He had not

kissed her goodbye.

Dora felt herself tense, but she looked down at Christine and her heart swelled. "It's you and me, I guess." She hugged her squirming baby a little tighter.

CHAPTER 45

9/15/72 – Friday

The phone rang at his desk and Hank snatched it up. "Yes?" he said anxiously.

"It's Maddie. Thought you'd want to know. Mike just told me the model is done. I can start showing it. The only thing is they're holding off on some interior painting and kitchen work depending on what the buyer wants. Thought you'd like to know."

"Oh, yeah. My God. Yeah, thanks."

"I already have some people interested, so I'm going to be showing it this afternoon."

"That's great. That's great. Thanks. And good luck. Let me know how it goes."

"You'll be the first to know."

Hank pictured Maddie smiling at the other end of the phone. God, she could make him feel good, he thought. "Okay, thanks again," he said, trying to project a confident smile of his own through the phone.

Maddie laughed. "See you," she said and hung up.

Hank sat still for a moment. He felt like celebrating, but it was the fifteenth of the month and he had to get going to Bridgeport.

He left his office in a better mood. He was feeling a little less anxious, buoyed by Maddie's call. He had forced himself to believe whatever happened between Generoso and the police would not involve him. He would be fine, he decided. He hoped.

****

It was early the next morning. Dora had been tossing and turning much of the night. She nudged Jared awake. He was in a netherworld between sleeping off his high and not yet needing a fix for the day. He looked up at her, with one eye open. "Yeah? Whadda ya want?"

"I want to talk… about us," she added after a pause.

"Yeah, okay. What about us?"

"Well…" Dora struggled to find the words. She was not happy with the life they had, not at all happy with Jared. "Well, you're hardly here. And when you are, you're high or you're asleep. And you want money all the time. I.." she tapered off, unable to finish the thought.

"I know. I gotta get my act together."

"Well, yeah. You do. I mean this just sucks. It's like it's me and Christine, and you're not part of it."

"I want to be part of it. I do. I mean, I'm just... you know, getting it together."

"Well," she felt her anger returning. "You never go to your job any more. Do you even still have that job? The job at the warehouse?"

Jared thought about lying but figured, what the hell, he was doing alright. He was making money. He was dealing drugs. "No, they fired me. Like yesterday."

"So what do you plan to do? Just mooch off us? Is that the idea?"

"No, no, I have my own money."

"You do? From where?"

"Well, I sell a little junk on the side, you know."

"No I did not know. Jesus Christ, Jared. You're dealing heroin? Are you for real?"

"Some, but mainly grass. It's okay. I don't do it here."

"Yeah but..." Dora sputtered. "Fuck this. I've got a record, you know. If something happens... Jesus." She felt no affection for him at that moment, only anger. And she was fearful for all of them.

"I know. I know. You need security. I get that.

Maybe we should get married. You wanna get married?"

"What! No I don't want to marry you. I don't even want you here anymore," she shouted. Christine started crying.

"Fine. Fine. I'll go. Christ. Fuck this. I don't need this bullshit." He gathered up a few loose items and put them in his pockets. He was already dressed. He slammed the door as he left.

Dora was breathing heavily. She climbed off the bed and picked up Christine. "It's okay, sweetie. It's gonna be alright."

****

Two hours later, Jared was back. Dora was seated in the chair, nursing Chrissie. "They said they might give me my job back," he announced as he walked through the door. "I'm gonna kick," he added. "And I'm gonna go to college too."

Dora stared at him, not hiding her doubts. "Uh huh."

"But first, do you have some cash? I just need like twenty bucks." He was scratching himself, bouncing on the balls of his feet.

"Jesus! No, no, I don't. Look, I don't want you here."

"All right, all right. Just let me..." He had picked up her purse and was rummaging through it.

Dora quickly put Chrissie down and stood up. Her shirt was unbuttoned, one breast visible. "What are you doing? Leave that alone." She reached for his arm.

"Just a second," he said, shrugging her off. He had found a ten dollar bill and promptly stuffed it in his pocket. "Okay, I'm going."

"Gimme that," she screamed, digging at his pocket. He pushed her away. She fell back on the bed. Christine's crying grew louder.

He slammed the door and was gone.

Dora stared at the door. *He wanted to marry me,* she thought. *I should change the locks.*

CHAPTER 46

10/8/72 – Sunday

Amy's life was a whirlwind of modeling and parties. She was picked up at her home in a limousine and transported to wherever the day's shoot was taking place. She was rarely left alone. Make-up people, prop people, hair stylists surrounded her, and mother accompanied her everywhere she went. Norma was captivated by all the activity. But Amy was numb. She had to drag herself out of bed each morning. She still tried her best, but it was hard. She went along with most of what she was told to do, at least in the modeling arena. She rarely objected. She would pose as told, wear her hair and makeup as it was applied, and smile on command. Every act took extra effort. It was as though she was a doll and everyone moved her about. She felt empty and lonely.

She had trouble sleeping and she still ate very little. None of her handlers mentioned her weight. They did however comment on how tired she sometimes looked. At one shoot, when her fatigue was showing, the photographer had pulled her aside and offered her cocaine. "This will perk you up," he had said. But Amy refused. She instinctively cringed at the prospect of drugs. Instead, she had lit a cigarette and said she'd be alright.

There were parties after the shoots on some days and often on weekends. Amy was urged to go, but she did so rarely. When she did attend a party, Norma would come along. Norma was usually intoxicated and sometimes made an embarrassing scene or she might sit quietly. Amy never knew which to expect. For her part, Amy would listen to the other girls, but she never felt connected to them. They were different than she. They were excited by the world in which they lived. Amy was not. She felt like an outsider. She did not enjoy or even understand what others her age seemed to enjoy. True, she had money and people fussed over her, but nobody really seemed to be interested in her. When they interacted with her, it was usually to adjust her in some way such as altering her hair style or rearranging the clothes on her body.

****

Jared returned again to Dora. He had been gone several weeks. He looked pathetic. He was emaciated and his clothes were dirty. Dora could not help asking him where he had lived.

"I stayed with my parents for a while, but I couldn't hack it. Can I stay here for a little while? I just need some place to crash."

Dora felt a twinge of guilt and compassion. "Okay," she found herself saying, "for a little while."

"Thanks, man." With that he fell on the bed and passed out.

Dora looked down at him. *What really goes on in his head?* she wondered. *What's it like to be him? Nobody really knows what someone else is like inside, do they? Is it dark for him? Does he feel scared? I guess you can't ever really know another person. Not completely. It's hard enough to know yourself.* She shook her head. She had loved him when they were in high school. She had loved him completely. She thought then love was absolute. Now she realized there were gray areas. You could love someone less.

Dora went to the living room and picked up the phone. She dialed the Appleton's number. Betty Appleton answered. "Hello." Gone was Betty's usual cheerful, singsong greeting.

"Mrs. Appleton, it's Dora."

"Dora! What do you want?"

"Well, I wanted to ask you about Jared. He said he was staying there."

"Yeah, he was. Then he left."

"That's it? What happened? Why'd he go?"

"He went because we are practicing Tough Love. He can't stay here if he's using. He's turned into a heroin addict you know."

"I know. That's what I'm calling…"

"You know! You know! Of course you know. You're why he is what he is now!" Betty Appleton was shouting and crying at the same time. "He stole from us. That's not my Jared. If he never met you..." Dora heard Betty dissolve in tears at the other end of the phone.

"No, this was his choice. He did it to himself." Dora felt clear about that.

"No he didn't. No he wouldn't," Betty sniffled.

"I can't.. I wanted to ask.." Dora struggled to find the words, but Betty interrupted her again.

"We tried to get him help, tried to get him into a program. They have these Methadone clinics now. He won't go. I don't know what to do." She started a fresh round of tears.

"Well, he's back here now. But he can't stay." Dora tried to sound firm. She wondered if she was in some way complicit in Jared's addiction. She really doubted Christine was his baby. Had she deceived him when they moved in together? Nothing was right and she was at a loss. "He can't stay here," she repeated.

"Oh he needs help. His father wants him to get help. Try to get him to get help." Betty pleaded.

"Yeah, okay," said Dora. She hung up. She did not like being blamed or expected to help. It was an impossible situation.

Dora heard Jared stir in the bedroom. She

walked in to find him again rummaging through her purse again. "Get out of there," she shouted.

"All right." He had found two dollars, but it was not enough. "All right, I'm going." He lurched toward the door. She watched him go and found herself wondering *when did he switch from getting high for fun to this?*

****

Sitting at his desk the next morning, Hank found himself feeling hopeful. Things were coming along at last. Maddie had interested buyers. Maybe it was all working out. His phone rang. Surely this was good news, he thought. And it was. Maddie told him she had a signed contract to sell the model home for $125,000. It was the first sale and the others would go easily, probably for more money, she said. The only thing Holden needed to do was some interior painting on the second floor, now that the buyer was known. Maddie said the buyer would need a mortgage and she had referred the couple to Hank's bank. She hoped there would be no difficulty getting one. They were well-qualified, she told him. Hank reminded her he was in commercial, not residential lending, but he thought Jenny Dwyer who handled that market would be fine. He'd speak to her, he said.

The buyers, Sidney and Audrey Levy, applied for their mortgage the next day. Hank had casually asked Jenny about it after the couple left. Jenny had wondered momentarily about his interest, but shrugged and told him it looked pretty straightforward. She didn't see any problem. In fact, she added, she would try to fast-track the application since they were hoping for a closing in a month.

Hank could not let on that he had a strong personal interest in the mortgage approval, but he asked Jenny about it again several weeks later. Sure enough, the loan was approved. Hank nodded and said "That's good. Good for the town to develop." Again, Jenny had wondered at his interest in this seemingly routine matter, but she gave it no further thought.

CHAPTER 47

11/1/72 – Wednesday

Amy's success continued. She was getting more work than she could do. Ginger juggled her schedule so she often had to fit two different location shoots for different clients in the same day. Amy felt tired and some people started to ask if she was well. She weighed no more than hundred pounds and without clothes, her 5'9" frame looked gaunt.

She continued to work hard and outwardly, she could flash a brilliant smile, but inside she was feeling bleak. It was all too fast for her. She wanted to scream "STOP!" But she stifled her fury every time she felt it. There was constant pressure.

More than one photographer told her they could do more with her if her proportions were better. She was too small up top, they repeated. She would look hopefully at her mother, wanting some support and understanding. Instead, all she heard was Norma explaining that breast implants would come as soon as Amy was old enough.

It wasn't all bad. There were some nice people.

Judy, one of the hair stylists, noticed how tired she looked and urged Amy to take some time off to rest or do something fun. Amy had smiled, thanked her and, lighting another cigarette, said she'd be alright.

****

Maddie told Hank the Levy's mortgage was approved, which he already knew. She told him the closing was scheduled for Friday, November 10th, which he had not known. That was only nine days away. Hank's spirits were high.

CHAPTER 48

11/7/72 – Tuesday

Jared was still staying with Dora, at least when he happened to sleep there. He repeatedly sought cash from her. She refused to give him any and instead urged him to enter a Methadone program. He was not interested. He was doing fine, he claimed. She knew he was dealing but it did not seem to produce enough money. She would find him searching through her purse or looking for something in the apartment that he could sell. The first week back there, he had stolen the only piece of jewelry she valued, a gold bracelet belonging to her mother. Of course she had stolen it in the first place, but still she felt violated. He had apologized and promised it wouldn't happen again. He claimed he would get it back for her. He never did.

Jared did not steal any other items, but only because Dora owned nothing else of value. She wanted him out of the apartment. She didn't like having him there, near Christine. And she worried the police might implicate her if they arrested him. She wanted him gone. She told him so, but he kept coming back, sniveling and pleading. She relented time and again, against her better judgment.

Finally, one evening he stumbled into Chrissie's crib where she was sleeping. He broke the wooden rail and nearly fell on the little girl. That did it. Dora threw him out for good. She had loved him once, but that was over, she told herself firmly. It felt like a turning point, an important step for her. She changed the locks the next day. In the subsequent weeks, he rang her bell several times, but she would not let him in.

In a corner of her mind, Dora knew she still longed for the love they once shared. But now when she would hear the buzzer, she would sit huddled in her chair, waiting for him to give up and go away.

****

In New York, Norma was on a downhill course. Some mornings she found she did not want to leave the apartment. In the previous weeks, for the first time, she had started to miss some of Amy's photo shoots. She felt aches and pains throughout her body that were only slightly relieved by vodka.

This morning, Amy looked at her mother and then observed herself in the mirror. *Neither of us look well*, she thought. Remembering the advice of Judy, the hair stylist, Amy decided to go out to Westport for a rest. She called and asked her father to meet her at the train station. He agreed and she went to Grand Central Station to catch the 10:08. Hank had gladly driven down to the Westport station to pick her up.

Now he watched as she exited the platform and

walked toward him in his parked car. She did not look well. It had only been a few months since he had last seen her, but she seemed taller and thinner than before. Her eyes had dark circles. She opened the passenger door, nodded at him, and sat down, immediately rolling her window down. As they left the parking lot, he glanced over at her. She fidgeted nervously and removed a cigarette from her purse. He wanted to engage her somehow, see what he might do to help, but she faced away from him, blowing smoke out the window. She seemed distant, watching the new, elegant stores fly by as they drove home on the Post Road.

"Are you going to see your sister while you're here?" Hank asked the back of her head.

"I don't know. Maybe. I hadn't thought about it." She continued to look out the window.

"I could drive you over there tonight, or over the weekend. Are you staying through the weekend?"

"No. I have to get back. I should be there now."

"Well, you'll spend the night at least, I hope. And maybe see Dora."

"Yeah, okay. Maybe."

Hank felt at a loss for words. He wanted to say more, to learn more. They arrived at the house. "I have to get back to work," he explained, "but you call me if you need anything."

Amy smiled wanly and said "Okay."

****

After her father left for work, Amy ambled upstairs to her old bedroom. Nothing had changed. She sat at her desk for a moment thinking how she used to sit there for hours struggling with her homework. Now, she had a tutor and schoolwork was a tiny part of her life. She was not given homework and it seemed nobody cared whether she learned any of her subjects or not. She slumped in her chair. She hated her life and felt powerless to change it.

She got up and wandered back downstairs. She realized the point of the visit was to relax, to get away from the stress of her New York life for a little while, but she felt as though the stress had come with her. She walked into the kitchen and opened the refrigerator. There wasn't a lot in it but she found a carrot which she removed. She took a peeler from the drawer and a knife as well. She cut both ends off of the carrot being careful not to scratch the counter. Then she began systematically peeling. She wanted none of the dark and pitted skin left on the carrot. So she peeled it multiple times until it was pencil thin. She sat down at the kitchen table and nibbled on it in tiny bites. As always, she was careful not to overeat.

But she could not sit still, let alone rest. She got up from the table and walked back upstairs. She went into her parent's bedroom and found herself examining everything she found there. She picked up objects from her mother's dressing table, figurines and odd pieces of jewelry. Each piece she examined and then put back where she found it. Without knowing why, she opened each drawer in both her parents' dressers. She studied her father's socks, his underwear, his neatly folded shirts. She came across an old license. He looked very young and confident in the picture. He was handsome then, she thought.

Later in the afternoon, she returned to her own room. She stood staring out the window at the backyard. A feeling of relief came over her momentarily as she thought of her favorite tree. There was a glimmer of hope. She smiled, turned and ran down the stairs, nearly tripping in the process. Outside, she arrived at her tree and touched it affectionately. She climbed it effortlessly, an old habit. At her customary branch, she settled in, feeling a bit better. *Yes, I can relax here*, she thought. But the feeling did not last long.

In the fading light, she gazed out over the yard and to the woods beyond, not really focusing on anything. She suddenly remembered the housing development back there, her father's development. Without really understanding why, she climbed down and began walking in that direction. *Nothing ever gets better,* she thought. *It only gets worse.* She passed through the meadow beyond their stone wall. It seemed undisturbed and as tranquil as ever. It was twilight, but she felt compelled to go on.

Arriving at the far end of the field, she glimpsed the construction site through the trees. It seemed quiet at this early evening hour. *My father is building this.* She felt a shudder of fear, but walked on anyway. Coming out the other side of the small stand of trees, she looked at the scene. Just to her right, she saw an empty in-ground swimming pool and beyond that, a fully built house loomed. It was tall and dark. To either side of it were two houses that were under construction. The ground was muddy and she saw the tracks made by a bulldozer. It was getting darker and there were no other people around. She walked through the mud, around the pool and up to the finished house. She stared in one of the windows. She trembled. She was looking at a finished kitchen. Its counters and appliances gleamed in the dim light. She thought *there used to be a little stream right here*. To her right was a door. On impulse, she tried the handle. It was unlocked. She felt drawn in.

There was mud on her shoes and she tracked it on to the shiny kitchen floor but she did not notice this. If she had, it might have jolted her out of the trance-like state she was in. She walked through the kitchen and came to a stairway. She climbed the stairs to the second floor. In the diminishing light, she could make out a number of rooms that opened off a wide hallway. She entered one. It smelled of turpentine. It was quite large. On the far side of the room, she could see an open door leading to a bathroom. She was in the master bedroom.

There were rollers in trays, cans of paint on the floor and paint brushes resting in open jars of turpentine. Stepping around these, she wrinkled her nose at the acrid fumes. Drop clothes were spread on the floor throughout the room. There was no furniture. Amy almost turned and fled, but her legs felt weak and she sat down for a moment, cross-legged in the center of the room. She lit a cigarette. She felt tired and light-headed.

CHAPTER 49

By the time the firemen arrived, the model home was fully engulfed in flames. They couldn't save it. It was all they could do to wet down the partially constructed homes on either side to protect them from further damage.

They found Amy's body in the charred remains of the second floor, in the master bedroom. She was sitting cross-legged on the floor in the position she was probably in when the fire started. Her hands lay by her sides, palms up. Her clothes were burned to tattered remnants. They hung in wispy black threads dripping from her damp, sooty body. Her head lolled to one side, her hair burnt off. The firemen walked gingerly around her, not wanting to disturb anything until the Fire Inspector and the police had a look.

Earlier, before the body had been found, the Fire Chief had called Holden knowing it was his site. Holden in turn called Hank and Maddie. All three had driven there almost immediately from their respective homes, arriving within minutes of each other. Hank had gotten there first and was staring at the steaming wreckage when Holden and Maddie walked up behind him. Emergency lights lit the scene. Together they watched silently for a moment as the Firemen gathered up their hoses and the police cordoned off the area.

They moved forward, encountering a waist-high line of yellow caution tape. "Step back," they were told by a young Patrolman.

"What's going on?" Holden asked.

"They found a body on the second floor, a girl," the cop said excitedly.

"A what? A body? Someone was in there tonight?" Holden shouted. He was only inches from the cop's face.

"Yeah, yeah. Back off. A girl, they think. It's hard to tell. We'll know more soon."

A girl? Hank felt dread. *Where was Amy?* She wasn't home when he had gotten there an hour ago. He thought perhaps she had gone to see Dora after all or maybe she even went back to the city. But maybe not, he thought anxiously. "Can I see her?" he asked.

The cop stood in front of them, holding up one hand. "No. The Fire Inspector is due, the techs, the EMTs, Medical Examiner, whatever. They can't even touch the body yet."

"Well, I want to see her as soon as they take her out, before they put her in the ambulance... when they move her."

"Maybe then. I don't know." The cop looked

behind him, as if seeking advice from the night air.

"I think I might know her…" Hank said softly.

To his surprise, Maddie reached over and squeezed his hand. "Let's not jump to conclusions Hank," she said. She let go of his hand after giving it a moment.

More official vehicles and an ambulance arrived. A small crowd was starting to gather. People had heard sirens in the night and had come to see what was going on. Hank heard chatter around him.

"Someone died here."

"It was a girl."

"Oh my God."

Hank held his breath and waited. It was all he could do. He watched as police and firemen entered and left the house. Eventually, he watched them wheel out a gurney carrying a small covered object. Somehow he knew it was Amy. He rushed under the police tape and up to the group.

"Is it Amy? Is it my daughter?" he shouted. They all stopped for a moment and turned as one to look at him.

"It's.. I think it's Amy, my daughter. I think. Can I just see her face? Please."

One cop, who seemed to be in charge, said

"Yeah. It's all right. Let him see."

They gingerly pulled back the tarp. Even in the dark, even without hair, even covered in soot, there was no doubt. It was Amy.

Hank gasped and his knees began to buckle. Holden had come up alongside him and held him upright. Hank caught his balance and said "It is her. I thought so. What was she doing here? How could this happen? How did she even get in?" He turned angrily to Holden and all his rage focused there for a moment. "How could you let this happen? Don't you lock up the site? Don't you make sure nobody gets in?" He shoved Holden hard in the chest. Holden stumbled back and then regained his balance, glaring at Hank.

Hank reached out and grabbed Holden by his shirt. Two cops stepped in and pulled him away. "Easy buddy," said Holden, catching his breath. "It's not Fort Knox you know. People can get in if they really want to. I'm sorry Hank."

"We have to take her now," an officer said. "You need to come down to the station with me," he added.

Hank was dumbstruck. As quickly as his anger arose, it was replaced by limp compliance. "Okay."

The cop took his arm. "You okay to drive? Can you follow me?"

"All right," said Hank.

"You want us to come?" Maddie offered, gesturing toward Holden.

"Nah. I'll be all right," Hank replied in a monotone.

The cop turned to Holden. "This is your site, right? You better come too."

"Yeah. Okay" Holden said. "Maddie, I guess you get to go home." Holden managed a smile.

"All right. Is there anyone I should call? Anything I can do?" she asked Hank.

"No. I don't know. Not right now."

"All right. Take care. I'm so sorry." She reached out and squeezed his hand again.

Hank looked down at their hands and then into her bright eyes, in the glaring light. He only nodded.

Hank and Holden spent the next several hours at the Police Station. Hank explained that earlier his daughter had seemed quiet, but otherwise okay. He had no idea she would do anything like this, if in fact she had deliberately set the fire. He did not want to believe she had. Holden told them they were completing painting and there may have been open cans of paint and turpentine. And rags, he added. Maybe they had accidentally caught fire. Amy did smoke. It was possible. Probably an accident, Holden and the police all agreed. Only Hank was left with a nagging tug of doubt that perhaps Amy had set the fire.

After the police interviews, Hank had been taken to the morgue in the basement of Norwalk Hospital to make a formal identification of the body. Standing in the cold room, before looking, he had asked the Medical Examiner how she died.

"We haven't done an autopsy, but it looks like smoke inhalation. No evidence the burns did it or anything else that we can see. Smoke. Better than burning."

Hank nodded.

"Are you ready?" he was asked.

Hank nodded and for a second time, forced himself to look under the tarpaulin as it was pulled back. Again, there was no doubt. Amy was dead. She was not quite sixteen years old.

CHAPTER 50

11/8/72 – Wednesday

The next morning, when Hank called Norma to tell her of Amy's death, Norma was barely able to comprehend what she was being told. "Amy's what? She's dead?" she had asked over and over.

"Yes, in a fire. She died in a fire. No one knows how exactly… what she was doing there, in the model home at Newport Lane."

"Newport? Where? Where is that?" Norma was having trouble catching up.

"You know. The housing development. In Westport. Newport Lane," Hank said.

"But we have a shoot tomorrow. For Sears. She's supposed to be back."

"Norma. She's dead. She's dead. She's not coming back. Not for a shoot. Not for anything. Amy's dead." Hank began to sob quietly.

"Oh my God! She's dead. She's really dead?"

"Yeah, she is. The funeral's this Saturday."

Norma finally seemed fully alert. She shouted into the phone "I want to come. I want to be there."

"Okay. Of course. Look, I'll pick you up at the station. Get the train so you're there at Westport at ten. You got that?"

"Ten. Saturday. Okay. Okay. Jeez, does Ginger know? I better tell Ginger. I, I gotta go."

"Whatever you need to do. But I'll see you at the station Saturday morning at ten." Hank was about to say more, but Norma had hung up.

Hank sat back. He felt dazed. His baby girl was dead. It made no sense. Sure, she had seemed troubled, distant. But this? *Did she kill herself?* Hank didn't know. He wasn't sure he wanted to know. For a moment, guilt and sadness overwhelmed him.

His next call would be to Dora. *No*, he thought, *I'll go see her. Better to tell her in person.* He dialed Dora's number. She answered on the first ring. He could hear Christine crying in the background. "Okay if I stop by? There's something I need to talk with you about. This morning. It's important."

Dora immediately thought of the money. "Okay, what is it?" she asked nervously.

"I don't want to discuss it on the phone. Will you be there if I come now?"

"Yeah. Yeah, okay."

"All right honey. I'll see you soon."

****

They sat facing each other in Dora's small living room. Hank felt outsized in the tiny space, his long legs stacked up in front of him as he sat on the low sofa. He looked around the room. It was dark and sparsely furnished. He looked at Dora and could not help thinking *she's an unwed mother, living in a dump, with that drug addict Jared Appleton.* He forced himself to put those thoughts aside.

Awkwardly, he began "It's about your sister."

"Amy?" Dora was confused. She had really expected this talk was going to be about the money she'd found in the garage. She sat up straighter. "Amy?" she repeated, "What about her?"

"She's... Jeez, there's no easy way to say this." Hank stared down at his hands. "Oh God. Amy died last night. In a fire. She died in a fire. She..." Hank looked up, tears filling his eyes.

"What! My God. She died? Amy?" Dora pictured her quiet, studious sister, the shy nature-loving girl she knew, not the fashion model she'd become. "How? Where?" she asked.

"Yeah, she was... for some reason, she was in the model home on Newport Lane, on the second floor where they'd been painting. There was a fire. A really bad one. Amy must have died from the smoke. At least she didn't burn to death. That's what they said. Smoke inhalation, they said."

"I don't understand. What was she doing there? Why wasn't she in New York? I don't get it."

"Well, she'd come home for a rest. Yesterday. She needed a break, I think. She was tired, she said. Your mom stayed in the city. She just wanted to come out to Westport for a rest I think. Why she was in that house, I have no idea. It was a construction site, for Chrissake. She shouldn't have been anywhere near it." Hank sounded angry for a moment. "She must have gotten in somehow and went upstairs. It was almost finished, except for the painting. That's what they think caught fire, the paint… open cans, rags, a cigarette, I guess. Oh Jesus. I don't know." Hank began crying.

Dora looked at her father with his face buried in his hands. She heard Christine crying. She wanted to comfort both of them. She got up and went to Hank. She tentatively touched his shoulder and his whole body shook. She bent over and put her arms around him and her head on his shoulder as he wept. In the back of her mind she suddenly thought *at least it's not about the money.*

"The funeral's Saturday." He looked up. "At St. Luke's. You'll come?"

"St. Luke's?"

"It seemed like the right place, I thought..." Hank was silent for a moment. "You'll come?" he asked again.

"Yeah. Of course."

Dora moved back to her seat. Hank seemed to gather himself. "Yeah, I can use some help. At the house, after, if you would... I could use your help."

"Whatever you need Dad. Of course." She walked over and picked up Christine who had been sobbing quietly in her crib. "We'll be there."

****

The model home was a pile of charred rubble. Of course there would be no closing. Holden had called Hank and Maddie to figure out their next steps. They agreed to meet that afternoon at Maddie's office.

A little after 2:00 pm, the three of them squeezed into Maddie's office. Hank and Holden sat uncomfortably in the low chairs in front of Maddie's desk. The mood in the room was grim. Maddie tried to find something encouraging to say. Hank sat there with his hands fidgeting on her desk. They would recover from this setback, she assured them. Feeling genuine sympathy for Hank, Maddie placed her hand over Hank's. He jumped as he felt an immediate electric spark cutting through all his misery. It surprised him and he looked up sheepishly at Maddie. She smiled warmly though she was a little puzzled by his reaction.

DEVELOPMENT

Holden for once refrained from jokes and said "This is so awful about your daughter. I'm sorry for you Hank. But we have a development to finish and sell. We have to figure this out now."

"Yeah, yeah, I know," said Hank.

"Okay, here's the story," Holden said. "We do have insurance. The policy will let us rebuild. But there is a $20,000 deductible. We're going to have to come up with that."

Hank was waiting for Holden to say the deductible would come out of Hank's share, since it was his daughter who apparently caused the fire, but thankfully Holden did not suggest that.

"So we'll file the claim. It happens. Accidents happen." said Holden.

"Yes, they do," said Maddie.

"All right... let's see... what else?" Holden asked Maddie. She looked at Hank.

"Well, I still have the payments to Generoso... and.." Hank was trying to think.

"Yeah, those can't stop. That's for sure," Maddie pointed out.

"And we still have the big payment to him due next November. He's not going to want to hear any excuses on that. So I guess the question is can we rebuild the one house and sell it and all the others by then?"

Hank looked at Holden.

"Yeah. We can do it," said Holden, who in turn looked at Maddie. "But we'll need that insurance money soon. I'll get going on that."

"All right. I'll talk to our buyers," Maddie said, "see if they'll stick around and wait. I don't know about that. I think they may look somewhere else and we'll have to refund their deposit."

"What a nightmare," said Hank.

"It'll work out. This is just a setback. Nothing fatal." Maddie immediately realized what she'd said. "Oh I'm so sorry Hank. I didn't mean that. I'm so sorry about Amy. Really I am. But don't worry about Newport. We'll get it back on track. I promise you. That will work out. You'll see."

"All right" said Hank. He seemed dazed. "I guess that's it then. That's it for now?" he asked, looking back and forth at both of them.

"Yeah. We're done." Holden got up and put on his coat.

"Okay." Hank did the same and followed Holden out. He turned at the doorway and gave Maddie a half-hearted wave. She smiled and nodded. He turned to go.

"Helluva thing" said Holden at the top of the stairway. "Hang in there." He slapped Hank on the back and walked down the stairs and out the door.

Hank stayed in place a moment. He thought of going back to Maddie but he had nothing else to say. He wanted to be in her company, but instead, he turned and walked slowly down the stairs after Holden.

****

Dora and Christine spent the night at Hank's house on Friday. Now, Saturday morning, the three of them went out and picked up cold cuts, cheeses, fruit and bread, as much as they could think of to stock up for whomever came back to the house after the funeral. On their way home, they stopped at the train station and picked up Norma. Hank had been slightly surprised that she had managed to get herself up and on to the train on time, but sure enough, there she was, waiting on the platform.

Dora and Christine climbed in back and Norma sat in front next to Hank. She looked over at him with bloodshot eyes. Hank realized that she had been drinking as usual. "When do we go to the church?" she asked.

"We'll get this food home and then go right out to St. Luke's," Hank explained.

"Okay." Norma fumbled in her purse for a cigarette. "I can't believe this" she muttered angrily, more to herself than anyone else.

Christine began to cry in the back seat and Norma turned to Dora and said "Shut that baby up, willya!"

"Christ, mom. She's a baby. There, honey." She pulled Christine to her. The little girl's cries subsided to a whimper.

Hank faced the road stonily. He had no use for Norma's anger. *This is no time to be fighting,* he thought, but he said nothing.

They arrived at the house. "You just stay here, in the car. I'll be right back," Hank said as he gathered the three heavy bags of groceries in his arms. He brought them to the kitchen and placed all three bags in the refrigerator. He returned to the car. "Let's go."

They drove to the church and arrived at 10:45. Though early, the church was surprisingly full. A lot of people had known and apparently cared about Amy. Norma searched the crowd, looking for Ginger. She could not see her, but she did recognize a number of faces. There were some of the models Amy had known and Norma thought she recognized photographers, stylists, assistants, people from the various shoots she'd been to. It was a busy blur to her and she suddenly felt nervous and shaky. She told Hank she'd be along in a minute. She found a little out-of-the-way enclave where she carefully removed the jar of vodka from her purse and took a long swallow. She recapped the bottle quickly and returned to the church foyer. She went in and found Hank and Dora seated at a pew near the front. Other people continued to pour in.

DEVELOPMENT

The service lasted an hour and a half. One of Amy's teachers gave a glowing tribute. People Hank and Dora had never seen before got up and spoke warmly about Amy's beauty and talent and how sad they were to lose her. To Hank, it seemed like they were not talking about the Amy he had known. He found himself thinking *Amy united this family. In a way, she held us all together. She was the common link among us, between me and Norma, and she was one of the links Dora had to us. She was the star around which we orbited. But she pulled us apart too, moving to NY, going with Norma. She didn't really want to go. She didn't want to pull us apart. It pulled her apart when she moved. We each became like stones thrown across a pond, each disappearing in our own circle of ripples.*

When he spoke, Hank tried to present Amy as he had known her, a girl who loved nature and died far too young. He had trouble keeping the anger out of his words. Norma did not speak, but to Hank's surprise, Dora wanted to say something. She spoke warmly about her younger sister, how she had always worked hard and tried to do her best at whatever she did.

After the service, a funeral cortege formed and about one-fourth of the attendees made the short drive to the Assumption Cemetery off the Sherwood Island Connector. The burial was solemn and brief. Only the Priest spoke a few words.

Back at his house, with Dora's help, Hank laid out food on a table that he had resurrected from the basement and placed in the living room. The house was crowded with well-wishers, few of whom he knew. Hank shook hands with many strangers and thanked them for coming. Many brought food. There were steaming casserole dishes, trays of lasagna, salads of various kinds, and several cakes and platters of cookies.

Dora sat with Christine on the couch. People she didn't know smiled sympathetically at her and moved on, chewing sandwiches and chatting among themselves. Norma knew more of the visitors, but only vaguely. She looked anxiously for Ginger but she was absent. Retreating, Norma settled in a kitchen chair and watched the crowd through bleary eyes.

Later, after most of the guests had gone, Hank walked into the kitchen carrying a stack of dirty plates. He found Norma sitting at the table, a drink in her hand. She looked up at him with empty eyes. He felt no connection to her, no urge to reassure her. Instead, the thought crossed his mind that she was the reason Amy was dead. It wasn't necessarily true, but he felt a sharp stirring of anger nonetheless. At the same time, he thought *without Amy, are we even a family?*

Walking around Norma, Hank angrily placed the dishes in the sink. Without saying a word to her, he turned and left the kitchen. But a few minutes later, he returned. Norma's back was to hm. He placed a hand on her shoulder and gave her a gentle squeeze. She looked up at him. She looked lost. "I'm sorry," was all he could manage. She reached for her drink and he pulled away.

By late afternoon, the last guest had left. Hank

asked Dora if she wanted to stay, but she declined. Hank said he would take Norma back to the station and drive Dora and Christine back to Norwalk if they were ready. Or, he proposed, they could all go have dinner somewhere. But both Dora and Norma said no, they wanted to go home. At Hank's urging, Dora decided to take the tray of lasagna and a large bowl of salad.

Hank delivered them all and returned to an empty house. He disconsolately cleaned up, putting away the remains of the food, storing unused paper plates and cups and throwing out the trash. It was over. Amy was gone.

CHAPTER 51

11/15/72 – Wednesday

After the funeral, back in New York, Norma could not bear the thought of Amy's death. She literally could not keep the thought in her mind for long. When she did think of it, it felt as though the ground she stood on was a sheet of glass. It would not support her and she crashed through it repeatedly. She would find herself collapsed on the floor or sprawled on the bed with no recollection of how she got there.

She would awaken at any hour in her empty rooms and her stomach would clench in agony. For a while, enough vodka had taken away some of the pain, controlled the fear. But now, a little more than a week after Amy's death, Norma was terrified. The vodka was not working. Alone, she had no idea what to do next. The confusion and pain were so unbearable, she considered killing herself. She stumbled into the bathroom and found an open package of razor blades in her medicine cabinet. As she removed these and examined them in her hand, she had a new thought. Ginger. She realized she wanted Ginger. Ginger would help. She decided she would go see her.

Without thinking much about it, she carried the razor blades back to her bedroom and put them in her purse. She quickly got dressed and staggered out her door. She thought *Ginger will know what to do.*

When she arrived at the Wilhelmina offices, Norma told the receptionist she needed to see Ginger right away. She had never learned the name of the receptionist and now the woman eyed her skeptically, noting her flushed face and disheveled clothing. "Just a minute," she said to Norma.

Norma watched as the receptionist rang Ginger's number. "Norma Latour is out here and says she needs to see you immediately." The woman looked up at Norma. "Yes, okay. I'll tell her." She hung up. "She'll be out in a minute. Why don't you have a seat."

Norma sat down, nearly missing the chair. She looked up to see the receptionist shaking her head. Norma fidgeted nervously with her purse. "It's about my daughter Amy," she said. The receptionist just nodded and said "Ginger will be right out."

Norma looked in her purse, fingering the package of razor blades. She felt the reassuring plastic bottle of vodka as well.

"Norma?" Ginger had appeared suddenly, startling Norma.

"Yes. Oh Ginger. Amy…"

"I know. Let's go to my office."

Sitting in the office, across the glass coffee table, Norma explained what she could about Amy's death. A few of the details were new to Ginger and she listened thoughtfully as Norma concluded by asking "What should we do?"

Ginger simply said "The poor thing. What a tragedy. Amy could have been so much more."

"I know!" Norma said angrily.

Ginger looked at Norma's flushed face. "Well," she said, "We've canceled her bookings of course. I'll send you her last check. I'm afraid that's it. I'm very sorry. Sorry for you. It's a tragedy." With that, she stood up. The meeting was over.

"Okay, but... What do I do?"

"Well, you'll have to go on with your life." Ginger strode to the door and opened it for Norma to leave.

"I was thinking of modeling myself."

"I don't think so, Norma. You take care."

Norma looked puzzled, but got up and left without another word. She walked back to the waiting room and sat down. She had nowhere to go. She could think of nothing to do. The receptionist eyed her curiously and returned to her work.

Norma had not moved. After ten minutes, the receptionist called Ginger and told her irritably that

DEVELOPMENT

Norma was still sitting there. Ginger said she'd come speak to her.

A few minutes later, Ginger stood in front of Norma.

"Norma, you can't stay here."

"But I…" Norma struggled to explain.

"I know this is hard for you, awful, but there is nothing we can do. You need to go."

"Could I, could I just have a glass of water first?"

"Okay, but then you have to leave." She turned to the receptionist. "Bonnie, can you get Norma a glass of water?"

Bonnie grudgingly got up, left the room and returned with a glass of water.

"Here," she said, handing it to Norma.

"When you finish, you have to go," Ginger said firmly.

"Uh huh. Okay."

"All right. Take care now." With that, Ginger departed for her office. Bonnie returned to her desk. Her phone was ringing.

For several minutes, Norma could not seem to move. She ignored the glass of water. Then she opened her purse and took out her bottle of vodka setting it carefully on the table before her. She contemplated it for a moment and then looked back in her purse where she found the package of razor blades. She removed one. She slashed her left wrist. It hurt less than she expected. As she began to bleed, she switched hands and cut across her right wrist in the same way, but deeper this time. She remained seated, bleeding in her lap, on the chair, and spilling blood on to the beige carpet. After a little while, she leaned back in her chair sleepily. Her leg bumped the table, knocking over the glass of water.

At the sound, Bonne looked up. Norma was covered in blood. "Oh! My God! Oh my God!" the woman shouted. "Help! Help!"

Ginger heard the heard shouts and saw Andrew Romano dash past her office. She got up and followed him to the waiting room. It took her a moment to comprehend what she saw there. In the front of the room, she glimpsed Norma at the center of a noisy crowd. People clustered around her, trying to stem the blood flow with handkerchiefs and facial tissue.

Norma was seated at the center of the group. Deep red blood covered her lap as well as the hands and sleeves of people trying to stanch the flow. Blood was spreading on the carpet. Ginger was shocked. It was a disaster. She turned and told Bonnie to call the police. She looked back at Norma in the bloody chair. She came closer to get a better look, feeling a mixture of disgust and pity. She watched as Norma's head lolled to one side. Ginger thought she detected a faint smile on

Norma's lips.

The police brought Norma to the Emergency Room at Bellevue Hospital, where her wounds were stitched and she was admitted for a psychiatric evaluation. After several days, she was moved to a detox program in the same facility.

****

For Hank, life gradually resumed. The old pressures were still there. Amy's death had left a dark hole in his life, but he could not walk away from his responsibilities. He had to go to work. His payoffs to Generoso still continued. Hank fretted as the deadline loomed to sell the homes and pay off the loan shark. He prayed to whatever God might exist that the houses would be built and sold in time and he would get through this ordeal.

When he learned about Norma's suicide attempt and subsequent hospitalization, Hank found he no longer cared much about what happened to her. *Amy was the last link that connected us*, he thought. *Now that link is broken and we're like two objects in outer space, no longer tethered together, drifting further and further apart.*

He wanted to put his former life behind him, to close that door and lock everything away, his home, his wife and his memories of Amy. Realistically, he told himself, he had to make some big changes. Perhaps, he thought, Amy's death was what he needed to prompt him to dig himself out of the hole he felt he was in. It was clear to him that Norma was part of his past and not in any future he could imagine. He steeled himself. He thought *Good. She's in detox. Maybe this time it will stick. But I don't much care anymore.* Even if she got better, he knew he had no desire to be with her. His love had just evaporated. He wanted to be out of their marriage and he resolved to divorce her.

Looking around his empty house, he felt equally sure he no longer wanted to live there. The memory of Amy haunted him. He decided he would get an apartment. *It will be cheaper and it will be simpler. This place is too big for me and it has too many memories.* Soon, he decided, he would get together with Maddie and he would list the house for sale.

CHAPTER 52

11/27/72 – Monday

On a cool drizzly morning, Hank sat across from Maddie, in her office.

"So you've decided to sell?"

"Yeah. I don't need that big place. There's really just me." Hank had been looking at his hands in his lap. He looked up and met Maddie's eyes.

She smiled sadly. "Well, that's what I'm here for." She was feeling a mixture of sympathy and pity toward him. *He looks so pathetic*, she thought.

Hank sensed her judgment of him and winced inwardly. He was torn. He wanted sympathy and support, but he hated appearing so weak. *Still,* he thought, *she's probably used to that from me by now.*

"I'm going to divorce Norma," he announced, seemingly out of nowhere. "I mean she doesn't live there. She's in New York. It's over."

Maddie was not really interested in the details of Hank's life. She was much more interested in selling his property. "Okay, I understand," she said. Then, after a pause, she stated "I need to get some comps to price it. And we need to think about what you need to do to spruce it up to sell."

"All right," Hank said, still wanting something more from her.

"Let's plan a walk-through. Is later this afternoon good for you?"

"Yeah, any time is okay, I guess."

"How 'bout we meet at your house at four?"

"Yeah. Four. Okay."

"All right. I'll see you then. And Hank… things will get better. You'll see."

"Yeah. Thanks." He sat for a moment, not moving.

Maddie was anxious for him to leave, though he seemed as if he had more to say. She waited. When nothing was forthcoming, she picked up a folder from her desk and opened it. "I better get to work," she said.

"Yeah, okay. Okay, bye." This time he got up, put on his coat and turned to her, hesitating in the doorway.

"See you at four," she said brightly.

"Yeah, okay." With that, he finally left. Maddie

returned to her paperwork, shaking her head slightly.

****

Hank's next stop was with Hennessy, the attorney. That had been his plan. First meet with Maddie to list the house. Then meet with the lawyer to begin divorce proceedings. He sat in his car in Maddie's small parking lot, the rain hitting his windshield, not moving for the moment. He was thinking about Maddie. He had an 11:00 am appointment with Hennessy, but he could not bring himself to go just yet.

Eventually, he shook himself out of his stupor. He started the car and headed to his next meeting.

The lawyer's office was spacious and thickly carpeted. Dark wood-paneled walls were hung with large prints of hunting scenes. The windows were covered with shades and bounded by heavy burgundy curtains. It was a dimly lit room other than the bright light cast by the lamp on a large oak desk. Hank settled in one of the soft leather easy chairs in front of the desk and looked across at his attorney. Tom Hennessy was one of those guys who could not sit still. As Hank started to discuss his reasons for divorce, Hennessy got up, stood next to his desk for a moment and then began pacing back and forth behind it. His small, thin frame and rapid movements seemed out of place in the dark, plush office.

"Divorce. Big step,' he said.

"I know. But it can't go on this way any longer. It's over. Over for me."

"You'll have to pay alimony, you know."

"I expected that. I mean, she's sick. That's how the courts would probably see her anyway... with the drinking and all."

"And she's been in and out of the hospital, suicidal. She needs support. So yeah, you'll have to pay."

"Well, I can't pay much. But..." Hank trailed off.

"We'll work out a manageable arrangement." Hennessy sat back down. His hands never stopped moving. He picked up a yellow legal pad and scrawled some notes on it. "Does she have an attorney yet?"

"What? No, no, she doesn't even know I'm doing this."

"Well, she'll need to have one, even if you have to pay for it."

"Oh Christ," Hank swallowed hard. This was not going to be easy and money seemed to be a constant problem for him. "I'm planning to sell the house. And move somewhere, rent something cheaper. So that should help, should give me some cash to work with."

"Good idea. You'd probably have to sell the house anyway, dividing up the property, so better to do it now. What about the children? You have two daughters, right?"

"Yeah. Well, no. Just Dora. Um, Amy. Amy died. She's gone. There's just Dora."

"She died? How?"

"In a fire. It was awful."

"I'm sure. Oh of course, the development. Yes, I heard. I wasn't thinking. I'm sorry. That was terrible."

"Yes, it was. Still is.

"I am sorry for you. All right, anyway, okay, there's Dora. How old is she?"

"Uh, let's see. Dora will be eighteen next month."

"Okay, so she will no longer be a minor at the time of the divorce."

"No, I guess not." It struck Hank that he had no family to call his own any more. Amy was gone; Norma was as good as gone, and now Dora was about to be an independent adult. He felt discouraged and somewhat disoriented for a moment. He was trying to change his life for the better, but it felt more as though he had lost everyone he had ever cared about. He felt deflated and wondered how he would muster any energy. "Well, what else do you need?" he asked.

Hennessy looked at has pad. "We'll need to work out grounds for the divorce and get a list of assets together. We should discuss timetables and fees."

Hank spent the next hour with Hennessy. Finally, they wrapped it up. To Hank, it seemed as if he'd been in that office all day. He felt more depressed than hopeful and he was glad to leave.

CHAPTER 53

1/22/73 – Monday

Hank had told no one but Maddie and Hennessy of his plans, but he decided he finally wanted to see Dora and explain what he was doing. Although he hated seeing her apartment and he sharply disapproved of her life choices, he wished to see her in person. He hoped Jared would not be there. He had no idea she had kicked him out.

Hank was pensive as he walked out of his kitchen to his car, thinking *someday soon I won't be doing this anymore, in this house.* It was a brisk morning. He knew he should go in to work, but his mind was elsewhere. He would see Dora first. He listened to his radio as he drove to Norwalk. The Supreme Court, he learned, had just legalized abortion in the United States. The world was changing, he thought. Birth control pills were approved for women everywhere, whether married or single. He thought of Dora. These changes had come too late for her. Had she become pregnant a year and a half later, she might not have had Christine. Or with birth control, she might not have become pregnant at all.

Arriving at her building, he rang the bell and

climbed the stairs to her apartment. He was there to explain to Dora about the divorce and the sale of his house, but standing in her doorway, the first thing he said to her was "abortion is legal now."

"Not that I plan to get pregnant again," Dora responded. "I'm on birth control pills, so it's not going to happen." She felt no need to add that she had not had sex in many months. She glanced back at Christine playing with blocks on the floor.

"Birth control pills? Are they safe?" Hank asked. He came in and they both sat down.

"Yeah, sure. Katie's been on them for a while. I just started, but they're fine. Nothing to worry about. They work."

"Well, Katie…" Hank started and paused. "Anyway, I need to tell you what's happening… with me and your mother."

Dora sat still, waiting. She knew things were not good between her parents. Her mother had lived in New York for some time now. So she was not surprised when Hank said "We're getting a divorce."

Dora nodded, waiting to hear more.

"Well," Hank went on. "It takes a while, but the process is under way. We have to sell the house. I'll be looking for an apartment."

For just a moment, Dora thought he was going

to say he would live with her. She just as quickly dismissed the idea.

"Your mother is going to stay in New York. She'll be provided for."

"And you don't love her anymore?"

"No." Hank considered it. "No, I don't. We did love each other once, of course. But somehow it all went off. I don't know. Her drinking... I don't know exactly."

Dora felt him searching for answers. It was uncomfortable for her. She didn't really want him sorting out his feelings here in front of her. *Just tell me what to do*, she thought.

Almost as though he read her mind, Hank said "You don't have to do anything. It's possible somebody might interview you, but you're an independent adult." He looked around the room. "I'll help you if you need anything. I'll have some money once the house is sold."

Dora wasn't worried about money. She still had a good deal left in her safety deposit box. But she did feel some anxiety. It seemed like a door was slamming shut behind her. Her family home would be gone. She had always thought of it as a place to go if she needed it. Now that would no longer be true. And her mother would be in the city somewhere, permanently.

"I'll stay in town," her father said. "Just need to find a decent apartment. There aren't that many in Westport. Anyway, gotta get the house sold first. That's my first priority. And the divorce of course. We should have a hearing in about a month."

"Okay, dad." Dora said quietly. Her father remained seated. He seemed lost in thought. Dora looked at him and a question occurred to her. "Do you think Amy can see us now? Does she know what we're doing?"

Hank looked at his older daughter curiously. "We don't know. I don't know. Maybe. You hope for something like that, Heaven. If there is a Heaven, I'm sure Amy is there."

"Yeah, that's what I think," said Dora. "She's looking down on us. She wants us to be happy. I hope she's happy now."

Hank stared into space. "There are two sides to every death," he said, "what happens to the dead and what happens to the living. We don't know about the dead, not really, but we know about the living. And we go on living."

"Well that's what I'm doing. I'm trying to be happy, to go on living."

"Me too," said Hank. He gave Dora a small, sad smile. She smiled back.

"Okay, then. I'll get going. You need anything? Money or anything?" he asked again. He looked around at her spare furnishings and the disarray. Dirty clothes, magazines and Christine's toys were all scattered on the floor. Hank frowned and quickly looked back at Dora.

"Nah. I'm all right," she said.

"Okay." He got up and kissed her on the forehead.

Dora sat in her chair and watched him leave.

CHAPTER 54

2/17/73 – Saturday

Since being discharged from the detox program before Christmas, Norma had been attending Alcoholics Anonymous meetings with some regularity. She had not had a drink in almost three months. But that changed when she received a thick envelope in the mail from Tom Hennessy. Her husband had not told her he wanted a divorce. She learned of it by mail from his attorney. When she read the legal notice standing in her kitchen, her eyes blurred, her legs felt weak and she slumped down into the kitchen chair.

She tried to read the notice… "irreconcilable differences… lack of consort…" She could not focus. The urge to have a drink was overwhelming. She put on her coat and walked down to the liquor store where she bought a quart bottle of Smirnoff Vodka. Back with it in her apartment, she eagerly gulped down a full tall glass. The familiar burning in her throat calmed her nerves and she smiled to herself. *Fuck him. I don't need that idiot anyway.*

CHAPTER 55

3/15/73 – Thursday

Dora had not seen Jared in months. She had thrown him out and he had at last stayed out. *Maybe he is truly gone from my life*, she thought. *That's a step in the right direction.* She felt she could focus now on making things better for herself and Christine. She started thinking about her future. *This is not the place for Christine, not for long. Norwalk is not the place for her to go to school in a few years.* Dora wanted more in her life, more for herself and more for her baby. She suddenly thought of Maddie. She admired Maddie. And Maddie had helped her before, helped her move out and get in apartment. Most of all she remembered that Maddie had not seemed to judge her.

Quickly, before she lost her nerve, she dialed Maddie's number.

"Hello. Hixon Realty."

"Uh hi, Miss Hixon. This is Dora. Dora Latour."

"Oh. Hi Dora. How are you?"

"Well, I'm okay. I'm fine. I wanted to ask you,

ask you if we could maybe like talk, like get together... I'm thinking about moving," she added quickly.

"Sure Dora. Sure. You want to come to my office? Or maybe we could meet for coffee. Would you like that?"

"Yeah, yeah. That would be great. But can I bring Chrissie? My baby?"

"Of course. I'd like to see her."

"Cool. Okay, so where do you want to meet?"

"How about Lily's? This afternoon?"

"Yeah, yeah. That would be great. What time? I can come any time."

"All right. Let's say four. I have a few things to finish up here."

"Okay, cool. So I'll see you at four at Lily's. Thanks."

"You're quite welcome. See you then."

Maddie hung up and thought about Dora. She liked Dora who reminded her a little of herself at that age. Maddie's father had left her mother when Maddie was ten years old. The subsequent years had been hard for Maddie and her younger brother, Billy. They had moved to a smaller apartment in a poorer neighborhood of Cleveland. Their mother struggled to make ends meet and Maddie and her brother were often left to fend for themselves.

Maddie dropped out of school at sixteen and worked as a clerk at a local department store. The following year, her mother married a man Maddie did not like. Billy seemed to like him, but Maddie felt uncomfortable in his presence. She was seventeen by then and did not like the way he looked at her when they were alone together. She mentioned her feelings to her mother who just scoffed. But when he placed a hand on her breast and tried to kiss her one Saturday afternoon, she knew she had to leave. With her meager savings, she moved to a small apartment that she shared with two other girls from work. She had a hard time trusting men and dated only rarely. But she wanted a better life and planned accordingly.

Now, Maddie and Dora were seated at a window table in Lily's diner. Christine sat in a high chair. Maddie was saying "I should have been a lawyer... all the money, none of the risk." She laughed.

Dora realized she was joking, but asked nonetheless "But you like being a real estate agent, right?"

"Oh yeah, wouldn't trade it for the world. I like finding homes for people. And I like being my own boss."

Dora nodded. She could understand that, being your own boss. She wondered what she might be some day.

"So what are your plans, at this point?" Maddie asked.

"I'm thinking I'll get a job. I threw Jared out. He's been using and dealing and stuff. And stealing from me. God, it was a bummer. So he's gone."

"Well, that's good. I'm sure it wasn't easy."

"Uh huh. I mean it was hard in some ways, yeah, but the way he'd been acting, he kind of made it easy. I mean there's no guilt like that or anything."

"Yeah, sure. And he was stealing from you?"

"Yeah, for his habit. He's a junkie.. and he doesn't want to get straight."

"Well, I'm sure you're better off without him."

"That's for sure."

"So you're looking for a job?"

"Yeah, I was thinking maybe at a daycare center. Some place I could be with Chrissie and get paid."

"That sounds like a good idea. A good next step."

"And then I want to move out, get out of Norwalk, before Chrissie is ready for kindergarten. I've got a few years yet, but you know…"

"Well that's a good goal."

"Yeah. That's what I'm gonna do." Dora smiled. She had a goal.

Maddie smiled back at her. "Well, I need to get back to work, but we should do this again. Call me whenever you want." Dora sensed that Maddie was sincere. She felt encouraged.

"I will. I will. And thanks."

"Oh it's nothing. It's nice to see you, both of you." Maddie looked at Christine sitting happily, gnawing on a french fry. She got up, looked down at Dora and said "Let me know what you do."

"Yeah, for sure." Just seeing Maddie made Dora feel better, more sure of herself. She watched as the older woman left the restaurant. "Okay, Chrissie, let's go home."

****

On Newport lane, the original model home was being rebuilt. The insurance company had determined the fire was an accident and Holden had received their payment. The two houses on either side of the burned home were almost done. One was to be the new model. In addition, three more houses were under construction. The first buyers were long gone, spooked by the fire, perhaps. But others were interested and Maddie and Holden were optimistic about sales.

CHAPTER 56

7/15/73 – Sunday

It had been five months since Norma learned of Hank's intent to divorce her. She had been assigned her own attorney, but she failed to show up at the February hearing. However two months later, she managed to get to a meeting with the attorneys and angrily refused to agree to a settlement. Since then, there had been another court hearing at which she again failed to appear. The lawyer Hank had found for her reached her by phone and explained that if she did not make the next appearance, the court would decide the outcome. She failed to appear once again and Hank was granted the divorce. He was ordered to pay her four hundred dollars a month, as long as Norma did not remarry.

During the latter part of that summer of 1973, Norma passed through her days in a drunken haze. She rarely left her apartment except to pick up her mail or buy some food or alcohol. Mostly she bought alcohol. Empty vodka bottles littered her apartment. She often passed out on her bed in her clothes and only rarely changed them the next day.

Finally one day in late August, she collapsed against the fence surrounding Gramercy Park. She fell there on the sidewalk on 21st street at the end of Lexington Avenue. As before, the police gathered her up and brought her to Bellevue Hospital's Emergency Room. Her cycle of detox and rehab was repeated once again. And once again, when sober, she vowed to herself to attend her AA meetings and cease drinking. And once again, it didn't last. She lacked the supports, the structure, and most significantly, the motivation to stay sober. Without Amy, she felt completely empty, adrift and alone. So she drank. The doctors warned her about liver damage, but she did not care.

That year, American troops finally came home from Viet Nam. 58,000 lives had been lost in what many viewed as a pointless war. The country too seemed to be adrift, divided and unhappy. Norma was not the only soul who felt directionless.

****

Back in Westport, Hank was doing his best to move in a positive direction. And in fact, things were looking up for him. He had gotten a good price for his house. He had some money in the bank because he was now only renting. True, it was a small apartment downtown, over a hardware store, but it was his; it was affordable and he felt a sense of freedom he had not felt in many years. He was finally able to make his payments to Generoso without feeling he was giving away his last dime. Better yet, the remaining houses on Newport Lane were nearly finished. Three were already on the market and they had interested buyers.

Only when he lay in bed, late at night, unable to sleep, did he think about his family. He felt a wisp of regret about Norma. Had he been a better husband, would she not have descended into alcoholism? He didn't know. Had he been a better father, would Amy still be alive? Should he not have allowed her to take up modeling, move to New York, smoke cigarettes? Could he really have controlled any of that? He didn't know.

And Dora, his remaining child, had separated herself from him too soon. He felt a sharp pang stab his heart as he thought of her. Could he have stopped her from moving out, from living with Jared, even maybe somehow prevented her pregnancy? Again he didn't know. He only knew he felt a welter of confused feelings when he thought about her. Her life seemed so degenerate to him. He suspected drugs and crime were part of it, and how could she be a good mother to her daughter? He knew very little of her actual life, but disapproved of what he saw.

At the same time, he smiled to himself as he pictured her listening patiently to him, sitting in her dark apartment, those many months ago when he told her of his plans to leave her mother. He remembered kissing her goodbye as he left. That was sweet, but he worried then and he worried now for her future. What would become of her? He didn't know. He had wanted to help; he had offered her money back then, but she had refused it. It had been all he could think to do. She did not need money, it seemed.

CHAPTER 57

9/17/73 – Monday

It had been a warm summer, but it had suddenly gotten cold and Dora wondered when Hitchcock would turn the heat on. She shivered a little and folded her arms around herself. *It never seems warm enough in this apartment,* she thought. She did not miss Jared. She was glad he was gone, but she felt lonely nonetheless.

The quiet was broken by her ringing doorbell. To her surprise, it was Figgy. As he came through her door, he sprang past her and circled through her apartment in seconds. Dora's first thought was that he was speeding. And he was. He was the same hyperactive, skinny speed freak he'd been the last time she had seen him. If anything, he looked worse.

"So, what's happenin' Dor? What's shaking? You doing good here?"

"Uh, yeah. Figgy. We're fine. What's up with you?"

"Nothin'. I just came by to say hi. See how you were doin' and all. You know."

Dora laughed. "We're good, Figgy." She bent over and picked up her daughter. "This is Chrissie. She's fifteen months old now. Say hi Chrissie."

Chrissie giggled and said "hi."

"Well, hi there. Wow. Look at that red hair." Figgy fingered his own lank reddish hair.

"Her grandma was a redhead," Dora quickly pointed out.

"Oh yeah, yeah. I can see that. Your mom. Yeah, right. So what are you doin' here? You workin' or anythin'?"

Dora put Christine back on the floor. "Nah, not right now, but I'm thinking about it. Thinking about daycare for her and work for me. I gotta do something. You still at the record store?" She looked him over. There was something wrong with his teeth and his skinny arms looked bruised.

"Yeah, it's like my home, man. My second home, I guess." He laughed nervously.

"That's cool."

Figgy had not sat down. He was constantly in motion. "You wanna…" His eyes drifted to her chest. Dora was braless, wearing a sleeveless tee shirt. "I got some good stuff," he grinned, digging his hand into the front pocket of his blue jeans.

"Uh, no… and no" said Dora.

"You're lookin' good."

"No, I'm not into that, not now." *Not with you.*

"Yeah, alright. That's cool. I gotta get goin' anyway. You know. Just thought I'd check you out and all. I'm outta here, okay."

With that, he was out the door. Dora stared at the space he had been before the door closed behind him. The idea nagged at her that he might think Chrissie was his baby. She almost mentioned it to him while he was there but realized there was no reason to bring it up. Nonetheless, the thought stayed in her mind poking at her, like a pebble in her shoe. She shook her head quickly as if to shake the thought loose.

It had been months since she had met Maddie at Lily's and still she did not have a job. In truth, she had not actually looked for one and she wondered how so much time could have gone by so fast. She jumped up and pulled her winter parka out of the closet and took Chrissie's coat out as well. She zipped Chrissie in and pulled on her own coat. Gathering Chrissie to her with right hand, she picked up her purse and keys with her left and rushed out of her apartment. She ran down the stairs and out the front door to her car.

She sat Chrissie next to her in her beat up little blue Honda Civic and drove to Time For Tots, the daycare center at the bottom of the hill. She'd seen it before, many times, but had never entered. This time, she walked in breathlessly and said to the heavyset

Negro woman who presided over a roomful of toddlers "I want to enroll my daughter. And would you have a job here for me?"

"Well, yes, sure thing," the woman smiled at her. "My name's Louise, Louise Hankins."

"Right. Sorry. I'm Dora. And this. This is Chrissie... my daughter," she added unnecessarily.

"And how old is Chrissie?"

"She's just fifteen months."

"That's fine. fifteen months is fine. We have a lot of little ones here."

Dora was suddenly afraid the woman thought she was abandoning Chrissie with her. "And I would like to work here, I mean, if I can, if you can use me."

"As a matter of fact, I could use some help. Do you have any experience? Other than with Chrissie?"

"Well, not really. I mean I used to babysit when I was younger. But I can learn. I can do anything. And I'm a hard worker."

"Well, we'll see. I can't pay you much. Just pretty much minimum wage. Not a lot of money in the child care business you know."

"No. I know. That's okay."

"Well, when do you and Chrissie want to start?"

"How 'bout today? I mean we're here." Dora smiled hopefully.

Louise laughed loudly, her fleshy arms jiggling as she did so. "Okay, sure we can start right now. Just put your coats over there." She gestured to a coat rack in the corner.

Dora put Chrissie down and took off the little girl's coat. Chrissie stood there a moment and then toddled over to another little girl sitting on the floor playing with blocks. Dora grinned at Louise, took off her parka and hung up both coats.

"The kids all go home at five, unless they need babysitting. We do that too. We have to straighten up, put all this stuff away, after they go."

So Chrissie and Dora began their weekday program at Time For Tots.

CHAPTER 58

11/3/73 – Saturday

True to his word, Holden completed the remaining houses on Newport Lane. And true to her word, Maddie sold them all, at an average price of $128,000. The closings went smoothly and on this windy morning in early November, Hank stood with Holden in the doorway of the little construction shack that still stood on the site. It was to be removed that afternoon.

Hank looked over the newly seeded lawns and turned to Holden. "You know, I remember it wasn't long ago this was all just an empty field."

Holden shrugged and said "No plot of land goes ignored for long anymore." He tapped Hank on the shoulder and handed him a heavy briefcase. It contained $400,000 in cash, their final payment to Generoso. Hank stepped back inside, shut the door behind him and opened the briefcase. It was filled with stacks of bills. It had been Holden's job to make sure the money was available in cash. They did not want a written record, hence no check.

Hank did receive a check from Holden for his

share of the proceeds. That check was $57,251. Since his initial investment was $50,000 and $25,000 had been deducted to pay back Holden, Hank's actual profit was only $7,251. It seemed awfully low to Hank. When he questioned why it wasn't more, Holden reminded him there were legal fees, architect costs, a lot of subcontractors to be paid, the extra loan expense and Maddie's commissions. He would have received more, but they had to pay the insurance deductible. "After all, your kid burned down the model," Holden added.

Fuck you, thought Hank, but he gave a tight-lipped smile, took the check and put it in his wallet, without further discussion. He would be happy never to see Holden again. He closed the briefcase, knowing he had to face Generoso one more time. He hoped that delivery would be the last time he ever saw that man as well.

CHAPTER 59

11/15/73 – Thursday

It was two years to the day since Hank had borrowed $300,000 from Rick Generoso and today he would pay it off on time and be done with the transaction at last. Maddie had called Generoso to set up the payoff meeting. They were to meet at the Delphi Diner on the Post Road at the Fairfield/Bridgeport line. Hank knew the spot. He arrived fifteen minutes ahead of schedule. He walked in clutching the heavy briefcase tightly.

He sat at a table in the back right corner, next to the bathroom. It seemed out of the way and somewhat out of sight. He placed the briefcase carefully on the floor between his legs and his chair. He looked around anxiously. Peering out the plate glass window, he searched the parking lot on the side of the building. He squinted at shadows in the Texaco gas station next door, fearing the Westport Police were lying in wait for him, but there were no officers to be seen. A dark sedan pulled into the parking lot and a man carrying a duffle bag got out and entered the restaurant, but it wasn't Generoso.

"What'll it be, honey?" asked a waitress, startling Hank. She seemed to have appeared out of nowhere.

"Oh, just coffee," Hank said. "Thanks." He didn't make eye contact and continued staring out the window.

"Okay," she said, "just coffee." She seemed about to say something more, but Hank had not turned to face her, so she left to get his coffee.

She returned a few minutes later, with the coffee and a small metal pitcher of milk. She placed these in front of Hank, who mumbled "thanks."

"Anything else?" she asked.

"What? No, I'm fine." He glanced around her. There were only a few customers in the diner. A young couple sat a few tables away. The man who had come in from the parking lot sat at the end of the counter quietly drinking coffee and reading the paper. Hank returned to looking out the window.

"Well, let me know if there is anything else you need," the waitress said, a bit huffily.

"Yeah, okay." He did not look at her and he did not touch his coffee.

Ten minutes passed. Hank looked at his watch repeatedly. Each minute felt like an hour. *Why don't I feel better about this?* He wondered. *This should be it.*

We should be done. Just get it over with and you can relax.

At last, he saw Generoso pull into the parking lot in his black Lincoln. Hank watched him get out, glance around and then walk quickly toward the diner. He entered, spotted Hank and sat down without a word.

Hank silently slid the briefcase across the floor to him. Generoso tapped the table with his knuckles, picked up the briefcase and walked out. Hank felt his stomach relax. He exhaled and took a sip of lukewarm coffee.

He looked out the window of the diner as Generoso strode across the parking lot. He watched in horrified fascination as four men seemed to materialize out of thin air and surround Generoso just before he reached his car. One took the briefcase from him. Another turned him around, leaning him against his car. Hank watched as they handcuffed him and marched him to an unmarked car parked nearby. The whole thing was over very quickly.

Hank waited a few minutes expecting the police to come for him next, but nobody came. After a moment, he got up, went around to the counter and paid his bill. The man reading his paper looked up at him and gave a slight smile, disorienting Hank for a moment. But nothing was said. *Maybe it's just a friendly stranger,* thought Hank hopefully. *Maybe they don't need me for this. No, I'm their witness. And this guy witnessed me give the briefcase to Generoso. They are bound to call me. They'll subpoena me. I'll have to testify. God, it never ends.*

Driving back to Westport, Hank decided he had better speak with Tom Hennessy about Generoso, the police, everything. He'd see what options he had and maybe find a way out.

As soon as he returned to his office, Hank called the attorney.

"I may have a problem," he said. "I'm not sure. I could be called upon to testify about um... a... a loan. And it could be dangerous."

"What are you talking about exactly?" asked Hennessey.

"Let's not discuss it on the phone. Can I come in?"

"Yeah, how's three o'clock?"

"Fine. Fine. See you then."

"Okay."

Hank was frightened. He imagined the courtroom and the police. After all, he'd borrowed the money from a loan shark. They knew it. They'd have to have him testify. How could he have thought otherwise? He was the victim. He was their witness, their most important one, he suspected. Thinking of his smashed phone and his two visitors that day almost two years ago, Hank shivered. Would they kill him to keep him from testifying? He doubted it. More likely they would intimidate him, threaten him. That was scary enough. And he doubted the police could really protect him. The thought of fleeing again crossed his mind. But first, he decided he would see what Hennessey might say. He hoped there was something the lawyer could do.

Hank arrived at Hennessey's office right at 3:00 pm. Hennessey was seated behind his big desk, but jumped up immediately when Hank came in.

"So Hank, what's up?"

"All right," Hank tried to slow himself down, control his breathing. "I'm scared. I paid off a loan shark today and he was busted, right in front of me, in the parking lot. I saw it out the window. And there was a man at the counter who might have been a cop, who witnessed the payoff."

"Wait, wait, back up a little. Tell me everything from the beginning."

"Everything? Okay. This is confidential, right?"

"Yes, attorney client privilege applies. I'm your attorney. I cannot repeat anything you tell me in confidence, but I have to know the whole story."

"Okay, okay." Hank proceeded to explain that they had desperately needed a substantial loan to go ahead with the Newport Lane housing development. He had been able to find only one source of money, Rick Generoso. "Jeez. They'd probably kill me if they knew I even repeated his name," Hank said shakily.

"It's all right. Like I said, you're safe here."

"Okay, yeah. Then, all right, we, I actually, met this guy Generoso at Lily's Diner."

"When was this?"

"Oh, like two years ago. Exactly two years ago."

"All right, what happened?"

"Well, he gave me a briefcase with $300,000. Told me to pay $1,000 interest, good faith payments, they're called, every month. For two years. And then, pay $400,000 at the end of two years. Which I did, which I did today."

"Okay, so you borrowed 300K and paid back a total of what?"

"A total of $424,000. Well, $424,500 to be exact."

"Over two years?"

"Yeah, like I said, two years of monthly payments of $1,000 a month, and then the $400,000 today. The extra $500 was a, uh, a late payment penalty." Hank gave a wry smile.

"And the problem is the police arrested this Generoso and you will be subpoenaed to testify. Is that it?"

"Yeah, that's it. That's the problem. These guys do not fool around. They scared the shit out of me once when two of his guys came to my office cause I missed a payment, made a partial payment, I mean."

"What happened?"

"Well, they smashed my phone, broke my pen… maybe it doesn't sound like much, but believe me, if you were there… they scared the shit out of me."

"Did anyone see them?"

"No, nobody saw them do those things, but my secretary let them in, heard the phone crash. She was scared, scared for me, and called the police."

"She did? All right. And the police came?"

"Yeah, after the two guys left. I told the police it was nothing. They asked about the crash, when the phone was smashed. I just said one of the men kicked a chair and it hit the desk. That was the noise. It was an accident, I said. I don't think they believed me, but they left. Things seemed okay I thought… but then, then a detective came the next day. Said they'd been watching me, knew something was up. I made up a story about these guys trying to start a pizza parlor. I know the detective didn't buy it."

"So the police were watching you? And that's how they knew where to bust Generoso today."

"Yeah, I guess. Or they tapped my phone," Hank

said gloomily. He looked up, hoping Hennessey might have a plan, a way he would not have to go to court.

"All right, Hank. Let me do some checking. There may be something here. I'll call you."

With that, the meeting was over. Hank was worried, but hopeful as well.

CHAPTER 60

11/19/73 – Monday

It was 9:30 in the morning. Hank sat at his desk nervously, unable to work. He was tired and anxious. The weekend had been hard. He had not been able to relax at all. He had barely slept. He drank coffee, drank scotch, and couldn't sit still. Several times, he had taken his car and driven around town, driving nowhere. He prayed Hennessey would call with a miraculous plan.

Suddenly, his phone rang. He jumped in his chair, answering it before the second ring. It was Hennessey.

"I think I have some good news for you," the lawyer announced.

"Really? What?" Hank felt a surge of hope.

"Well, here's the story. You borrowed $300,000 and paid back $424,500 over two years, right?"

"Yes… so?"

"So, that may not be illegal, for the lender."

"You're kidding. Why not?"

"By my calculations, that is a nineteen per cent annual interest rate."

"okay…"

"And Connecticut has a maximum allowable interest rate of twelve per cent per year. It is only a serious crime when the interest exceeds two times the maximum allowable rate, so it would need to be over twenty-four per cent annual interest to be a Class D felony. Bottom line, I don't think they'll prosecute this when they know the amounts involved. Unless they can prove you were intimidated, if you were threatened or harmed. That's a different crime."

"Well I was threatened that one time."

"But nobody saw it. They heard a crash, your secretary heard a crash. That's it. That's pretty thin."

"Okay… This is amazing" Hank said after a pause. "It would be great if it… if the whole thing just gets dropped."

"Well, we'll see. The police probably will want to talk to you, confirm the amounts, question you further about the threats, but I'll be with you. You won't say anything to bolster their case. And I think they'll have to drop it. Let me talk to the DA. You may not even have to be questioned."

"Okay, okay, thanks. You know, I was

wondering why he didn't charge more interest. I mean as loan sharks go, this wasn't all that profitable, was it?"

"No, it isn't typical. Maybe he kept it under twenty-four per cent for this exact reason. Or, maybe he was doing a favor for your friend Maddie. That's possible. We'll never know."

"No, I guess not. All right, let me know what happens with the DA."

"I will. I'll reach out to him today."

"All right, and thanks. I can't tell you what a relief this is."

"Well, don't celebrate quite yet, but it looks good."

"All right, yes. I'll wait to hear from you."

"I'll get back to you as soon as I know."

****

Hennessey called Hank again several days later.

"Good news. The DA doesn't see a case here. He is not going to prosecute. You're out of the woods."

"Oh my God. What a relief. You mean this whole nightmare is really over?"

"Yes, except for my bill," Hennessey laughed.

CHAPTER 61

12/25/73 – Tuesday, Christmas Day

Dora celebrated her 19th birthday quietly with Chrissie. It had been a wet, cold December and they huddled inside blankets in their chilly apartment. Nobody called to wish her a happy birthday or a Merry Christmas. Chrissie seemed happy enough seated on the rug, a blanket draped around her shoulders. She was coloring in a book with her crayons. Dora stared at her daughter and thought about their lives together. They still had about half the money from Dora's discovery in the garage two years ago. Chrissie seemed happy in day care and she was healthy. For the present, their life was stable, but Dora worried about their future.

She rarely thought now about Jared. She did not miss his selfish ways and was glad to be free of his endless demands for money, rifling her purse and taking what he found. But she knew she missed companionship. She missed having a boyfriend on these lonely cold days. The winter frightened her. Her money would not last forever and the $1.65 per hour she made at her job barely covered their groceries. Looking at Chrissie and the few toys scattered about, she thought *I need to get somewhere better, better for both of us.*

Time For Tots was closed. It would be closed the rest of the week and only reopen the following Monday. The time stretched before Dora like a canyon. She thought about calling her father. She had half expected him to call her on her birthday, but the phone never rang. *What is he doing now?* she wondered. *Was he seeing someone? Did he talk to mom?* She shrugged and told herself *I don't really care too much. I have my own family to think about.*

****

January 18, 1974 was bitterly cold. That morning, the temperature was five degrees. In Dora's apartment, cold air seeped in from the edges of the windows. The radiators did their best to fight it, but the apartment was chilly. Dora had wrapped Chrissie in every blanket she could find. The little girl did not complain and seemed content to sit swaddled in Dora's lap. Dora shivered. On impulse, she picked up the phone and dialed Maddie Hixon's number.

"Hixon Realty. Maddie Hixon speaking." Dora paused a moment, hearing Maddie's upbeat voice. "Hello?" said Maddie.

Dora almost hung up, but then plunged ahead. "Uh hi. This is Dora. Dora Latour. You remember me?"

"Yes, of course. Hi Dora. How are you?"

"I'm fine. I just wanted to call. I don't know. I wanted to ask you…"

DEVELOPMENT

"Sure. Good to hear from you Dora."

"Well, yeah, I mean, remember you said how you wished you were a lawyer. Remember that?"

"Not really. What did I say?"

"All the money and none of the risks. That's what you said."

"Oh right," Maddie laughed. "Well, I don't know about *no* risks," she clarified.

"Well, I thought maybe I could be a lawyer. You know? If I was a lawyer, I could help girls who were in trouble," Dora said. "And I'd make more money," she added hopefully.

"Right. And none of the risks," Maddie laughed gently.

"But how would I do that, become a lawyer?" Dora asked seriously.

"Well, first you'd have to go back to school Dora. You didn't finish high school, did you? How old are you now?"

"I just turned 19. I'm 19."

"Okay. I think the first thing is you need to get your GED. You need to finish high school. Then college, and then law school. That's a lot but you could do it if you really wanted to. You really could, I think."

Dora loved hearing that, someone who believed in her. That was why she had called Maddie, she realized. "Yeah, yeah, I could. So I need to finish my last year of high school. That's when I left. So I'd graduate with the GED, right?"

"Yes, you would. You should call the school system there in Norwalk, or maybe Westport, since that's where you were going. See what they tell you about the GED. The next steps."

"Okay, okay I will. Thanks!" Dora said brightly. She felt excited.

"Well, great. Is there anything else? How's your daughter?"

"Oh well, except for practically freezing to death here, we're both fine. She's in day care, you know."

"No I didn't. That's good. Should give you some time to study."

"Well, I work there too. But I'm thinking of stopping, so yeah, I can do my schoolwork. That would work out. That's what I'm gonna do."

"Sounds like you have a plan, Dora."

"Yeah, yeah, I do. So, uh, thanks."

"Okay. I'll see you some time. Let me know how you're doing."

"Yeah, thanks. Thanks I will."

Dora hung up. She felt better. She had a new plan, or the start of one.

****

In New York, Norma was drinking again. On this cold January day, she did not notice the temperature. A group of worn, glossy magazines lay sprawled in front of her, across her kitchen table. These were the old magazines with Amy's pictures in them. Poring over them, Norma would cry and she would drink. By late afternoon, the light was fading. She put her head on the table, on a full-page photo of Amy and fell asleep. Her tears and spittle left damp pools on the paper, warping it. Norma's apartment was like a darkened cave. She could not climb out, nor did she want to.

CHAPTER 62

8/9/74 – Friday

Dora completed her GED the second week of August. That same week, President Nixon resigned as a result of the Watergate scandal. His own presidential tapes implicated him. *He was a lawyer who broke the law*, thought Dora. *Well, I'll be a good lawyer. I'll help girls.*

One week later, Dora applied to Norwalk Community College, which was nearby and affordable. She was accepted and would start that Fall.

The school offered a two year Associates degree. Dora could not afford to go full time, so she took classes as often as possible and resolved to finish as quickly as she could. Chrissie would remain in her day care center where she seemed to be happy. Dora worked at Time for Tots as often as possible, but it was difficult with school. So she juggled her life, gradually and carefully, tapping her shrinking savings.

CHAPTER 63

1/15/75 – Wednesday

In New York, Norma continued to spend most of her days and nights drunk. She would sit on her couch and watch television with bleary eyes. Sometimes she stared out her kitchen window, thinking angrily about what might have been. Her alimony allowed her to keep a small single-room occupancy apartment, in the east 20s. She had become familiar with the neighborhood and she had no intention of leaving. But one morning in late September, she woke up thinking of Dora and Dora's little girl. She could not recall the girl's name, but she felt the wish to see her. She got dressed and managed to catch a train to Westport. She realized she did not know where Dora lived or her phone number. She knew Hank had sold the house, but she realized she could call him at the bank. It pleased her that she somehow remembered his number there. Dorothy put her through and Hank picked up his phone.

"Hello"

"Hank, it's Norma. I'm in Westport. I'm at the station."

"You are?" This was a surprise to Hank who had not heard from Norma in over a year and certainly didn't expect her to be in Westport. With a start, Hank realized he still felt angry with her and did not want to talk with her at all.

"Yeah. Can you pick me up? I want to go see Dora and her baby."

"No, I can't pick you up. I'm busy right now. Why didn't you call before you came?"

"I don't know. I just came." Norma said, her voice quivering.

Hank gritted his teeth for a moment. But he was torn. She sounded so helpless. At the same time, he had no wish to see her. Fair or not, he told himself, Amy is dead because of her.

"Can't you take a cab? There are taxis there at the station. A taxi stand right there."

"I know. I… I… I don't know where she lives. I don't have her number or anything."

"Oh Christ. So you don't even know if she's home. She's taking courses now at the community college. She works some of the time. You should have called first."

"I'm sorry." Norma whimpered.

"Oh for Christ's sake. I'll see if she's home and if she's there, I'll pick you up."

"Okay. Should I call you back or what?" Norma could barely speak. This whole thing was not a good idea. She wanted a drink and fumbled in her purse as she stood there.

"Yeah, give me ten minutes. Call me back in ten minutes." He hung up.

Norma stood by the phone. She had found her little bottle and took a reassuring drink of vodka. Feeling a little better, she put the bottle back in her purse and lit a cigarette.

After a few minutes, she called Hank back.

"I just got off with Dora. She is home. She has to go out in about an hour, but if I come get you right now, you can see her for maybe twenty or thirty minutes."

"Uh okay. Okay, yeah, I guess."

"You guess? Jesus. All right. I'll be right over. Stay put."

Norma looked around for a place to sit and found a bench on the platform. She sat down and continued smoking as she waited for Hank.

He showed up about fifteen minutes later. She got into his car. Her hair was tangled. Her clothes were wrinkled. Her face was blotchy. "You look like a mess," he said to her.

"I know. I know. Let's just go, please."

Without another word, Hank drove to Dora's building. They walked up her steps and Hank rang her bell. Dora buzzed them in.

Climbing the stairs was difficult for Norma, but eventually she arrived at Dora's apartment. "So this is where you live now." she said, as Dora let them in.

"Yeah," Dora fidgeted. "This is home." Toys were scattered about. Chrissie was not there.

"Where's your daughter? Where's …?"

"Christine" Dora filled in. "She's at day care."

"Oh, I wanted to see her."

"Well, maybe another time, mom."

"All right. So how are you?"

"I'm fine. Everything is fine."

"All right. You still with that guy, what's his name?"

"Jared. No, we broke up. It was for the best, believe me."

"So what are you doing? Your father says you're in school."

"Yeah, getting my Associates. I've got at least a year to go, at this rate. But yeah, I'm doing that. You wanna sit down? You want some coffee or something?"

"No, no. I can't stay. I know you have school and I should go. I just wanted to see. That's all."

"Yeah, well okay. You take care, mom."

Norma staggered back out the door. Hank looked at Dora and shrugged. "Bye dad," she said.

Outside, Norma said "Thanks. Thanks for the ride. It was good to see her, you know. She looks good. She's doing good."

"Yeah, she's doing okay. I didn't realize she'd split up with Jared. That's good. He's a drug addict. He was just dragging her down. I hated that guy."

"Really? I didn't know that. So yeah, it's good he's gone. And the baby, is the baby… Christine, okay?"

"Yeah, she's fine. She's, I think, two and a half now."

"Two and a half," said Norma in a state of drunken wonderment.

"Well, let's get you back to the train. You're going back, right?" Hank had no wish to be with Norma any longer than necessary.

"Yeah, yeah, I'm going." Norma spit back, a little bit of her old fire returning.

"All right. Let's go." They got in his car and headed off. He left her at the station, not caring how long she would wait for a train and whether she had a ticket.

He wanted to be rid of her.

Norma climbed back on the New York bound platform carefully. Her walking was not very steady these days and she was afraid she might fall. She did have a return ticket in her purse and she sat quietly on the bench waiting as Hank drove off.

****

Riding back on the train, Norma thought *I have to get better. I want to be able to see my daughter and my granddaughter. That's my right. I know I have to straighten out.* But when she got back to her apartment, it was gloomy and half a bottle of vodka sat on the counter. She could not resist and soon she had passed out on the sofa.

She awoke there the next morning and remembering her trip to Connecticut, resolved that this time, today, she would straighten out once and for all. Despite an agonizing desire for a drink, she made herself walk to Bellevue Hospital and ask for admission to the detox program.

She was admitted and once again went through a three week period of drying out, getting treated medically and attending AA meetings. She was placed on a new drug called Anabuse. It was designed to make her sick if she drank while taking it. That was supposed to be an effective deterrent to drinking. After her discharge, she took the drug for a few days, but then she stopped and resumed her drinking again. At first it did make her very sick. She was terribly nauseous and she stopped drinking. The Anabuse stayed in her system for another week, but after that, she found she could drink again without the ill effects and she resumed her alcohol consumption.

A few weeks later, she awoke one morning in agonizing pain. She clutched her stomach and staggered out on to the sidewalk, trying to get to the hospital. She fell there, in front of her building. Neighbors who knew her slightly shook their heads and one called the police. They picked her up once again and brought her to Bellevue. She was near death.

CHAPTER 64

3/16/75 – Tuesday

Like Norma, Jared had tried to straighten out. He had entered a Methadone program. It had been nearly six months now. He had gotten his old job back, at the warehouse. He was trying to get back on track. He had tried to see Dora and Christine on a couple of occasions, but Dora had not even let him in the apartment. He told himself he was fine without her.

Dora was doing well. She had her own plans and did not want Jared to be a part of them, whether or not he recovered. She doubted he was Christine's father anyway. Christine had Fig's coloring and build. It did not matter to Dora. She had never wanted the blood test for her daughter that Vince Appleton had long ago demanded. Both Jared and Figgy were in her past, not in her future.

Dora did not know if she would ever again have a man in her life. She was taking birth control pills, but so far, had no need for them. There were boys at school, but they were younger than she for the most part and seemed to shy away when they learned she had a little girl at home. Dora tried not to let that bother her. She had all she could handle with Chrissie, her schoolwork and making ends meet.

She heard from her father that Norma was back in the hospital. Apparently Norma had nearly died of cirrhosis this time. If she drank again, Hank said, she would die. He added that Norma was again in Alcoholics Anonymous and maybe she would get better this time. Dora could tell he didn't believe it and that he did not seem to care very much one way or the other. But Dora wanted to believe there was hope for her mother. She still hoped Chrissie might someday have a healthy grandmother.

CHAPTER 65

3/31/75 - Monday.

Three weeks after her latest discharge, Norma had remained sober. She had apparently accepted AA this time. She called Hank asking for Dora's phone number, which he reluctantly gave her. But when she called Dora, she was told no, it was not a good time for a visit. The truth was Dora was afraid to believe her mother had recovered. She did not want her daughter to meet her grandmother in the condition Dora had last seen her. Despite Norma's protestations that she was indeed better, Dora did not want to risk it. Not yet. She told her mother "Maybe someday." Norma had hung up, disconsolate, wanting a drink.

CHAPTER 66

9/12/75 - Friday

Dora had not seen Jared in a long time when she and Chrissie bumped into him one September morning while out shopping. He was clearly using again. Dora could tell he was high. He lurched toward them, looking as emaciated as he had years earlier.

Stopping before them on the sidewalk, he looked at Dora with bloodshot eyes. His clothes were filthy. Dora reached down and pulled Chrissie close to her.

"Hey Dor. Hey. Hey, how ya doin'?"

"Hi Jared." Dora cringed, the fear and anxiety etching her voice.

"Hey, can you help me? I'm a little short. Like I could use some help here."

"What do you want? You want money, right?"

"Yeah. Can you give me twenty?"

Dora looked around. Two people had paused on the sidewalk, looking at them. "All right. I don't know.

Let me see." She opened her purse. Jared lunged for it and she jerked it back away from him. "Stop it!" she shouted. "Just give me a minute, will you!"

"Yeah, yeah okay," he said, catching himself. He had nearly fallen over when she pulled back.

Dora fished out a ten dollar bill. It was all she was willing to part with. "This is all I have. Don't ask me again."

"I won't. Just need something to get by. You can't give me any more?"

"No. Hey, what happened to the program you were in? The methadone program?" She couldn't stop herself from asking.

"Oh, that place. Man, I quit. Well, I mean they kicked me out. My urines were dirty. Too many rules. It sucked."

"Too bad." Dora realized Chrissie had seen more than enough. "Well, we gotta go."

"Yeah, see you around."

Not if I see you first, thought Dora.

EPILOGUE – TWO YEARS LATER

10/25/77 – Wednesday

Two months shy of her 23rd birthday, Dora received her Associate degree. She decided to transfer to the University of Bridgeport to complete a four year bachelor's degree.

As she explained very seriously to Maddie "I need to get a four year degree to go to law school."

Maddie laughed in spite of herself. "Yes, you do. Good thinking," she said. It was what she had explained to Dora years ago.

"I know," said Dora. "I'm going to be a lawyer, like we talked about."

Maddie, who had never married and never had children said "I'm proud of you, Dora."

"Thanks. I still have a long way to go, I know, but I'll get there."

"Yes, I think you will."

****

The following January, Dora entered the University of Bridgeport as a full-time student. She had only enough money left from the garage discovery years ago to cover her first year. But she believed she would figure something out. Chrissie was in public school now. There were scholarships; there was work; maybe her father would help; she would manage somehow.

She nervously called her father to tell him she had been accepted and she was going on to get her Bachelor's degree. She admitted she was hoping to become a lawyer. Hank had sniffed at that, at the time, dismissing it as a foolish dream. She had hung up, hurt and angry.

But later that night, as he thought about her, Hank realized he had been wrong. He thought about her progress with amazement. He no longer viewed her as a degenerate failure, as one more example of his own shortcomings. Instead, he suddenly saw her as a brave soul, who had fought difficult odds and was achieving success. He felt a burst of pride. He wanted to see his daughter and his granddaughter. He dialed Dora's number.

"Hello"

"Hi honey. It's your dad."

"Uh huh. Hi."

"Well, I wanted to say… I wanted to tell you…" Hank struggled for the words.

"What?" Dora asked impatiently.

"Uh, well I wanted to say how proud I am of you."

"You are?"

"Yes. I am. What are you doing now? I thought I might visit you. Maybe we could go out to dinner?"

"Now? It's already seven o'clock. Chrissie's going to bed soon."

"Right. Of course. Well maybe I could come by and see you for a bit. Just a little while."

"Sure. I guess. Okay."

"Great. I'll be right over."

When he got to her apartment, Chrissie was sleeping. "Shhhh…" said Dora as she let him in. "C'mon in here." They sat at her kitchen table.

"Thanks," said Hank. "I've been thinking about you, what you've accomplished, what you had to overcome. I don't know how you did it, but you did it. You're doing it, and I'm proud of you, Dora."

Dora's eyes misted over. "Thanks dad."

"I know it hasn't been easy, raising a child. You're doing a great job of that by the way. And dumping Jared, getting him out of your life. That must have been hard."

"Not as hard as you might think," she said, laughing.

"Well, yeah," he chuckled, "maybe that wasn't so hard. Jeez, what a bum."

"I know. Who knew? He was so smart and everything in high school."

"Yeah, you can't tell about people. They'll fool you. Your mother... well never mind. Anyway, you're doing great. I guess we've both been through a lot."

Dora paused, thinking about her father, Amy, their mother. "Yeah, you have too."

"The thing is how could you afford it? I mean, this apartment, child care, school..." Hank trailed off, looking around the small kitchen.

"Well, we get by," Dora answered evasively. She did not want to discuss money.

Suddenly Hank looked directly at her. "That money from the garage. You found it. You took it, didn't you?"

Dora bit her lip, startled. She looked down at her lap. Barely audibly, she said "Yes."

Hank reached over and covered her hand with his own. "It's okay. I'm glad."

ABOUT THE AUTHOR

Paul Backalenick has worked a variety of jobs including: psychiatric counselor in a methadone clinic, information technology strategy consultant, Director of Admissions for a psychiatric hospital, founder of a web development and Internet marketing agency and Wall Street day trader, among others. He graduated from Brown University with a concentration in Psychology and later obtained an MBA from Boston College. He is a supporter of animal rights, ecology and conservation causes. He enjoys playing piano, poker and golf, and traveling as much as possible. He grew up in Westport, Connecticut and now lives in New York City with his long-time love, artist Karen Loew. DEVELOPMENT is his first novel.

Made in the USA
Middletown, DE
11 February 2021